CHILEAN WRITERS IN EXILE

CHILEAN WRITERS IN EXILE

Eight Short Novels
edited by Fernando Alegría

 THE CROSSING PRESS / Trumansburg, New York 14886

Library of Congress Cataloging in Publication Data
Main entry under title:

Chilean writers in exile.

    1. Chilean fiction--20th century. 2. Chilean litera-
ture in exile. 3. Chile--History--Coup d'état, 1973--
Fiction. I. Alegría, Fernando, 1918-
PQ8076.C5   863   81-12567
ISBN 0-89594-059-0   AACR2
ISBN 0-89594-060-4 (pbk.)

Contents

Foreword

After the military coup that overthrew the constitutional government of President Salvador Allende on September 11, 1973, a brutal repression began in Chile against all forms of democratic expression. Universities were taken over by the military; newspapers, magazines, and books were subjected to drastic censorship; student organizations were abolished, and a net of espionage was established to ensure that forces still struggling for freedom of speech would be permanently stifled.

The consequences of this ruthless onslaught against Chilean institutions and individuals have been devastating. Thousands of university professors, intellectuals, artists, and professionals went into exile. Chilean literature, prospering during the years of the Popular Unity (1970-1973) when Quimantu, supported by the government, published Chilean authors in editions of one hundred thousand copies, suffered heavily under the fascist repression. Quimantu was confiscated by the military and a general was appointed as its new director. For a while books by Nobel Prize winner Pablo Neruda were banished. Such famous Latin American writers as García Márquez and Cortázar were outlawed. More than a hundred writers left Chile to live and work in exile.

The story of Neruda's death and the destruction of his house in Santiago is well known. Priceless books and manuscripts were burned or stolen. Neruda's remains, buried in the mausoleum of a distinguished Chilean family, were ordered removed by the Junta and reburied in a wall-niche.

Some distinguished Chilean authors who decided to stay have been submitted to interrogations and searches. Unable to protest, they have maintained a proud and painful silence, sending out coded messages through the channels of the underground press.

Writers and artists in exile have waged an incessant struggle against the oppressors of the Chilean people. Numerous magazines have sprung up in Europe, the United States, Canada and Latin America: two have become the official voice of exile: *Araucaria* and *Literatura Chilena en el Exilio*. Modest but dynamic publishing enterprises are making known the works of young Chilean poets and novelists in Mexico, Canada, and France. Playwrights and actors have founded successful companies in Caracas, San José de Costa Rica, and Madrid. There are also many film-makers, painters, sculptors and musicians working in Cuba, Sweden, Belgium, Holland, England, and other nations. Chilean culture is very much alive and productive, acting as guardian of a magnificent humanist tradition that the military dictatorship has been unable to destroy.

This anthology is the expression of a group of writers who, in spite of all the hardships inherent in life in exile, are producing vigorous statements on behalf of the Chilean people. Three generations of writers are published here: Fernando Alegría represents the Generation of 1938; Poli Délano, Ariel Dorfman, and Claudio Giaconi speak for the Generation of 1950; Juan A. Epple and Leandro Urbina represent the younger writers who have matured in the years of exile. Alfonso González Dagnino, a physician, and Aníbal Quijada, a civil servant, became writers as a result of experiences in Chile during and after the coup.

Introduction

Chile is renowned for the poetry of such extraordinary innovators as Gabriela Mistral, Pablo Neruda and Nicanor Parra. Chilean novelists, on the other hand, tend to assimilate the literary traditions of other countries. During the first half of the twentieth century, Chilean novelists developed "social realism." Their work faithfully depicted life in the rural areas, on the coast or in the cities, their stories portraying the conflicts of the emerging middle class as well as the social awakening of the lower classes. Society was seen as unstable, confused, contradictory; the necessity to create a more authentic and dignified life seemed more a dream than a possibility. Social realism with its critical analysis of the present was not capable of blue-printing the future. In fact, the literature of this period is characterized as being fatalistic.

After the experience of the Popular Front Government in 1938, however, writers became more hopeful. In the literature of this generation, which included Fernando Alegría, Guillermo Atías, Volodia Teitelboin, Francisco Coloane, Oscar Castro, Nicomedes Guzmán, Reinaldo Lomboy, Andrés Sabella and Juan Godoy, the search for a national identity coincided with an historical experience that was *new,* full of changes and promises. Characters ceased to be isolated entities and became typical figures of a collective process. The characterization of the world took on a new coherence.

Later, in 1964, when the popular movement that would become the government of Salvador Allende in 1970 began to coalesce, three novels narrating the days of 1938 were published. Fernando Alegría's "Tomorrow The Warriors" (Mañana los guerreros), Luis E. Delano's "The Battle Roar" (El rumor de la batalla), and Guillermo Atías' "The Day's Shade" (A la sombra de los días) were the closing works of a rich period of apprenticeship and creation.

The realistic tradition now incorporated the innovative advances formerly reserved for Chilean poetry, especially the inspiring and visionary statements of Vicente Huidobro, Pablo de Rokha and Pablo Neruda. Novelists enriched their works by exploring the poetic possibilities of language. This was accomplished through a narrator who no longer merely described the world but who created a universe of multiple meanings. The narrated world became the space onto which the creative consciousness of the narrator was projected. In this way the literary work becomes simultaneously history and poetic adventure. This dialogue between narrative and poetry became the most outstanding feature of later Chilean literature. As a perpetually renewed symbol of this creative alliance, one can hear Neruda's song resonating in recent novels by two authors of the 1938 generation: "War Chorale" (Coral de guerra, 1979) by Fernando Alegría and "The Internal War" (La guerra interna, 1980) by Volodia Teitelboin. Neruda himself seems to haunt these pages in order to converse with the future.

In the 1960's and 1970's there were rapid changes in Chilean political life: the conservative government of Jorge Alessandri (1958-1964), the Christian democratic government of Eduardo Frei (1964-1970), and the so called "Chilean road to socialism" under Salvador Allende (1970-1973), followed by the military coup of 1973 with its dictatorship. Chilean literature, naturally, had to confront these political and social changes.

In the middle of the 1960's young writers like Poli Délano, Antonio Skarmeta, Ariel Dorfman, Carlos Olivares and others, began to give Chilean literature a new rhythm: a revitalization in which experiences and challenges are expressed in more uninhibited language. As opposed to the cautious rationalism of the previous generations, the new writers expressed their dreams of freedom and solidarity. It was an act of affirmation in which the individual is celebrated in a kind of Promethean expansion of the will. The exploration of a new aesthetic language —impulsive, irreverent, and deliberately disordered—came as the natural and necessary result of the exploration of the possibilities of living and dreaming a different world.

This new, vital literature has matured remarkably in recent years. Initially, these works were an open invitation to adventure, a shared experience perceived as a collective challenge. It is more important for them to expose in a poetic way the immediacy of life than to present a fixed interpretation of reality.

The military coup, however, paralyzed the cultural development of Chile. Most of the intellectuals and artists were forced into exile and those who continued to live in Chile had to confront censorship and the scarcity of literary outlets. In describing this situation with its new challenges, Antonio Skarmeta points out:

"For Chilean writers, liberty had been so obvious, so self-evident, it seemed a natural blessing. The precipitous loss of liberty, for whatever cause, means much more to a creator than mere deprivation of a certain dimension of civic life. Strictly speaking, this loss is essentially a metaphysical crisis. It demands of the poet a respiratory adjustment to a new climate, a response to the problem of trying to understand it and of trying to survive in it. Some writers stayed in Chile and continued to create within the frontiers of tension, managing to express their outrage in humor, metaphors and parables but in language that is exact. Others write in exile. Whether a text deals with love, nature, dreams, the city or introspection, one cannot help noticing in it an overwhelming sense of the finite, the impermanent, of incipient nostalgia, absurdity, risk. Our literature is becoming an exile *obra*, and not primarily in the geographical sense. The land missing under our feet—missing not only from under ours but from under those of our compatriots living in Chile as well—is nothing less than life itself, and the concept of life with which we grew up, confidently and spontaneously." *

Contemporary work from inside Chile comes either from underground presses or from government-sanctioned publications. The former literature is essentially testimonial and denunciatory; the latter is heavily metaphorical and symbolic, full of codes and allusions that the reading public can relate to the reality of Chilean life. Literature in exile must face equally tense obstacles and concerns: the dialogue with other cultures, the problems of translation, and, above all, the quest for meaning in the life of the Chilean in a foreign country.

All this recent literature, whether written in Chile or in exile, is the expression of a culture trying to fly in the same direction but with a broken wing. Those who write inside the country grow isolated from the international audience they want to address. The literature of exile has reached that audience but is evolving displaced from its natural habitat.

This paradox is stated in a recent issue of "The Bicycle" (La Bicicleta) a magazine edited, with great dificulties, by a group of young writers in Chile:

"The freedom of expression that the exiled Chilean artists enjoy is precarious if their work can express only the loss of the homeland. They face censorship in the sources of creation just as we suffer from a censorship of the ways we can express ourselves artistically. We need to ask for permission to express what we are experiencing and they need authorization to come here to live what they want to express." **

Immediately after the coup an impressive testimonial literature emerged describing the political repression and the life in the concentration camps. Among these works which explicitly separate themselves from fiction, the most widely

---

*Antonio Skarmeta, "Words are my Home," *Review* 27 (1980), p.8.

**Cf. *La Bicicleta* N. 5, Santiago de Chile, 1979, p. 16.

read are Tejas Verdes, 1974 by Hernán Valdés (already translated in several languages and "Barbed Wire Fence" (Cerco de púas, 1977) by Aníbal Quijada.

In contemporary fiction one can see development from an initial descriptive account of the new Chilean reality to another perspective that is searching for the deep causes of this historical nightmare. This process is clearly shown, for example, in the recent novels of Fernando Alegría, "The Chilean Spring" (El paso de los gansos, 1975) and "War Chorale" (Coral de guerra, 1979). Finally, this literature is incorporating the unique and complex experiences of life in exile that open new horizons for Chilean writers who have become exiled ambassadors of their country. They are finding a receptive public with whom to share part of that collective history retold in literature.

Translated by Steven White   Juan Armando Epple
                                             (University of Oregon)

CHILEAN WRITERS IN EXILE

Part I

The First Days

By Alfonso González Dagnino

Translated by Carmen D. Alegría

I

The car headed toward the mountains. Slumped in the back seat, Gormaz saw the mercury street lamps wrapped in halos of mist. Nicanor had already commented on the uselessness of their meeting, and Gormaz had responded that there was no way left to avoid the crisis. Every day they had the same conversation, with slight variations. The circumstances had given them a mutual trust that went beyond Party camaraderie.

"When the coup comes, I'm going to join the workers at the factory near my house," the driver had said, "at least I'll blow away a couple of fascists before I leave this world!" he laughed . . . "When the shit hits the fan, we'll need fighters, not bureaucrats."

Gormaz looked at the driver, and thought of the bureaucrats, sweating it out to prepare everything, organizing it all, and then paying the bill afterwards for all the broken dishes. "I'm a poor bureaucrat," he thought, amused.

"We're almost at your house," said Nicanor. "Shall we circle around once?"

"Yes."

They always did that when Gormaz came in late, to make sure there was no one suspicious around. He was getting bomb threats everyday. Not that he gave it much importance—the same thing happened to everyone in leadership positions. But he had to take some precautions. A little further up the street they turned and headed back to the house.

"What time shall I pick you up tomorrow?" asked Nicanor when they reached the iron gate.

"Don't come by. I'll go to the Ministry in my car. I want to get up a little later tomorrow," answered Gormaz.

Gormaz opened the gate as the car drove off. With his hand on the butt of his pistol, he checked around the garden, as he always did before entering the house. In the back yard, the swimming pool reflected the blue light of the colonial lanterns; along the wall, the birch trees looked like powdered masks. This was a place like any other where death could be hiding. Had things really come to this? He looked at the flowering peach tree; it was natural for it to be in bloom, but that thought hadn't occurred to him. A few petals had fallen and they made a circle of bluish snow around the tree.

"What's wrong?" whispered his wife through the living room window. "What are you doing there?"

He felt awkward at being caught by surprise.

"I'm coming," he answered.

When he walked into the house, his wife was back in bed reading an Agatha Christie novel; she was listening to radio station Magallanes. Lately they slept with the radio on because Magallanes would be the only station giving true information about the coup.

"Any news?"

"Nothing special," she replied. "In Bitacora they announced the new list of terrorist acts. That permanent complaining only discourages people."

She didn't ask where he had been, they had a tacit agreement that there would be no questions. Gormaz began to undress. He placed the pistol on the dresser, half out of its holster. He barely felt strong enough to take off his pants. All of a sudden, his wife let out a little laugh.

"What's so funny? What are you laughing at?"

"I don't know, it's just so grotesque."

Gormaz shrugged his shoulders. He couldn't tell if she was laughing at the political situation or at his bare ass. If it were up to him, he would have thrown himself on the bed fully dressed. It had been days since he'd slept. Putting on pajamas made him anxious and kept him awake. It happened every night, but there was nothing he could do about it. Then his wife would ask him, "What's wrong, are you sick?" That was even worse than not being able to sleep.

They listened to the voice over the radio: "This tango is dedicated to all the workers standing guard at the Summar Factory tonight—how's it going out there? Pretty cold, huh . . . "

The voice sounded comforting. "Everyone in the Party is on guard tonight," thought Gormaz, "one more night; let's see if we make it through this one." They turned off the light. Salinas had such a happy laugh! "You communists take everything on the bad side, man. We have a constitutionally established Army here, and your enemies are the extremists—MIR and the Fatherland and Freedom Party." He almost believed him. The Congressman's lip stuck out like a race horse's when he talked: "We're all in this game, and the name of the game is Democracy, that's all. We're the opposition, and we want to be the government; that's legitimate." His thick lips stretched: "Don't expect any help from us!"

But that was why they had come—for help. "We've come to begin a dialogue with you . . . " No wonder the opposition had found them so amusing. On the wall hung a portrait of Frei in his funeral suit, with his embalmed face. He began to perspire, and his heart beat violently. He knew that soon would come the feeling of emptiness in his sides, the terrifying sensation that time was running out. Fortunately, the psychiatrist had explained to him that these moments of anguish were normal reactions. "A little Valium or Librium, and you're on your way!"

He turned on the light and looked on the night table. He found the Valium and took a 10mg. tablet.

"Aren't you feeling well?"

His wife, propped up on her elbow, looked at him attentively.

"No; it's to help me sleep. I've been having a hard time falling asleep." He turned off the light.

"It's all this uncertainty," she said, "we'll lose our minds if things go on this way. Just waiting here with our arms folded for the fascists to do whatever they want!"

"We can't give in to provocations," he was about to say, but kept his mouth shut. She was right, after all. He changed the conversation. "How've the children been?"

"O.K. They did their homework and then went to bed."

Gormaz remembered that he hadn't been in to kiss them goodnight. "To think that I used to lie down with one on each side of me and read them stories."

The radio was playing Mexican music.

"What are you thinking about?"

"About tonight's meeting with the Christian Democrats."

"What was the meeting for?"

"To try to reach a truce, gain a majority and hold off the strike called by the Medical Association. We went with the Undersecretary and Juan Bravo."

She laughed again, "I can imagine the response . . . "

"Yes."

They were silent. Gormaz noted that the Valium was beginning to take effect. Something inside of him was loosening up.

"After the President made all the concessions that they asked for," he said, "they let the fascists continue the strike. Now they're saying that they can't help us because they are the opposition. You should have heard the Congressman talk about Democracy. Even their voices are phony."

4

"Doubletalk, that's all."

"Pluralist expressions," Gormaz corrected her, "Salinas has a picture of Frei with a dedication. When I asked him if Frei was also involved in the Coup, he laughed and said, 'You never know . . . that gentleman hides behind the door and only sticks his nose out when everything is ready.' "

"Cynical bastards!" exclaimed Maria Luisa. "Of course, you also have to be an idiot to go talk to them."

Gormaz didn't want to continue the discussion. Maybe his drowsiness had something to do with it.

II

The telephone was ringing insistently. Maria Luisa awoke with a start and looked at the clock. It was 8:15. She jumped out of bed yelling, "We overslept again! We can't keep these late hours every night. Children, get up, you're late already." She picked up the telephone. It was Tito asking if Alfredo had left for the Emergency Ward yet. "Hang on, I'll wake him up," she said. "Alfredo, it's Tito, he wants to know if you're going to the Ministry!"

Gormaz grumbled, "Tell him I'm just getting up and I'll leave right away." He headed toward the shower, his eyes half closed. The rush of hot water shook his whole body. The phone rang again.

"It's Tito again, and he wants to talk to you directly this time!" his wife yelled.

"Tell him I'm in the shower, that I'll be on my way in 15 minutes."

"He insists on talking with you now."

"Shit!" growled Gormaz dripping water everywhere on his way to the phone.

As he walked by, Maria Luisa explained, "He says he won't be able to call you back, the phone lines are jamming up."

He picked up the phone brusquely, "Hello Tito . . . I told you I was on my way."

"Asshole! Haven't you been listening to the radio? Haven't you heard the radio?" Tito's voice sounded exasperated.

"No, no I haven't heard anything." He realized then that the radio wasn't working.

"Downtown is burning up, gunfire everywhere, the big ones. Why don't you have the radio on?"

"What else?" he said. He wasn't about to start arguing about the radio right then. "So, it's begun?"

"It sure has begun." Tito was extremely excited.

"Did Carlos call you? What's happening?"

"That motherfucker hasn't called me! What'll we do?"

"Let's get together over at Fernando's."

"In how long?"

5

Gormaz paused for a moment to think, but he couldn't think of anything. "In an hour."

"O.K. Chao!"

He jumped back into the shower to get the soap off, shouting, "The Coup, The Coup! Mama, get the kids dressed and let's get out of here."

His wife was already moving fast. She went to wake up the kids who had fallen back to sleep. Without alarm in her voice, she said, "Don't be frightened. Go get dressed so we can leave immediately."

They began to cry.

"There's nothing to cry about. We have everything ready . . . remember we've talked about this, we have to get out of here because this neighborhood is full of reactionaries, and it will be taken over by them. Trust us to know what we're doing; now hurry."

The children got dressed as fast as they could. Maria Luisa wanted to turn the radio on.

"No!" shouted Gormaz, "We'd only be wasting time! We know what we have to do."

He finished dressing as Maria Luisa folded the blankets. Suddenly a thought struck her: the papers. They had forgotten the papers. She ran to the desk and pulled out a box that was hidden behind it. In it were three files. If they fell into the wrong hands, not only would they hang Gormaz and dozens of other compañeros, but it would also cause disputes within the Popular Unity.

She put the files into the fireplace then went out to the back porch and brought back a tin of paraffin. She tore up the files, poured paraffin over the paper, and lit it. A reddish flame with black smoke rose up. She moved the papers around with a poker—"damn papers won't light." She hadn't taken the files completely apart. She had to wait for the fire to die down to detach the papers and try again.

As Gormaz removed the skeletons of the charred paper, she tore up another file. The first section had their Party cards. They hesitated a moment before throwing them in the fire. After the cards came certificates, letters, address books, telephone numbers. Everything was in those files. They had put them together and classified everything ahead of time. Nothing was left in the house that could endanger them; not a single fragment of that dramatic three-year period. Again: paraffin, fire, poker.

"Papa! Soldiers are passing in trucks!" cried the little girl.

Maria Luisa opened the iron gate and started the car to warm up the motor. Gormaz stirred the papers a few more times. Just to make sure nothing was left. Now he felt a strange kind of peace. He got into the car. His wife gave him the driver's seat and he drove the car out of the garden, stopping at the path to close the iron gate with the same care he gave it on weekends when they went to the beach. It was Tuesday, but they could explain to any policeman that they were off to visit their parents, or some such thing. There were no visible packages, the children were in their Sunday best, and the pistols were in the little box under the seat, inaccessible to any routine inspection.

They took the road down through Las Condes, toward the center of town, driving at a medium speed, and careful to stay far to the right so as not to interfere with the military trucks on the road. At the Airforce Hospital, the Guards had already stationed themselves behind the gates. They wore berets instead of helmets, and carried only their machineguns. Maybe the heavy arms were on the roof. They turned into Kennedy Freeway, but the police had detoured traffic, and the cars were circling around to get onto the main road. Only there did they begin to realize that nervousness permeated the entire city. The cars shot by like bolts of lightning over the freeway. On the side of the road a number of cars had already turned over or crashed.

As they reached Archbishop Bridge, a string of cars held them up; dozens of trucks filled with soldiers were passing by on the sides of the road. When traffic started to move again, they crossed the Mapocho River and followed the line of traffic toward Las Lilas. They had studied the route beforehand, in order to be prepared for whatever obstacles they might encounter.

They had to make frequent detours, directed by soldiers and police. Surely the soldiers were isolating combat areas from the public, although no shots could be heard. The passersby didn't seem affected by the madness of the drivers. They walked more slowly than usual, apparently without any direction. As they crossed certain side streets, they had to honk their horn at crowds of little children playing ball. Gormaz was worried that they might have a problem with the car and end up stranded in the immense city; he drove very carefully. In this kind of situation everything seems to go wrong: the gear shift gets stuck, the steering wheel loosens, tires blow out. With all the broken glass strewn about from accidents, this last possibility was a real one.

They finally reached Gallardo's house as planned. His blind grandmother was waiting for them. Gormaz didn't get out; he urged his family off, his voice under control. The entire operation lasted only a few seconds. Just before leaving, he kissed each one good-bye.

He took the road through Santa Rosa towards San Joaquin, then he headed toward the main Boulevard: la Gran Avenida. He passed by in front of "Fernando's" place to see if anything was wrong. Everything seemed o.k. so he turned around at the corner, and stopped the car about half a block away. It was in a poor neighborhood of one story houses. Small groups of people stood around talking on the sidewalks: no one paid much attention to him.

He walked toward the corner. A woman in a red dress was leaning against "Fernando's" door. He walked through the door onto a little cement patio. An old woman sat on the stairs feeding soup to two little children. She said hello to him, and continued with her business. Gormaz didn't have any idea what he was supposed to do so he just stood there and waited.

"Inside there's a place to sit down," said the old woman.

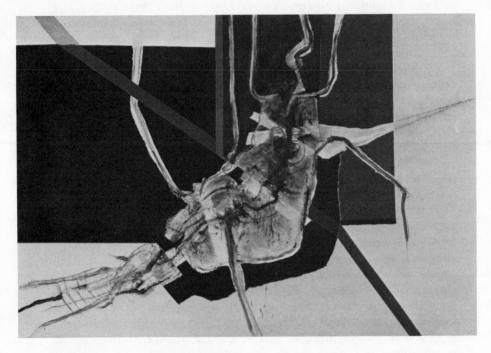

"Silent Mouth," acrylic on canvas by Guillermo Nuñez.

Gormaz entered a room without windows. He had never been in this house before. Through a door he could see a bedroom in disarray.

"Would you like a cup of tea?" asked the old woman from outside.

He gave a vague response. The room was cold and everything seemed so detached from his tasks that he didn't know where to begin.

"Has anyone been here?" he asked finally.

"No one, sir," answered the old woman.

"But I had expected a message!"

"Oh dear . . . " The old woman continued to feed the children their soup. At that moment, the girl walked into the room. Gormaz felt that he could speak freely with her.

"I was to meet two people here. Hasn't anyone been here yet?"

"A man came and left."

It was clear that they were being cautious; they didn't call him compañero.

"He didn't leave a message?"

"No."

"How long was he here?"

"Just a short while."

"Oh. Didn't he say when he'd be back?"

"He didn't say anything."

"How long ago did he leave?"

"Maybe ten minutes ago."

It must have been Tito who arrived before him. He had probably gone to talk to his people in order to save time and would be back soon. There was nothing much else Tito could do since he also had no other instructions. Carlos was bringing the instructions and Tito, from what Gormaz had gathered during their phone conversation, hadn't seen Carlos yet. There was nothing left to do but wait. He went to the door, "O.K. I'll have some tea."

"What a mess!" he thought. "But my only alternative is to wait." He smiled at the old woman. "I'm going to the corner for a moment to take in a little sun."

The old woman nodded her head.

On the corner was a newsstand with a small group of people gathered around it. He could see the headlines clearly. On the lower part of the stand the large red letters of "El Siglo" stood out. Across the page he read, "Each one to his combat position." "O.K." thought Gormaz to himself, "I'm at mine."

He circled around the newsstand. Inside, a boy straddled a wooden bench listening to a transistor radio. It was difficult to understand what came over the radio: maybe the mobile transmitters had been put into action, and perhaps they were giving orders over the radio. But Gormaz knew that his orders would come directly to him through Carlos. And even if the person who came had been Carlos, he'd still have to return. His job was to give Tito and Gormaz their instructions. Each person had his part to play in this thing, unknown to everyone save the person playing the part. They had taken all the necessary security measures.

"How's it going?" he asked the newsboy.

The boy shrugged his shoulders. "The big mess is on."

He looked at his watch: it was 10:30 a.m. Gormaz walked away.

A huge number of people had begun moving through San Joaquin toward Santa Rosa. Men and women in work clothes, the women wearing the typical woolen sweaters; they walked without talking. "They're going to work," thought Gormaz. But right away he realized what a stupid thought that was. "On the contrary, they're probably leaving work to go home . . . " Gormaz stood on the sidewalk with a group of onlookers, as the lines of people grew larger. Suddenly Gormaz recognized Mandiola—it was Mandiola for certain with his washed-out blue eyes and half smile. Mandiola approached him.

"What are you doing here?"

"Waiting for a contact who hasn't arrived . . . how about you?"

"I'm going to the newspaper offices. You're the first compañero I've run into. I'm coming from my house in San Bernardo. We were sent through Santa Rosa because they aren't allowing the buses on the regular route."

"What are you going to do at the newspaper offices?"

"Well, I'll wait to receive orders but I'm sure we'll be putting out an Extra."

"Are you crazy? Orders were not to go downtown. What kind of paper are you going to be putting out if the office is in the middle of a combat zone? You'd be better off not going down there. You'll create problems more than anything else."

"I'll have to go . . . we'll put out one page, something, even if it's on the mimeograph machine. What's the situation like?"

"Downtown there's open combat. But we have to act according to instructions, otherwise there will be confusion."

"Right, my instructions were to show up at the offices. Can you help me?"

"To show up at the newspaper offices in the middle of the fight is crazy," thought Gormaz. But then he said, "O.K. I'll give you a ride in my car, then I'll come back here. Let me go tell them at the house where I'm supposed to meet my contact." Gormaz walked away.

When he returned, Mandiola told him that Allende was in the Presidential Palace, La Moneda, and that he had announced that he would neither resign nor give himself up. That's what people were saying at the newsstand.

"It seems like they're going to bomb the palace," he added.

They looked toward downtown. Two aircraft were visible, taking dives over the same area, one after the other. They swooped down coming from the ocean-side and ascended again up by the Cordillera. They made a turn, probably toward the north because they seemed almost to disappear in the distance like two black dots only to return and repeat the same maneuver again, like a game. There were no sounds of explosions.

"They're getting ready," said Mandiola.

"It'll be easy to down them," replied Gormaz. "A cross-fire from a couple of machine guns could get them as they swoop down like that."

They went to the newsstand.

"They think they're going to bomb the palace," said the boy. "Lies . . . with two airplanes?"

"It was about time they knocked the shit out of that old shithead," yelled a young man with a violent look on his face.

Some people nodded their heads in agreement, others remained expressionless. The young man probably wanted to pick a fight and seemed very excited but nobody appeared to notice and he finally left.

"The old man will put up a fight," said Gormaz.

"They won't be able to get him out of there no matter how hard they try," chimed in the young newspaper boy.

They moved away.

"Our people are also preparing, that's for sure," said Mandiola.

Gormaz continued to watch the airplanes. Each time they dove, he expected to see only one return, or neither one, but that didn't happen. The distance between them didn't even change.

They walked toward the car. Gormaz extended the antenna and turned on the radio. They picked up instructions from the military: "Band four, we repeat, also we repeat Bands one, two and three of the Governing Military Junta." He nervously moved the dial to pick up another station. All the stations were carrying the same thing.

"They've taken over the radio stations," said Gormaz somberly, "there isn't even a sign of the emergency radio transmitter. And this guy never shows up! Who knows what the hell happened and here I am waiting!"

"Let's go to the newspaper offices," Mandiola said, "we have to make the best of our time."

They started the car and headed down toward San Joaquin. From that point they turned toward Santa Rosa in silence. On the corner a policeman was stopping traffic.

"The same thing is happening on Gran Avenida," said Mandiola. "We'll have to continue on foot."

Gormaz made a U-turn and they ended up facing Gran Avenida. "See you later," said Mandiola. "Be careful. They've begun to arrest people they consider suspicious. Don't stay on the corner."

Gormaz shrugged his shoulders. "The worst thing to do would be not to follow orders. Then everything would really go to hell."

III

At that moment, the workers were finishing up their preparations, and were talking amongst themselves. Some felt that the defense of the factory was dependent upon receipt of the weapons, others felt that if the arms arrived late, they could resist with what they had: a machine gun, fourteen pistols and a double-barreled shotgun. The factory was small, and access to it was difficult. Only one side of the factory had houses across the street that could serve as cover for the soldiers. The building was also surrounded by a high cement wall.

They climbed up onto the roof, and from there were able to keep watch over one of the access roads; it was on that road that the truck with the arms was to arrive. All the numbers they dialed on the telephone sounded busy, which confirmed that the weapons were being distributed to the most important factories at that moment. Two radio receivers had been keeping them informed, but now they paid little attention to them since all radio stations were in the hands of the fascists. The last broadcast they heard on Radio Magallanes had been Allende's speech announcing that he would fight until the end.

Nicanor had just arrived and was helping to board up the windows so that the soldiers couldn't throw tear gas canisters through them; he carried large bags of grain to barricade the front entrance and other places. He still had to go move the paraffin. Four compañeros were in the kitchen boiling water in huge cauldrons that later would be useful in treating the wounded and also as part of their defense to pour over the soldiers' heads. In the kitchen they had set up a small emergency room with a couple of tables with mattresses on top. Next to the improvised hospital beds, they had placed cotton, hydrogen peroxide, bandages, cough syrup and belladona. They had also taken everything from the clinic across the patio because once the exchange of fire started it would be impossible to retrieve anything.

As time passed, tension grew and protests could be heard about the late arrival of the weapons.

"All right," said the boilermaker who was acting as head of operations, "it's pretty clear: if you don't like it, then leave."

His attitude bothered the workers.

"No!" said one. "We all have to defend the factory come hell or high water."

"It's worse to have discontented people," insisted the boilermaker.

"So let's vote then," said a few men, "so everyone can express their opinion."

"Quit bullshitting," exclaimed the boilermaker. "Why does everything have to be decided by vote? Majority rules here, and that's that!"

"Well, that's what the vote is about."

"Let's get this over with," insisted others.

They called everyone into the patio. As they waited for the people on the roof to come down, some sat around smoking while others did calisthenics to get their circulation going. They had somber expressions on their faces, and although once in awhile a joke would echo from a small crowd, the laughter was short and cutting.

When everyone was gathered in the patio, the boilermaker explained that the issue they were voting on had to do with whether those who didn't want to fight could leave or not.

One worker said, "I'm one of the ones who wants to leave and I want to explain my reason to you. This factory won't last more than ten minutes in a confrontation with the army, I know because I did my military service. We should have the machine guns set up by now, the sharpshooters on the roof up front, and a system of communications functioning so that reinforcements can be requested when necessary, or a call to retreat if the situation demands it. What will we get out of burning down the factory if we can't get out? Nothing but being burnt to a crisp! None of the preparation has been done and it will be a slaughter. My compañera is pregnant and I have two little children. I'm willing to fight, but this is a deathtrap. They'll kill us all for nothing."

"O.K. We heard you out," said another. "This is no time for speeches. Let's vote."

"Those who support the motion to allow these people to leave raise your hands," said the boilermaker.

Twenty hands went up, among them Nicanor's and four of the women workers. Only eight workers didn't raise their hands.

The boilermaker was disheartened. "Man, some comrades we have here!" he said sneeringly, "they all cool down when the fire gets hot. We might as well all go home and take care of the kids," he paused. "Now those who will stay of their own free will, come what may, raise your hands!"

Twenty-six hands went up. Only the person who had spoken first and another man didn't raise their hands.

"Goddamnit," the boilermaker said after a long pause, "here we'll stay! Let's go. Each person to his task. We still have sacks to carry and paraffin to distribute."

The workers ran off to do their various tasks. They felt joy filling up their hearts. One of the women workers was there with her little daughter.

"Why are you crying, mama?" asked the little girl as they walked toward the kitchen.

"You wouldn't understand, sweetheart," she said.

Nicanor walked up to them. It was senseless for a woman to be there with a little girl under five years of age.

"Listen, compañera . . . " said Nicanor, "there's still time. Why don't you take the little girl home?"

"What for?" she asked raising her eyebrows, "it's just the two of us alone anyway. This way we'll keep each other company and we'll both feel more at ease. Anyway, one's fate is the other's fate, too."

Nicanor moved away from them understanding her intentions. Everything had boiled down to the nitty-gritty. He leaped over the three steps leading up to the building and began his task of distributing the paraffin. He started at the farthest end of the factory from the third floor on down. He would take the caps off the tins of paraffin then cover the opening with a wet cloth. At a safe distance he would leave the wads of cotton and a box of matches. The problem area was at the other end of the patio beyond the access door because it was not possible to reach that place under fire. He went to discuss the problem with the boilermaker who decided that one of the persons who had no weapon would be assigned to that task. The man grumbled, seeing that the possibility of recuperating the weapon of one of the wounded went up in smoke, but he obeyed.

Soon everything was ready and each was at his post. It was 11:30 a.m. The boilermaker ordered all the radios turned off. "Anyway, we aren't interested in any of the fascists' babblings." Finally, they raised the nation's flag above the iron gate. The two workers who had decided to leave said goodbye. The door opened and they slipped outside.

Nicanor stood by two compañeros posted next to the windows on the third floor. There wasn't a sound; the workers meditated as they smoked stocky cigarette butts.

They felt the sound of trucks. They thought it was the weapons arriving, but from the roof they were informed that it was four military vehicles.

"Maybe they're not coming here," commented one.

The trucks stopped at a certain distance. They spoke to the workers over the megaphones: "Attention, attention! Those of you in the factory: we will proceed to break into the building in accordance with orders from the Supreme Government. If there are people inside, come out immediately with your arms above your heads and nothing will happen to you."

Inside you could hear a pin drop. The announcement was made twice and since there was no response, the soldiers got off the trucks and approached the building flush up against the wall. From the rooftop and windows the workers opened fire. Three soldiers fell, and the rest retreated. A few minutes passed without a single shot fired. Afterwards, a few soldiers began to cross the street toward the houses in front, spreading out into combat positions. Pistol shots could be heard each time one of them crossed the street. Some shots had apparently hit their mark because blood could be seen on the pavement.

All of a sudden shots were to be heard from everywhere but especially from the houses in front of the two far ends of the factory. The soldiers had installed machine guns on the roofs and the crossfire grazed the building. Desperately the workers from behind the sacks in the patio pushed to get them closer to the wall to cover themselves.

The workers concentrated on the ends of the building so they could shoot at the machine guns. It was difficult because they were such a small target. Suddenly there was a jubilant uproar: a body could be seen falling over the front of the machine gun . . . the body was quickly moved away, and the machine gun was silenced. But the joy was short-lived: instants later, the fire broke out once again. Other machine guns fired now from the roofs of the houses in front.

A number of workers had already been killed and wounded. Those nearest by had taken up their arms right away. Nicanor had gotten hold of a pistol and some bullets, and had positioned himself at a strategically located window on the third floor. The woulded were taken to the kitchen by the compañeras.

Nicanor shot, aiming carefully. He chose the soldiers who were advancing toward the main entrance as his mark. He decided to wait until there were soldiers directly in front of him, in order to make sure he hit. He pulled out the clip and blew into the pistol, which had heated up with the last round. Then he loaded it again, and waited.

Nicanor peeked out through a crack in the window and his heart skipped a beat: just a few feet away and directly in front of him, three soldiers were hiding behind an open door. They had placed themselves in a hallway across the street in order to slip through the line of fire coming from the rooftop. They were waiting for an order to assault the side entrance. He aimed very carefully at the soldier he could see the best. He chose the chest as his mark and shot. Both the soldier's legs bent and he fell forward. Rapidly, Nicanor emptied his clip on the other two soldiers. Another one fell, and pulled himself into the house until he could no longer be seen. He couldn't tell whether he had hit the third one, too. Immediately, bullets hailed onto the window and he felt a dark blow, like a heavy blunt object on his left shoulder. He felt a strange sensation growing inside. There was no pain, though. He looked at his hand: a string of blood flowed onto the ground from his fingertips. He tried to move his hand and his arm, but he couldn't.

At that moment, the soldiers began their assault on the entrance. The shooting from the factory had slowed down considerably. With a spray of machine gun bullets they made a hole around the door lock, and pushed. A couple more rounds were fired at the hinges and that finally knocked it down completely. A number of soldiers ran in and were hit with shots fired by the workers barricaded behind the sacks of grain. Two or three fell, and others who closed in on the sides of the door were riddled with bullets. Screams and yelling could be heard as the infuriated soldiers shot from the patio at the building as they advanced on the few resisters who remained inside. The hunt had begun. The soldiers seemed to have gone mad; the workers were shooting from the hallways, but were falling from the bursts of machine gun fire.

Nicanor got up and walked to the corner. He poured three tins of parrafin out, took the wad of cotton, lit it with one hand, since his other arm hung immobile, and he threw it in the middle of the little lake. A huge flame went up. He didn't wait, but ran up the ladder they had set up to get to the attic. Right at that moment, he felt a first fainting spell. He was able to get to the top by leaning against the railing. His legs felt a little weak, and he was being overcome by a feeling of stupor. He put the small ladder away, and closed off the smooth ceiling with its cover. Then he went through the same motions with the paraffin in the attic. It took him a little longer this time, because it was harder for him to pour out the tins. The energy it took to throw the burning cotton wad made him faint. He made an effort and felt for his pistol in his belt: he had to get to the opening that led to the patio before the soldiers could get into the attic.

He felt better lying down, so he decided to drag himself along. He could hear the fire crackling behind him, and that comforted him. The distance was no more than 15 meters. He would stop to catch his breath only when absolutely necessary and then continue; he couldn't lose any time. As he passed the boilermaker's post, he saw him hanging head down, with his eyes open. The machine gun had fallen from his hands, and lay a short distance from Nicanor. He picked it up, made sure the clip had bullets in it, and then went on.

Outside, the soldiers had stacked up the bodies of the dead and wounded against the wall and had made the four compañeras, the little girl, and two surviving workers stand on top of the pile. A number of soldiers stood in front of them and seemed to be talking, although Nicanor could not hear them. He leaned the machine gun against the frame, aimed at the group of soldiers, and then emptied the clip on them. He dropped his weapon, and fell, half of his body hanging out of the opening. Cries of rage and machine gun fire could be heard . . . Nicanor's dead body was uselessly pumped full of holes.

A column of fire rose up from the other side of the patio, and a man could be seen crossing through the flames with his clothes ablaze. He was also shot full of bullets and fell dead at the feet of the soldiers.

"Leave them to me, Lieutenant," cried the soldier, "I beg you, please leave them to me!"

"O.K. damn it, everyone ready to shoot!" yelled the Lieutenant.

And the machine guns discharged over the group of dead and living, leaving a pile of arms and legs and blown-up heads. The body of the little girl couldn't be seen, it must have ended up covered by those that fell on top.

"And with that piss-ass bunch of weapons that they had, look at how many of our men they killed!" yelled the soldier.

"Lieutenant!" said a soldier who arrived out of breath, "they burned it down from behind, the flames are coming from the rooftop!"

"For the piece-of-shit factory it was, let all of those bastards cook in there with it!" answered the Lieutenant.

IV

After Mandiola got out, Gormaz drove the car back very slowly, since the streams of people had increased. At "Fernando's" there was no message, and nobody had been there.

He went and stood at the corner. Once in awhile he would take a walk to the street on the side, and sit down on a stone bench. He looked at the hour: noon. The airplanes continued with their pirouettes. Obviously, something unexpected had happened. "Maybe they got Tito and Carlos," he thought, "but someone should be coming with the instructions anyway." The thought passed through his head that he should be in one of the hospitals offering his services as a physician . . . the hospitals must be full of wounded people. But he knew that would mean a departure from the agreement they had made in the Party about his particular situation: immediately after the Coup, he was to go underground and wait for orders from the leadership. He kept repeating that word over and over to himself: wait . . . wait.

The others were probably in the same boat; "they must think I'm an idiot," he thought bitterly to himself. He got up and went back to the corner. Less people were going by now but the ones who *were* passing by, ran.

"Why are they running?" he asked the newsboy.

"They announced a curfew."

"Who did?"

The boy looked at him with distrust. "Who do you think? The Military, of course . . . "

"So, they're in control?"

"Are you stupid or something? Haven't you realized what's happened?"

Gormaz gazed distractedly at the boy. The planes were no longer visible.

"What time does the curfew start?"

"They said 6:00 first, but now they say 3:30."

Gormaz looked at the time. It was already 2:30.

"Is that why they're running?" He pointed at the people.

The boy didn't answer him. Gormaz went back to the house.

"Has anyone come by?"

"Nobody."

He went back to the stone bench. Now he was sure that no one was coming. He felt both a knot in his throat, and a sense of total indifference. His eyes filled with tears, and he thought about Maria Luisa and the children. His life seemed to be a dream. And Allende? Surely he wouldn't be captured . . . they couldn't kill him, obviously. Again he felt hopeful that his instructions were forthcoming.

There was no one on the street now. He looked at his watch: 4:30. Remembering the curfew, he walked back to the house only to find the door closed and locked. He knocked until the woman opened the door. She seemed very frightened.

"Don't you know what the curfew means? Anyone out in the streets after the hour can be shot on the spot. You better come in and stay in."

"Thanks . . . any message for me?"

"No! How many times have I told you that nobody's been here?"

Now it really seemed impossible that any instructions would arrive.

"I'm leaving. I'll be back tomorrow, so if anyone does come, tell them to wait for me or to leave me a message. I'll be back in the morning."

He went to the car, started it up and took off towards Santa Rosa. As he neared Gallardo's house, he pulled up to a corner and stopped. From there he went on foot. Gormaz knocked at the door. Almost immediately, the door flung open and Maria Luisa and the children seemed to be embracing him all at once.

"We thought you'd been killed," sobbed Maria Luisa. "It's 5:00 p.m. and the curfew started at 3:30 and they announced that anyone out past that time would be shot and killed."

"Calm down," he said, "I haven't been in any danger . . . I'm just a little late."

"You don't understand anything," said Maria Luisa. "You're in a daze . . . the Coup was successful . . . they killed Allende . . . they've been saying vicious things over the radio!"

"I know," said Gormaz, lying—"I'm really tired and want to rest for awhile."

He went into the bedroom. He lay down, pulled out his handkerchief, wrapped it around his head to cover his eyes so that he would be in total darkness, and then said to himself very slowly: "They killed Allende . . . we must understand what that means . . . they killed Allende."

V

He woke up with his ears burning and his feet cold. It was dark already. He could hear the sound of silverware tinkling in the dining room. In a low voice his wife was telling the children to keep their conversation quiet. Gormaz sat up on the bed for a moment and then stood up. He saw his pajamas, a ghost in the fog. He picked them up and studied them carefully. The world had caved in and his pajamas were awaiting him in the usual manner. It was funny. It seemed that the entire situation had created a strange kind of humor.

He walked toward the dining room. Everybody was at the table, including Gallardo and the blind grandmother.

"We made some soup," said his wife.

Gallardo smiled from the head of the table. His graying British Commander's moustache gave Gormaz a good feeling inside. His wife gave him a reproaching look and made a gesture, opening her eyes in the direction of the children.

"You know what the night curfew exercises are about," she said emphasizing the tone of her voice.

Gormaz thought about his wife . . . she was truly admirable.

"So where are the exercises to take place?" he asked with a crooked smile on his face.

"All over the place," explained Gallardo making a circular gesture above his head with his right hand as if to indicate his halo . . . "but they aren't taking it bad." He lifted his moustache.

"Ah ha!"

They heard a truck outside.

"It's the patrols," explained Gallardo.

"No—that's the sound of a helicopter," interjected the blind grandmother.

They all went to the window but couldn't see anything. Gormaz and Gallardo went to look through a skylight that opened up onto the roof. Sure enough, with red and green lights brightly lit, the helicopter passed by. Suddenly it threw out a bright spotlight and a huge area seemed to glow with the yellow light.

Shooting could be heard louder. The noise rang in their ears.

"It sounds like it's right next to us," commented Gormaz.

"Get down!" screamed Maria Luisa. "They're shooting this way!"

The men laughed. "What would they be shooting in this direction for? They're trying to scare people, that's all."

After a while, the light began to fade . . . Maria Luisa continued screaming at them to get out of the way.

"This is a good place for a lookout," they both shouted back at her.

"What are you going to look out for up there, you idiots?" Maria Luisa was angry now.

Gallardo and Gormaz paid no attention to her. "My boy sleeps up here," said Gallardo.

The light was completely out now, and the sky was pitch black. They came down. Maria Luisa and Gabriela were washing the dishes, and the old woman sat in the middle of the living room quietly listening to everything around her.

"Move over here, Mother," said Gallardo. "I'm going to light the stove."

Everyone sat around the stove now, Gormaz with his feet stretched out to take in the heat, and the children all rolled up in their blankets. The little girl sat on Maria Luisa's lap and the little boy on Gormaz'. They turned out all the lights; in the darkness, they could hear shots ringing in the night air . . . Gormaz felt his dry mouth and commented to Maria Luisa that he hadn't even been able to smoke his pipe—a habit he never gave up. They talked in low voices for a short time and then everyone went off to bed.

The next morning the government announced an extension of the curfew for another twenty-four hours. Gormaz thought angrily that this meant another day with no chance of receiving his orders but he didn't say anything. For breakfast, they had some dry bread and then went up to the garret. The children played on the back patio and Gormaz joined them in a ball game for a while. It was a beautifully bright, clear spring day. The sun was hot and burned the skin.

"Don't yell," said Maria Luisa. "The neighbors musn't know that we're here."

Suddenly three airplanes flashed past them with an infernal noise. They were bound due North and were apparently coming from El Bosque base. Shots could be heard from every direction; it seemed impossible to guess what the situation was out there.

"The planes are going to Summar," said Maria Luisa with a sense of sureness. "The workers are letting the Army have it over there," added Gallardo.

Gormaz slipped out into the street. If there were fighting all over the city then the curfew would surely go down the drain. He walked to the corner and stopped: not a person in sight. "What fighting?" he said to himself, gazing at the paved road, stiff with solitude. He turned and went back to the house.

Maria Luisa and the old woman were listening to the radio. The TV stations weren't on the air yet. All they could pick up were military broadcasts on the radio. Gormaz did his best to avoid hearing the radio . . . his uneasy conscience couldn't stand it.

"How long are you going to be listening to that bullshit!" he exclaimed.

His wife turned off the radio.

"So, there's nothing we can do about it now, eh?" Gormaz almost mumbled.

A moment passed and Maria Luisa got up. "I'm going to get lunch ready."

Someone banged at the door. It was Gallardo's wife back from the Gonzalez Cortes Hospital where she worked as a cook. With her was an orderly: both wore white uniforms and seemed in high spirits. They had hitched a ride on one of the ambulances to go to their homes and see how things were going and ask if there were any news. They told the household that as far as they knew, things were going well, that their Committee had received information that Allende was alive, although slightly injured. They said he was with the Palestros in San Miguel preparing a counteroffensive.

The discussion continued for a while with the newcomers contending that the tide would take a new turn in the morning and Gallardo joining in. Maria Luisa and Gormaz knew better. Soon afterwards, they returned to their work at the Hospital and Gormaz, Gallardo and Maria Luisa all agreed to get up early the next day: the curfew was to be lifted by 7:00 a.m.

The next day they got up early and had breakfast. At the sound of the clock striking seven, they were off into the streets to explore. It was agreed that only Gallardo and Gormaz would leave the house, and that upon their return, together with Maria Luisa, they would discuss a plan of action based on the information they had gathered.

As soon as they had walked a short distance, they could see that the car had been broken into. The police had obviously searched it, but luckily, the box with the pistols in it was intact. When Gormaz tried to start the car, the motor wouldn't even turn over. Upon closer inspection, they realized that electrical cables had been yanked out. In vain they tried to pair them up and reconnect them again.

"Man, what luck," said the British Commander. "All we've got is our feet now."

They locked the car and left it on the sidewalk, then headed up toward Gran Avenida.

In the distance, through the emptiness of the street, they could see a small black dot approaching. As it came nearer, they saw that it was a bus full of people. As the bus got closer, they saw that the people were soldiers, Air Force, and that they carried a huge machine gun on the top of the vehicle. The soldiers yelled something at them as they passed by, but Gormaz and Gallardo didn't understand what they said.

Suddenly each one felt the cold barrel of a machine gun at the base of their necks. Two cops had jumped out from behind a wall.

"And where are the little motherfuckers going?"

"To work," answered Gallardo with difficulty.

"Didn't you hear that the curfew was extended till noon?"

"No sir."

"O.K. wiseguys, on the double . . . go back where you came from before we crack you open."

Gallardo and Gormaz trotted away, their elbows bent and movements agile; they could feel the machine guns aiming at them.

"We better turn here," said Gallardo without turning his head, "or they might fall into temptation and blow us away."

They walked down a solitary street. Gallardo fixed his tie and wiped his face with a checkered handkerchief.

At noon they went out again. As they approached Barros Luco Hospital, they saw that it was being broken into. The bursts of machine gun fire and reports from the cannons almost made it impossible for them to exchange comments. The attackers were Air Force men—they were shooting at the entrance door to the Hospital and the wall right next to it, and they had reduced them to what looked like a strainer. They shot from the pavement or from behind cars that were blocking the street, and some were hiding inside the shrubbery in the park on the Avenida. Gormaz couldn't understand what was going on, since the door was open and no one was responding to the gunfire from inside the building.

"They're just trying to frighten people," said Gallardo, "see how they're just shooting into the air?"

At that moment, two airplanes flew over the Hospital almost grazing the rooftops. Gallardo and Gormaz felt it would be safer to walk on the other side of the street until they got downtown. From a corner, a group of soldiers shot a machine gun through the treetops. Gallardo and Gormaz stood next to them waiting for them to stop before passing. The soldiers looked at them with disdain.

"What're you doing there?" they asked.

"We're on our way to work," replied Gallardo, "we're waiting for you to finish so we can pass."

"Go ahead then," answered the man at the trigger, a little disconcerted.

From Avenida Matta, they went up toward Santa Rosa to see what was going on at the Food Distribution Center. The iron gates to the entrance of the Center were perforated with enormous holes, and the walls full of small pecks at regular intervals, from the very top to the very bottom. Through the windows, a big mess could be seen: furniture turned over, papers all over the place, burned curtains, and various objects still smouldering.

"Let's go to the Constructora," said Gallardo. "I have a key to the architect's offices. That's where our cell's documents are: it's best that we burn them."

"O.K. I hadn't thought about that."

It didn't look like the Constructora had been attacked, even though the doors were wide open. From the corner, a police patrol watched them go inside; they were posted to watch toward the center of town, and were heavily armed; they didn't pay much attention to Gormaz and Gallardo. They walked upstairs and opened the office. Gallardo pulled out papers, leaflets, old Party cards, some other material, and put everything on the table. Afterwards, he searched the drawers.

"What luck!" he exclaimed, "here's a whole carton of cigarettes!"

He filled his pockets with packs of cigarettes.

On the table were a number of notebooks with phone numbers in them so they called as many of their compañeros as possible, but nobody answered. Only Dummel from the National Health Service Archive.

"How're things going?" they asked him.

"Perfectly," replied Dummel dryly from the other end.

"And our people?"

"Each cell is active."

"We're on our way over there."

They went down to the basement and burned all the papers. This took a while because they had no paraffin and the plastic coating on the cards wouldn't burn. Finally, they left.

"You got away," said a man they vaguely recognized as they passed the corner, "the police were on their way to get you, but got called on the radio."

They decided to separate in order to draw away any suspicion. Fifteen minutes later, they met again at the corner of McIver and Monjitas. Gallardo turned right, and Gormaz went on to Forestal Park.

Gormaz decided to go to the Mapocho River and then turn back through Mosqueta before heading for their meeting place. As he walked by the Palace of Fine Arts, he saw a group of women who were yelling and laughing at the river's edge . . . he approached them. They had on dark "fly-like" sunglasses; some wore gloves and jewelry. Gormaz got nearer to the railing. What was provoking the screams and laughter were the cadavers dragged along by the water downstream. They floated by singly or in groups of two and three, bouncing like dolls. Their wet faces were blown off. Some were nude, and others dressed in poor clothing, sometimes patched with colored pieces of cloth, like a clown's outfit.

Gormaz saw, but didn't understand . . . that laughter, those dead watery bodies passing. It was a strange party. Suddenly he felt afraid . . . not of the dead but rather of those women. He left the place running.

"All of them without faces," he said to himself, "all of them faceless; all the dead fit there." He thought about Gallardo's son. At that moment he was passing the Ministry of Health. He lifted his head to catch a glance at his office, but instead of an office, all he saw was a huge black opening. Gallardo was just a few feet away, standing there waiting for him.

"You should see your face," said Gallardo. "Looks like you saw a ghost."

A truck passed, full of soldiers pointing their machine guns in all directions. Gallardo was surprised that all the cells in the National Health Service were still functioning and they had decided to investigate. As soon as the truck went by, they crossed over to the main entrance. A man with a dark coat emerged. As soon as he saw them, he opened his eyes wide and began to make faces. At the place where his pocket was he moved his hand about as if he were shooing away flies.

"Is it o.k. to go inside?" asked Gormaz in a friendly tone when he was a few feet away.

"Yes, but you can't come back out because they're arresting anyone that goes in." His lips barely moved as he spoke, and he walked right past them without even looking at them.

"We had better leave," said Gallardo.

They went off toward the Plaza de Armas. There were lots of people there, walking around as if they were in some kind of a ritual.

"These people can't go to work," stated Gormaz.

"No . . . they're our own people, looking for their contacts."

They joined the walk. Angelica was approaching from the opposite side; she joined them, and they continued going around in circles.

"We don't know what to do," said Gormaz, "we've lost contact with the Party."

"Orders are to show up at work," she responded.

"We tried to but we were warned that inside everyone was being arrested."

"In the morning it wasn't at all like that. Some compañeros went, but they came back because there was nothing to do there. We agreed to meet here to make contact and receive instructions."

"It wasn't a very original idea," chimed in Gormaz.

"They say that Dr. Marino was shot to death," she said.

Gormaz felt his heart stop.

"Someone brought the news from Barros Luco Hospital."

"It must have just happened."

"That's right . . . "

They kept strolling. People went around very quickly, they seemed to be in a hurry. While he was here being a tourist, his friend was being assassinated. These things are not easy to understand at the beginning.

Before leaving Angelica, they agreed to meet here every day at the same time.

"It's best that you don't go back to work until you can consult with the Party," said Gallardo, "you see what happened to Dr. Marino."

"Let's go to the Central Committee," said Gormaz in the same tone of voice he used when he was about to propose a serious idea. Gallardo agreed.

The Central Committee Headquarters had been destroyed. Black smoke came out of the windows. A pipe had broken and a gush of water flowed in front of the main entrance.

"Let's go to the Presidential Palace," proposed Gallardo.

What they saw at La Moneda was even worse. The only things left standing were the outside walls and they were covered with black smoky dirt. Inside, some large pieces of wood still smouldered . . . the roof was gone, and a few burnt beams extended into the emptiness like stiff fingers. Outside the main entrance there was a big pile of debris. People looked at the ruins in complete silence. Some older couples walked around arm in arm. Gormaz looked at them, trying to detect a gleam in their eye, a facial expression, something that would show that they were not robots . . . but he found nothing. The only thing they expressed was an oppressive, ugly silence.

They went back to Plaza de la Constitucion. Gormaz wanted to go to Allende's office, where they had met and spoken so many times, but the office had disappeared. "Maybe there's something left that we can't see," he thought to himself, and then, "as if that would change things any!"

They started back. Outside the downtown area, some stores were open and people were stocking up. At a cafe, two men were talking at a little table. There were no other people in the cafe and the men spoke very excitedly. He stood at the door to observe them more closely.

"Come on now, compañero, don't stand there like that . . . nobody likes to be stared at." Gallardo was a little surprised at his friend.

Most of the houses had put flags out, and all the neighborhoods looked as if people were celebrating Independence day. In the streets children were playing ball, taking advantage of the new school holiday. Some young people, large paintbrushes in hand, were painting over the Popular Unity slogans. They carried out their task with the same enthusiasm that young UP militants had shown as they painted the walls. The swiftness with which the marks of the UP were being wiped out was surprising.

They ran into a ragged old man who was half drunk. Gallardo said hello to him respectfully and offered him two cigarettes. The old man quickly hid them in his clothing. They talked about the weather. The first little heat waves were rolling in already.

"Maybe tomorrow we'll be over to see you, and then we can talk over half a bottle of wine," said Gallardo as they took leave.

"Who is that old man?"

"I don't know what his name is. They call him Don Filo. He knows a little about plumbing so he makes a living from it but he spends his time doing little more than drinking. The thing about him is that he knows everybody and can fill us in on what's happening here. I'm on good terms with him because I always send him a couple of beers or a good half-liter when there is cash on hand."

When they got home, they told Maria Luisa what they had seen but gave it little importance in order not to alarm her. They even joked a little in the middle of their talk about the robberies in broad daylight carried out by the soldiers at the Socialist Party Headquarters. It was funny to watch these soldiers, sweating like horses as they carried furniture and typewriters on their shoulders with their helmets still on and their machine guns slung over one shoulder. But Maria Luisa closed her eyes and wept in silence, a handkerchief covering her mouth.

"Is it true that they killed Allende," asked the children.

"No one knows for sure yet; that's only a rumor," replied Gormaz, "we just have to wait." He surprised himself by the optimism with which he had used the word "wait." "Lying is getting to be a habit with us," he said to himself.

That afternoon, two boys from the neighborhood came to pay them a visit. The fatter one had bulging eyes and talked incessantly, flitting his eyes back and forth from Gormaz to Gallardo. He was talking about the car; it was the soldiers who had tried to catch someone who was breaking into the car. The soldiers had chased him away with gunfire. It was better not to mess with the soldiers. Maria Luisa tried to change the conversation but the fat one kept bringing it back up.

"Well I guess it's because you aren't from here and that's why you don't know anything," he said. "This neighborhood is full of thieves. Where are you from?"

"Chillan."

"That's why. In the south, nobody steals. Now, in order to cover up they're saying that the car was full of arms and munitions and that the soldiers had shot it out with the extremists. When they found out that the car belonged to some of Mr. Gallardo's guests, they started a rumor that a communist doctor was hiding our with him. A communist doctor! You're not a doctor are you?"

"I'm an accountant," he answered. "I keep tabs on everything. Doesn't it show?"

The fat boy was startled. His companion didn't utter a word. Finally they both got up to leave saying goodbye. They went out and closed the door behind them.

It was Maria Luisa's opinion that they had come over to check things out and get whatever information they could use to nail them with.

"No," said Gallardo, "they were frightened. They're the ones who tried to break into the car and they're afraid that we'll press charges against them."

"Pluto is a thief," said the grandmother, "he always has been. He has always had the voice of a thief although now it has gotten much worse."

The next day they saw a foot sticking out of a little area of unploughed land. They thought it was probably a drunk but as they approached, they realized that it was a body full of bullet holes. The body was covered with blood and the head was completely destroyed.

"It's Don Filo!" cried Gallardo. "He has on the pair of pants I gave him last month. My God!"

"Someone turned him in," thought Gormaz, "it looks like the end is coming for lots of people . . . the informers have begun to spring up."

"We're better off leaving," Gallardo finally gave his opinion, "since there isn't much we can do and if we take the dead man with us who knows what kind of mess we'd be in."

The young people who had been painting the murals over in white had gone. It was surprising that they could be painting over such beautiful murals and that passers-by wouldn't so much as bat an eyelash. Gormaz and Gallardo understood that the reason was fear; the entire city was terrorized. If the policemen who had aimed their machine guns at the back of their necks had been in a worse mood, chances are they would have killed them right on the spot. Later on, their bodies would have appeared in some deserted area and people would have moved away immediately upon seeing them.

They did their best to avoid the police and Army patrols. Around the neighborhood people were saying that sometimes they shot for no reason. Angelica and other compañeros had warned them to be especially careful if they happened to come upon soldiers ransacking a place because they would surely shoot immediately. They had also been told by these same people that none of the Party cells were functioning at the National Health Service. There was no contact with the local committee but there were assurances that this tie would soon be re-established.

For a few days in a row they repeated these trips downtown without making much headway. At every chance they had, they would go by "Fernando's" but there was never any news. Finally, Gallardo recommended that they stop going: it was obvious that the contact had failed.

Despite the fragmented nature of the information, when pulled together it indicated some definite characteristics of the situation: uncontrolled violence, shootings, rapes, nighttime assassinations, cruelty toward foreigners, even toward children . . . these occurrences were in everyone's reports. Apparently, there were massive detention centers set up in two places: the National Stadium and the Estadio Chile.

Every day it became more dangerous to go downtown. Once, Gormaz found himself face to face with a doctor he knew who belonged to the fascist Fatherland and Freedom Party. They guy froze and Gormaz escaped into a crowd. On another occasion, a woman pointed a man out to a soldier. The man was walking just a few feet in front of Gormaz. The soldier shoved his gun up against the back of his neck and took the man away just like that. It had been a violent experience for him, a brush against death, right at his side. Later on he remembered where he had seen that woman before. She was one of the women who had been standing at the edge of the river watching the corpses float by.

Burning all the notebooks with telephone numbers in them had turned out to be a disaster: he could only remember two or three numbers, among them Tito's. But each time he called a woman's voice at the other end would say, in a cutting tone: "He's not here," and hang up. He tried to remember other numbers but his mind was blocked. He never had a good memory for telephone numbers, addresses, bank accounts or birthdays. He chided himself for that fault.

Rumors flew around the neighborhood. The assassination of Don Filo had caused them to multiply. Gallardo's wife, who had returned, told them that she overheard people at the store speculating that a group of extremist doctors were hiding at their house.

Gormaz and Maria Luisa understood that someone was sure to turn them in. She thought they should call Juan Bravo, whose phone number she remembered, so Gormaz called him. The situation was forcing them to move on; they had to find another place to stay. They agreed with Juan that they would meet the next day.

They decided with Gallardo to keep meeting at the Plaza de Armas: probably the meetings would be with Maria Luisa instead of Gormaz . . . it was safer. The contact with the local Committee was essential if they were to know what to do. Gallardo wasn't sure whether he should show up at work or not, but in any case, he was not a well known communist. Maria Luisa thought it would be a mistake to go since sooner or later he would be turned in. Who didn't know the communists in every workplace and neighborhood? Their names were published even in the local press . . . it was impossible to suddenly become an unknown person especially for people who had played a role in the UP government.

The day they left, Gallardo took him aside. "Compañero, I know I don't have to tell you this but you know you can always come back here. We will receive you gladly no matter what the situation.

"Thanks," said Gormaz.

"What's going to happen to my boy? I haven't heard anything from him since the Coup. Since we saw Don Filo, I haven't been able to stop thinking about him. My mind's a little mixed up, compañero. After everything that we've seen, it's as if we didn't exist any more. I don't know exactly how to explain it but sometimes I have that sensation. I don't talk about this with my wife . . . she cries every night about our boy. And now, on top of everything, you're leaving too. What am I going to do if they have killed my boy?"

Gormaz suddenly felt that this man was his brother. "What can we do . . . ? I also feel sad at leaving you . . . we were keeping each other company but life pushes us forward. We've lived through some strange days, like dreams. The world turned upside down." Gormaz put his arm around Gallardo in a friendly gesture and said to him, "Your son will return again for sure. You have to have everything ready for him when he returns." He felt that he was about to weep but he continued. He saw hope begin to glow in Gallardo's eyes. "And by the time he returns, the Party will be reorganized. By then, it will already have taken the offensive and we will all be pushing forward."

"Yes," said Gallardo, "we musn't give up. I'm going to do what you have suggested. I'll go South with my son. Then we'll come back when it's time to deal with these bastards. That's right, we have to begin preparing ourselves right now."

Gormaz stretched his hand out to him, "Chao . . . "

"Chao," said Gallardo and stretched out his hand. "We'll see each other again."

VI

The buses moved through the city full of people with expressionless faces, while soldiers with machine guns looked into the buses as they passed. Gormaz couldn't understand why there was so much surveillance.

"They took the counteroffensive rumor so seriously," he thought, "and they were so stupid."

In order to take the bus on Irarrazabal St. they had to cross Bustamante Park on foot. There they ran into Arcadio and his friend taking in some sun. They had been going to the same place every day in search of a contact. Viola told them how a police officer had said, "It never occurred to us that this would be so easy. We even felt badly about arresting the leaders. They're falling like flies. And as far as the possibilities of resistance go, how can there be a resistance if there are no organizations left, and all the leaders are being killed?"

"Only the international situation continues in our favor," she added.

Juan was waiting for them and took them home in his car. He was a bachelor and lived with his parents who spent the greater part of the year in Osorno, where his father had large investments. The house was a beautiful Spanish mansion with a huge park surrounding it. Juan bemoaned the fact that all the servants had left so he had to do all the housework.

They all went to sit down in the living room filled with antique colonial furniture. Juan was a bit tense and went to prepare some cocktails. Gormaz, following what was almost a habit, went into the library.

"Juan," said Gormaz, coming to the point. "We're on the run. We aren't sure yet whether anyone is on our trail but we think it's better to hide. All kinds of people are being arrested."

"I think that in your case, it's a good idea," said Juan. "They hate you at the Medical School. My case is different. My only political activity has been to work at the Commission for the Distribution of Milk. If there were any misunderstanding it could be cleared up rapidly."

"Who's worrying at this point about clearing up misunderstandings?" said Maria Luisa.

"Well," said Juan, "I have supported the government because it gave milk to the children. I would have done the same with any government. I was temporarily laid off my job, but I'm going back on Thursday. People are very frightened and sometimes they exaggerate," he said, "but I have nothing to fear. I haven't done anything wrong."

They remained without speaking for a few moments.

"I don't like the faces of the Military and I don't like people's silences either," said Gormaz. "Behind both there is something terrible."

Juan felt weak. "Yes," he said, "it's true. It's hate . . . my father went upstairs to have some champagne while the Presidential Palace was being bombed. My father—you know him—was always a good man."

"We don't want to put you in a spot," added Gormaz, "but there just aren't very many houses where we can go. There's really just you and my father but it's much more dangerous at his house because all of his friends are fascists and so is he . . . in theory only; he's 77 years old. That's why we're better off in this situation. What do you think?"

"I gladly welcome you into my house and I will protect you insofar as the situation is under my control," said Juan with a kind of violence.

Gormaz just shrugged his shoulders. "We'll just have to get used to this," he replied, "we'll stay till tomorrow, and then we'll be taking off."

"I'll call Jeronimo, maybe he'll have some ideas," said Juan.

He returned right away saying that Jeronimo was on his way. Just then the front doorbell rang. It startled all of them. Juan went to the window and peeked through the curtains.

"It's Marcos Villarroel," he said. "He told me he would pay me a visit."

"Try and get some information out of him," said Gormaz, "ask him if they killed Marino."

"O.K., but hide. Make sure the children don't come out."

Both men went into the living room. Villarroel noticed the glasses on the table. "Have I interrupted something?" he asked.

"No, just a couple of friends who left a moment ago."

Villarroel sat down looking around the room very slowly. "This really is a beautiful house," he exclaimed. He radiated an almost aggressive calm. Then he glued his eyes on Juan. "Juanito, you had better cut out the social life. Remember you are under house arrest."

"The professor didn't say anything about that."

"I'm the one who's telling you now." The "I'm the one" seemed pretty decisive.

"Why are you here then if I'm under house arrest?"

"Don't be difficult Juan . . . and don't get off the track. I can go wherever I want. I respect you and I want to help you but you have to do your part."

"I suppose I can see my family."

"Naturally. They are honorable people. But you can't receive any other people. Don't think about having anything to do with Gormaz. That guy's a dead man." He made an expressive gesture. "They'll let him have it wherever they find him. If he calls you on the phone, don't answer."

"Are they looking for him?"

"Why do you want to know?"

"It's just a question . . . so they will continue with the killing then. They already killed Marino and he's only a technician."

"Yeah, only a technician in the underground hospitals. Besides I can assure you that he has not been killed yet. He is under arrest and will have a trial. This government respects legal procedures. Think about what I have said to you and show up on Thursday. I have to leave now."

After Villarroel had left, Juan sat and drank down his cocktail. Gormaz and Maria Luisa came back into the living room.

"Jesus," Juan said after a while. "I thought I wouldn't be able to keep my cool."

Soon afterwards, Jeronimo arrived. "I suspected that there was some important person here," he said happily. "Juan spoke to me of a seriously ill patient and of a doctor's meeting. We all talk in code now over the phone. If the soldiers are listening, they're going to think that half of Santiago is sick." He rubbed his hands and looked directly at Gormaz, "And you haven't asked for asylum yet? This is fascism! People spoke of fascism but they didn't know what it was. I'm Jewish though and I do know. The ovens are the conclusion of a process that starts slowly . . . each day a little turn of the screw. Initially, people are terrified . . . then they get used to it until they get to the ovens. There's another wave of persecution coming very soon and if we don't get caught in that one we'll surely go down in the next. We have to take advantage of time while we're free. To-morrow I'll start dealing with the passports and then we're leaving this country. What we have to do is buy dollars and get the hell out of here. There's nothing to do here now . . . the Popular Unity is wiped out. Fascism has no future. They still believe in Santa Claus. They called us all to show up on Thursday but I'm telling you we'd have to be really simple minded to go. They'll catch us all! Me, just for being a sympathizer of the Popular Unity and having voted UP in the elections. For not having participated in the Medical School strike, or anything else. I've told Juan. But he's truly naive. He thinks the soldiers aren't bad. Try to convince him! And as for you, take asylum immediately."

"I hadn't really thought about taking asylum," said Gormaz. "First time I've heard anyone talk about it. In any case, it's pretty sad to understand that you are nothing but dead weight. To abandon what you love is like destroying your-self and then in addition, fill out forms, ask for interviews with the Ambassador and deal with bureaucracy even in defeat."

"You're crazy. All you have to do is go to the Embassy and knock on the door for them to let you in. Otherwise, to seek asylum would be meaningless.'

"Do what you have to," said Maria Luisa. "We can't lose anything by getting prepared."

"Come to my house on Thursday, early morning. I'll spend the next two days making all the necessary arrangements for the both of you and for myself. Are you staying here?"

"No," said Gormaz, "just for tonight and tomorrow we'll be staying at my father's house."

"I'm not going there, I already told you," said Maria Luisa. "And my children aren't either."

"So what are we going to do then?" asked Gormaz, "can you tell me where we're going tomorrow?"

"I have no idea, but I refuse to go there." Her eyes were glistening with tears of anger and sadness.

"Don't say another word. Tomorrow, Maria Luisa and the children are coming to my house. Two beds are enough for you aren't they? And anyway it's better for you not to be together in the same place." Jeronimo seemed to be in control of the situation. He was making decisions for everyone.

VII

When Maria Luisa went out in the morning to meet Gallardo, she had decided to talk to him about the possibility of seeking asylum for her husband, herself and the children. Maybe a contact had already been made. They met at the corner of Plaza El Portal. They walked through the center of town without much concern. The city had returned to normal within a few days. People were having coffee at the soda fountains and others were out doing their shopping. Miraculously, what had been missing in the stores before the Coup suddenly appeared in abundance. It was a kingdom of abundance. Some were shopping with a radiant expression on their faces while others looked deathly somber. If at one moment it had seemed that the scarcity was artificial now here was the real proof. But nobody wanted to think about it: here was everything people had needed for so many months and could not find. Gallardo and Maria Luisa watched the spectacle.

"It's a circus," she said. "Let's have the clowns come out now."

"Let them laugh," said Gallardo. "Let them laugh at their own jokes while they still can, damn it. Because we'll take up our struggle again, and we won't stop until we've blown all their heads off." Gallardo spoke with assurance and all his movements revealed energy and conviction. He had shaved his moustache and dyed his grey hair; he looded noticeably younger. "It won't be easy for us," he continued, "but in the end, we'll get rid of every last trace of them. The military won't be able to last indefinitely. We'll meet face to face. I just want to be alive for that moment."

Maria Luisa felt perturbed. She found before her a force she had not encountered since the Coup and for the first time she doubted that taking asylum was the right thing.

"He's a worker, and can go by unnoticed," she was thinking about Gallardo. But then she remembered that the National Stadium and the barracks were all full of workers. Finally she came to the conclusion that even after having considered all of this it was still right to leave and she felt happy because afterwards there would be no doubt in their minds no matter what conditions being in exile brought about. It was in this spirit that she broached the subject with Gallardo.

He agreed to consult within the Party, despite the fact that this type of request took time to be answered. It had been just recently that even the local committee had been contacted and the Party was having to deal with a myriad of things. Maria Luisa understood that a real militant would have to resolve many things alone now without consulting the Party. She said this to Gallardo who was in agreement with her. "Even the question of asylum," she said.

They said their goodbyes agreeing to meet the next day. But Maria Luisa did tell him that the issue of seeking asylum might affect the picture sooner than they thought depending on what opportunities arose, and on what Gormaz finally decided. As she watched Gallardo move away into the crowd, agile as a boy, she felt an unexplainable joy and tenderness.

When she returned, Alfredo was talking with Veronica. They were concerned about Jeronimo. Despite the fact that he had warned everyone of the danger involved in going, at the last minute he had decided to go to work himself, just to witness whatever happened. At that moment they saw his car approach. Jeronimo jumped out of the car and came into the house almost running, as was his habit. But his eyes were full of tears.

"They attacked the hospital!" he said in a low voice. "They told me that the soldiers have put all the Popular Unity people to one side. But I was able to escape. As I approached the building I ran into a Christian Democrat who is an intern there and he warned me not to go inside. Some other people told me that Saavedra and Fuentes had a list of doctors and other personnel and were pointing them out to the soldiers. Among them is Mrs. Muñoz, the surgical nurse. They were turning their compañeros in! They have all of them against a wall in a corner of the patio; that's where all the workers are assembled, their legs wide open and their arms behind their heads and they are beating them, and shouting insults at them. Juan is one of them. They beat him savagely; he's really bleeding. The intern told me that they're taking all of them to the Stadium. But we warned Juan, we warned him!"

Maria Luisa cried with anger, "Slime! They'll pay for this."

Jeronimo took Gormaz aside. "The situation is extremely bad . . . much worse than we can imagine. They're combing the city. Now they're looking for me too . . . our time is getting shorter. I'm leaving Saturday with all my family. But I want to leave with a passport. You too, you can't lose a moment. The Ambassador is waiting. I've got everything arranged. Here are the aprons and the medical kit. I'll tell you the plan on the way . . . the Ambassador himself worked it out. He's a wise old man who's taking all kinds of risks to save a great number of people. Who would have expected that of the Ambassadors? Not all good has vanished from the face of the earth!" They got into the car swiftly. "The success of this mission depends upon us acting with absolute calm . . . "

On a streetcorner the Ambassador was waiting in a very luxurious car. He had the children get in next to him and put Gormaz and Maria Luisa in the back seat. He told them to put the aprons on. They had barely said good bye to Jeronimo when the car took off. As they arrived at the Embassy, Gormaz felt goosebumps all the way down his back. There was a strong force of armed guards at the door and a little ways down, there were a couple of tanks.

The Ambassador stopped at the gate and descended from the car with dignity. He opened the back door of the car.

"Here we are, Doctor. Come along with me."

A sergeant approached. The Ambassador didn't even flinch. He walked straight toward the door and opened it.

"This way, Doctor." They walked in with composure. The Sergeant didn't dare ask any questions.

"Señora Maria Luisa," exclaimed the Ambassador, "bring the medical bag and the stethoscope."

Maria Luisa got out of the car quickly. She was wearing a Red Cross uniform and carried the doctor's bag in her hand.

"Don't forget the stethoscope," called Gormaz aimiably from inside.

She turned around and walked toward the car as if she were walking on a cloud. She picked up the stethoscope like a sleepwalker, thinking only that this was another example of her husband's sadistic sense of humor. The soldiers opened the door for her and right behind them came the Ambassador.

"They'll just be here a moment," he said courteously to the Sergeant.. "The last woman who took asylum has just had a fit of hysteria. Come with me," he said to the children, "we'll see whether the peach trees have flowered yet."

When he returned alone after a few moments, the Sergeant approached him respectfully.

"Will the Doctor and his wife be much longer, Mr. Ambassador?"

The Ambassador looked down at him from the hierarchies of the Diplomatic world.

"As long as is necessary, Sergeant . . . as long as is necessary. I provide the best possible medical attention and the best doctors for those who have taken asylum in my Embassy. Please inform your superiors of that. Good afternoon, Sergeant . . . "

"Yes sir," said the Sergeant, and lifted up his hand in a salute.

Of Flights and Abidings

By Juan Armando Epple

Translated by Stephen Kessler

The streets were beginning to fill up with honking horns, squealing brakes, shouts of vendors, people passing from here to there in a nameless hurry, for one more day that didn't know what to do with its air, still cold. Only the little square retained something of that provincial intimacy he was already homesick for, scarcely two weeks in Santiago and he still hadn't seen any of the important places the others had told him about on their return, putting on airs and looking down on the uninitiated. The light turned green and he waited a moment to see if anyone else was crossing. No, he had to go it alone, without looking at the line of cars with their menacing motors, but moving with an absentminded caution that only relaxed when he reached one of the iron benches in the square. One time I was caught in the middle of the Alameda when the light changed (Catullus had told him, raising his eyebrows), and you know what you have to do then? (said Oscar, a fencer of sorts), you'll never guess, you have to stand dead still, not even wiggling your ears, and the cars just whiz by, missing you, see?—till they all pass and leave you an opening, okay, I did it like that (Catullus, grumbling), but you don't have to theorize so much: just hold your ground in the little wind be-tween the machines.

He opened his shirt a bit to let the sun come in and warm the hairs that were starting to sprout on his chest. The breeze carried dirty papers and dust, and the pigeons seemed to run happily after their first crumbs, totally detached from the few passersby wandering across their territory. Suddenly a helicopter appeared in the sky, he couldn't tell from where, it made a couple of passes as if looking for some point in the city to set down and then flew off. To kill time, he went over his little mental, outdated tourist list: the Diana games, you have to be care-ful because it's full of fags and mafiosos (Oscar again), Santa Lucía hill, take a good-looking girl and show her Santiago naked (Catullus, who thinks he can get them anywhere), the Cinerama Theater, it's like being part of the show, or the Zoo, only watch out they don't mistake you for an animal and lock you up (Gringo, witty as ever), a soccer game at the National Stadium, the Alameda, psst, but in the afternoon (Catullus, inclined to invent another story), you always see weird things going on there, and don't forget the old bookstores on San Diego street (Gringo, jumping to entrust you with what isn't there). But from there, sure enough, had come *The Magic Mountain* and the mile-long volumes of *Jean Cristophe* which his father persisted in making him read when he went each sum-mer to the isolated place the old man stubbornly kept as a house, there in the South, and that could have been a field of juicy alfalfa to chew absentmindedly watching the German girls going by to tan their delikatessen on the beach—a fish-ermen's cove when the haddock were running or a regular graveyard if it started to rain. And you really set in to reading that? (Gringo, ordering a beer in the Viennese), I didn't have to, but I used the covers to throw him off the trail, be-cause the old man didn't know I'd got hold of a copy of *Lady Chatterley's Lover.*

Uneasily nostalgic, he imagined his father glued to the radio, or wandering along the dock in search of some boat that would take him upriver to the Tru-mao post office. He wanted to tell him that the coup had been more terrible than many people suspected, to speak to him of the roar of the planes and the bombs, of Chicho Allende fulfilling to the letter what he'd already written, only by filling me with bullets will they obstruct . . . , the three shut up in his sister's house, the ones who fell fighting desperately and were then just one more number in the ten-dentious count of the military gangs, and of the strange impassiveness of this city he was visiting for the first time, and which he knew was not the same as it had been. But he wrote only that everyone was all right and that he would return south soon—he was missing classes.

He stopped to stretch his legs, holding the book with the beaten-up blue cover inside his jacket. He walked toward the corner, trying to retain the image of some old buildings—tell me about skyscrapers, the electric buses that went by throwing sparks off the overhead cables, San Cristóbal hill with its virgin on top, a bit blurred by the smog, tell me about skies, Mapocho Station raised at the end of the avenue like a cathedral covered with soot. He let himself be carried along, in-different, behind the figure of a girl who stood out in the crowd and disappeared

too soon. If you come to Santiago don't forget to call me so we can go out together. And then, tender and theatrical: let's say goodbye here, in the middle of
the countryside that taught us how to be happy, I'll never forget this summer, will
you? This nature so far from the city's alienation. Luckily the months pass quickly, another summer and we'll relive this love under the same sky. Dice thrown for
romanticism's sake (Gringo, sure of himself), and did she write you? The only
thing she sent me was a stupid record, the kind they put out in the bourgeois era,
you know, on the beach, your skin tasting of salt, the sea gulls and the other cli-
chés. And how did you take it? You know, man, one gets used to these things. . .
the playboy has to take it lightly. Although, to be honest (another beer, on me)
the first few days I was a bit knocked-out, because the truth is I still liked her. It
can happen to anyone . . . besides, she had that way of acting amazed at everything she saw, with those little gestures that seem so important. Dropping a few
strong words of course that leave you sort of stunned. Always the same wave:
they come south to discover the wonders of the country, bored with the capital,
their heads full of canned landscapes (Gringo's meditations), man is a naturally
unhappy creature (Oscar, picking up the philosophical drift), a collective change
must be proposed (Catullus, pissing, missing the urinal), okay pals (Gringo, noticing his glass is empty), so the compañero explained his summer disappearances,
and in short: he made out better than we did, who hardly laid hands on home-
fries, after all.

Standing in the middle of the little square, forgetting the surrounding noises
for a moment, the lines that had seemed so right he'd memorized them once
came back to him: *Your presence is far off, strange to me as a thing.* / *I go over
my life before you.* / *My life before no one, my harsh life.* / *The cry facing the
sea, among the rocks,* / *running free, crazy, in the sea spray.* / *The sad rage, the
shout, the sea's solitude.* / *Broken loose, violent, stretched toward the sky.*
He started reading the signs on the buses, looking at his watch now and again, as
if to justify waiting. The streets showed no particular movement, nothing special.
He took a deep breath, expanding his lungs to get a little fresh air, and again he
had the sensation that he'd somehow flown off course, that he'd fallen into a cement valley where the people and things were dragging themselves against the
grain of life, in a thick formless swarming: unsmiling faces, trees in a daze of dust,
footsteps crumbling in a rush to get nowhere, loose sheets of newspaper blowing
around. I came to Santiago at the wrong time, he thought, and with my luck it
looks like I've come to the wrong square.

Then he saw the cortege. Coming out of a side street he hadn't seen like a little
shadow disoriented by the traffic on the main avenue and then finding the right
course, it was coming along in a slow undulation which little by little allowed the
black train to be seen, covered with wreaths of flowers, and behind it the heter-
ogeneous group of workers, women, students, and a lot of others, whose pictures
he'd seen in the papers.

With sudden fear he noticed a police patrol following the procession at a slight
distance, carefully driving their big motorcycles, stopping to look back and setting

their boots down indifferently, as if their only concern were to open the way for more of these people who march down these streets toward some transcendent appointment, to be applauded and forgotten. But here there must be others in plain clothes, he thought, locating people and taking pictures. He began to walk along the sidewalk, at a distance that seemed perfectly ambiguous, looking at the people as one observes some gratuitous fact, one more curiosity among those a person can be struck with in any city at any time of day. He tried to ignore the butterflies in his stomach, but his attempt at whistling sounded stupid.

In the first row he recognized the redhaired woman, whose wide smile, large teeth and firm, fleshy lips, had appeared in numberless photos during the poet's last years. Everyone knows her name, he said to himself. She walked with a certain assurance, her hair falling slantwise across her forehead, revealing an absent look in her eyes. She hasn't had time to cry, he thought. He imagined her wandering through the house, among the windows smashed by the military thugs, picking up ruined books or cracked sea shells. He also noticed another woman in mourning, who at times stepped out in front of the second row and with a hoarse voice, almost shouting, recited long fragmentary passages he couldn't make out, but they seemed to be pieces of the kinds of stories that people would know in the markets or public squares. She was a short brown woman, with thick glasses that made her gentle and at the same time energetic face appear more round than it was. He figured she must have grown children, that she washed clothes in a trough, and that she must be well known and admired in her neighborhood. He couldn't guess what her work might be, but he was sure she'd lived every year of her life, that she'd read other things and she wasn't afraid.

When the cortege reached the next corner, stopping while the police diverted the flow of traffic, he took advantage of the momentary confusion to join the line and mingle in among the crowd like a bird. He looked at the people beside him, but everyone seemed to be concentrating on the van at the head of the march, and that had started moving again flanked by the police motorcycles. At first the group had appeared fairly small, but being inside it he felt it growing and branching out with people who leaned out their windows and then came out and closed the shutters, or with those who followed along for a while, walking along the sidewalks like indifferent passersby, and then got lost on some corner, surreptitiously looking around. He put his hands in his jacket, feeling the book. Then he felt a hand softly toughing his shoulder.

"What's that you've got in your pocket?"

He looked around mistrustfully, and saw at his left a man who gave him a wink and then threw a careless glance toward the front rows.

"It's a book," he answered, not looking at him.

"By the poet?"

"By the poet."

"It must be one of the ones that's not banned. That you can carry in your pocket without any trouble."

"It's the twenty love poems." He tried to answer without getting tangled up in the adolescent shame that gripped his kidneys.

"It's a fine book," his companion said, softening his voice. And smiling at him: "A book I read once just like you: I've been in love too."

He scratched his nose and took a good look at the man. He was wearing a dark suit, fairly old but carefully pressed, a white shirt with a folded lace front and a thick dark necktie. His face, very tanned and with strong lines that smiled when he squinted his eyes, showed a man who's worked in the open air and whom no one takes into account. He thought he must be a construction worker, a stevedore, a merchant seaman. He noticed the man was moving with an uncomfortable seriousness, with his thick stubby hands crossed near his waist, as if posing for a photograph, and he thought of an 18th of September, of little kids waving balloons and little flags in the park while the older folks went looking for a place to eat.

"But I'm not," he defended himself. "It's just a coincidence I'm carrying it. Besides, this is no time to be walking around thinking about girls and praising their pretty faces ..."

"There's always been time for everything," the man said to him, as if speaking for his own benefit, "the important thing is to know how to live it. And the poet has a lot to show us about that."

They went along in silence. The sky cleared up in bits and pieces, with clouds scribbling over the ashen layer of air till a little sunlight came through.

"Where are you from, if you don't mind my asking," his companion said suddenly, continuing the dialogue—"I mean, before the coup ..."

"I'm from the South, from Rio Bueno," and trying to be more specific, "between Valdivia and Osorno, where the river divides ..."

"Ah, Rio Bueno," the man's smile widened, "you can find good ducks and trout going down toward La Barra ..."

"You know it?" the boy looked at him open-mouthed, as if he'd had a revelation.

"You could say I'm familiar with it. But it was a while ago, when I came back from the North, when the blasting in the saltpeter works got tough, and I thought that in Chiloé or Aysén things would go better. Then I went back to try my luck in the port, in Valparaíso."

The boy felt he was getting close to someone who had something special to offer, something that went way beyond the day and its closely watched streets but at the same time was nearer than the words and questions of the conversation.

"And where do you work now? I mean, before the coup ..."

The man breathed a long sigh and gazed off into the air:

"That's a difficult question. The truth is I've been lots of places. Like: I've worked in the saltpeter refineries, as a fisherman, a farmhand, I worked as a baker right here in Santiago, and so on. You could say I've been around: on the coast and in the mountains." He gave him a look as if sizing him up. "I've also worked as a union organizer, and other jobs beside the point right now."

"And haven't you had trouble these days? I mean, all this that's happening . . . "

The other tightened his jaw, threw a sharp look at the kid and erased the smile, pressing his lips together like an oyster:

"Trouble, sure, plenty of trouble. Let's just say I'm out of work."

"Just asking," the kid excused himself.

"Anyhow, the important thing is that we're here," the man's glance passed over the marching people—"besides, my friend"—and the boy felt the friendly thick hand on his shoulder—"what can water do to a fish, right?"

The young one noticed that the crowd was growing. Some people he'd seen earlier had dropped out of sight. But others had joined in, coming off a street-corner, a bus stop, out of a department store, a bar with its doors ajar, a news-stand.

"Changing the subject," his companion said, after picking his teeth for a second with his little finger, "did you manage to hear that compañera who came along reciting some of the poet's things? What a memory!" he shook his head in admiration.

"Yes, I heard her," and he dared ask, "but what poems were those?"

Not looking at him, the man dropped a dry reply: "The *Canto General.*"

The young man saw himself leafing desperately through pages and pages of a Losada volume, skipping over things that didn't seem his own, looking only for those verses which connected with his condition of a poor clumsy lover seren-ading a window that would open any minute. Messing around with a married woman is no easy job (Oscar, axiomatic), they give you a rabbit punch and if you're no good in the clinch you're down for the count (Catullus, scratching wounds of his own), but it all depends (Gringo, the peacemaker), at best the woman's little heart has a beat of its own. And finally, as Plato said (Oscar, that is), there's nothing like a good face in a bad time.

"I don't think I've read the *Canto General,*" he said, challengingly, "but I re-member *España en el Corazón* pretty well. There's a poem where Neruda recalls his friends, three friends that lived in a neighborhood in Madrid, sharing every-thing, until fascism came and destroyed the wine, the songs, the flowers . . . The one where he says: *and one morning everything was burning,* and at the end ex-plains *come and see the blood in the streets,* and before *but out of each dead child a gun with eyes is born, / but from each crime bullets are born / that one day will find their way / to your heart.* What can you tell me about that?"

"I was living in the South, in Puerto Montt," said the other in a slow voice, as if scraping up the memories, "I was younger than you and we believed the direc-tion of the revolution was being determined in Europe. When the civil war broke out, we were hanging on every bit of news from Spain, and since we'd had our own Socialist Republic and were more united than an octopus's arms, we dreamed of the mother country like little kids. One time a group of us were waiting for a boat that was coming to pick us up as volunteers for the International Brigades. You won't believe me. We'd collected bread, jerky, potatoes, our rifles . . . The problem was the boat never showed; we all had to go back home. But then the Popular Front came, and from that time on we took on the struggle—it's cost us so much now."

"Maybe you've just had more than your share of seasoning. And don't you think this defeat was due to the fact that our leaders were incapable of going beyond the programs of the Popular Front and following a different course? That these were other times and demanded different strategies?"

The man threw him a quick glance. He scratched an ear, as if the words were hard to come by.

"You're a good talker. I see you've read the newer stuff. What could I say to you now? All I know is that leaders don't make plans on pure inspiration; that methods don't arise out of reasoning alone nor out of pure willpower."

"But there have been mistakes, there have been. And from the top down. We didn't know how to defend the process, and now we're paying the price."

"It's true, it's going bad for us. What do you want me to tell you: they're wiping us out"—he'd raised his voice unintentionally, and noticing someone in front of them turn their head, he toned it down—"but it doesn't mean we're done for. The worst thing that could happen to us is to fall into defeatism, you especially, you younger ones. Although sometimes, when you don't have much experience in the things you're forced to face, I'll tell you that . . . "

"If you want experience, we've had our share up to now: the mummy government of Alessandri, the earthquake of sixty, Frei's revolution, another earthquake, the road to socialism, and now this. Does that seem to you like so little?"

The man looked at him sideways, and far from getting angry, he seemed pleased with the boy's irritation. The boy started looking up at the half-open windows, preferring to ignore the old guy.

"It's true these years have been awfully heavy," he nodded his head and clicked his tongue in respect, "so much has happened in so little time! But you know what else?"

The boy threw him a detached glance.

"I haven't been on vacation all these years."

The boy was going to say something but the old man made a friendly gesture:

"What I want to tell you is that the important thing is our being here. You're here for the same reason I am, and we're here for the same reason all these other compañeros are. It's better to discuss these things at a meeting or over a glass of wine at the corner bar, having a big debate, each one offering his own little cure for our problems. But that's not the case. It's true, the coup's been a rough one; it's true we're losing a lot, some more than others"—his voice broke, he wanted to say something but he held back—"but somehow we're walking along together and we keep talking: me to a snotnose like you and you to a stubborn old bastard like me."

The boy felt a lump in his throat. It was like suddenly going back to the family table where the misunderstood one jumps up at the most inopportune moment, for example when the mother walks in with the sherbet dessert and stands there with the tray in her hands, saying, "See if they come back to their right minds, or maybe it's better they get up and leave, they're already big enough to know when to argue and when we should share the time we can be together."

The boy finally said, "We can't prove anything by arguing now. Besides, what can we solve? We're not going to change the world with words."

"Yes, you're right. I don't deny we've made mistakes, some very serious ones. And that we didn't know how to defend this process, which was a dream for many years, since before you were born. But when there are two, three, ten people getting together, who begin to recognize each other, to do something, it's because all isn't lost. Alone we can't do a thing: we end up talking about ourselves, licking our wounds, and wind up looking at our own bellybuttons or sitting around in a funk. But if you trust the people's capacity to overcome their mistakes and get back in the fight, then you can start living again. I've always thought 'the people' was more than a word to be used in a speech; that it's like a plant that can sprout up anywhere, anytime, even if it's shut off from the sun or rain, even if they take its name away. Haven't you noticed that the mummies, with all the food they can buy, can barely raise a couple of big bony kids like buzzards, that they live hidden away in their fancy houses and don't dare go out on foot in the street, while in the villages the compañeros bang on each other like bass drums during fiesta and the kids spring up like mushrooms? If it goes on like that, despite all the repression, martial law, curfews, detentions, we'll still have reserves left over!"

The cortege reached La Paz Avenue. In the distance the yellow mass of a hospital loomed up, and beyond that the madhouse.

The boy wanted to ask him something, but now the other was looking toward the faded houses, as if the world had been reduced to a familiar landscape that his eyes went over with as sharp a curiosity as ever.

Suddenly he said: "Getting back to the poet, you know the poem of his I like best?" He closed his eyes a little, as if it didn't matter what the kid answered. "One called 'The Flowers of Punitaqui'—you know it?"

"No," said the boy, excusing himself again, "he wrote so much . . . "

"Maybe it's because I was there once, I don't know. You know the North?" His gaze hung there a minute, as if savoring an intimate landscape, and he said softly: "The Flowers of Punitaqui."

The crowd seemed to press closer together, but without stopping. Several trucks full of soldiers passed, circling around on a side street. The people marching seemed to be focused on their own steps, yet in their skins they were aware of what was happening around them.

The boy had the sensation of stepping across a threshold into a strange territory, a voluntary prisoner of unforeseen facts which sent a shudder through him. He thought of his friends living out their anxieties, their own adjustment to the times. He remembered that this was the poet's city, but even though he was walking the same streets the poet once walked, he was starting to feel the abyss between love and the world and he knew that sooner or later the separation would come. *Abandoned like the docks at twilight / It's the hour of departure, oh abandoned one!*

He noticed his compañero had gone ahead to the next row, exchanging a few words with another person and then returned to his place with a hard, pensive look on his face. He fell into step without looking at him, with no need to talk, looking only for closeness, the new intimacy that could be felt in the group like a necessary discovery.

I don't have time for my own pain / Nothing makes me suffer but these lives / that gave me their pure trust / and that a traitor turned under / into a dead hole, out of which / the rose will raise itself again.

"Were you at the poet's house? They say they destroyed everything . . . " the kid was trying to pick up the thread of the conversation.

"No, I couldn't look. But some other compañeros were there. The floor was flooded, the windows broken, his things trampled. As if they were trying to sink the house."

In you the wars and flights piled up / From you the songbirds' wings went up. / From tomb to tomb you still flamed up and sang / Standing like a sailor at the prow of a ship.

"But they couldn't stop this leavetaking. Even though the notices were banned from the newspapers, people found out anyway."

"It's a leavetaking all right, but it's also a demonstration," his compañero whispered, "the first demonstration after the coup. I already told you the people don't put their heads on the chopping block just like that, they can make their presence felt when that's what's demanded."

When the hangman imprisoned the judges / so they could condemn my heart, my determined swarm / the people opened their vast labyrinth / the cellar where their loves were sleeping / and there they kept a close watch over me / until the arrival of the light and air.

The procession slowed down; a dark heavy silence hung in the air as if the earth had suddenly opened its mouth; the latecomers started looking for a way out. There shouldn't be much further to go, the boy thought. He remembered his old man had told him once, recalling the capital, where he'd lived and had been married for the first time: the biggest thing in Santiago is the cemetery, it's like a city within a city.

Just then, somewhere in the rows of people someone ventured aloud: "Compañero Pablo Neruda."

There was a sense of disturbance in the lines, and a few voices answered: "here." From the rows up ahead a woman's hoarse voice repeated again: "Compañero Pablo Neruda!"

And now a determined chorus, reassembling their voices over this silenced time of bullets and decrees, shouted louder: "Here!"

The troops started climbing down from the trucks. The officers gave quick nervous orders. One of the vehicles took off ahead of the cortege, speeding up the march.

42

"The whores—the shit's about to come down," said the kid half-aloud, looking around, worried—"they're going to slaughter us all."

Two or three people tried to leave the lines. But they were too scared to be casual about it.

"Stay together, compañeros," someone said, not looking back, "if we're together they don't dare do anything, but if we start to split up they can pick us off like chickens."

Another voice went up: "Compañero Salvador Allende! "

And this time the response was a shout of defiance which seemed to echo with the sounds of countless marches, years of affirmations and defeats, streets that filled and emptied with waves of footsteps and voices which kept on precariously retrenching, but with the strength and certainty of shared dreams, that would come back in the hardest moment; seeking to rebuild the sense of the time:

"Here! "

"Now! "

"And always! "

The young man looked around at the faces of the marchers, and knew he was present at something important, something more important than the poet himself, something that wasn't in books nor in his friends' fabulous conversations, and that one day it would be necessary to tell of it simply, without adjusting history for the words' sake, because it sprouted like a truth as small and hard as a seed: he knew that all these people, paradoxically, were denying death in the breath of their own nostrils, and that the funeral was a celebration of life, an act of regaining all those dreams, cut off or isolated, that can fuse and be recreated in the prophetic mirror of poetry.

A murmur began to spread out over the heads, a murmur of clenched teeth that were now remaking a familiar melody. The boy bit his lips, half-opening them for the last words, *world,* feeling a cold breath on his back, *bread,* while he looked sidelong at his compañero, *united,* who shamelessly shed a couple of big tears he managed to wipe away with his hand, *international.*

He breathed deep, took a look toward where the soldiers were posted, and he could tell this time they wouldn't do anything, that their guns were even more precarious than the voices rising from this unarmed crowd.

When the procession approached the cemetery gates, some flower vendors spontaneously abandoned their stands and tossed a thick rain of petals over the hearse, throwing them from their baskets by the fistful. Several persons from the cortege went on ahead toward the grave site for the final ceremony, and others approached the van to pile wreaths on.

The moment the column stopped and the mass of people began to swarm through the gate, the old man left the group and headed off toward the central city.

The kid looked surprised, then caught up with him on the run: "What's going on? You're not going to stay for the burial?"

The old guy stopped, threw a look around and scratched his head as though he'd been caught in a serious lapse: "The truth is, I've never been good at burials," he said, and glancing at a nonexistent wristwatch, "besides, I'm already late, I have to get back to work."

The kid watched him walk away, shook his head strangely, then cracked a smile.

A couple of big strides and he was beside him again, not looking at him, and kicking a little rock out of his path, he said: "Since we're headed the same way, we can go on together a few more blocks. I'm late too."

Their footsteps, or the wind, lifted a few loose petals that drifted to the ground like a farewell offering. Or a welcome.

Barbed Wire Fence

By Aníbal Quijada

Translated by Jo Carrillo

Plus One, Minus One

I woke up startled by a strange dream. It was already late at night. I had gone to visit my older brother who lived in a house surrounded by gardens and tall trees. I wasn't alarmed by seeing a few people strolling through the pathways. I imagined that he was having a party or a get-together with his friends. I rang the doorbell and a strange man with a hat opened the door. My brother came out from behind. He smiled. "It's my brother," he explained to the stranger. "Come in," he told me, grabbing me by the arm. "We're talking things over so you should go away," he whispered. Then, raising his voice, he said "We're eating with Dr. Chavez. You know him." He introduced me to him again. Yes. I remembered this Dr. Chavez, an old friend from the past. He was still the same. I looked into the dining room. The family was standing close to the wall. A few others, strangers with their hats still on, were rummaging through boxes and throwing things on the rug. My brother motioned to me and I went back to the garden. Still unsure, I waited for a few minutes. All of a sudden the door burst open. Dr. Chavez was thrown outside. He fell close to me. A few of the men caught up with him and kept hitting him. Chavez's yells were frightening. He curled up. Because of the strong kicks, he rolled from one side to the other. He rolled toward the door. There another man waited for him with an open canvas bag. He went in without a word. I could see part of his face, his wide scruffy mustache and one of his contorted hands. The man skillfully dragged the bundle and put it into the trunk of a car. The stifled screams could not be heard anymore. I remained paralyzed. I felt a cold sweat run down my back. A tall man with a scarf around his neck came close. Without looking at me he walked, turned around and stopped behind me. I felt how his hand grabbed me by the collar and his eyes, like machine gun barrels, stuck to my neck.

Then I woke up.

I owed this dream to a talkative, slightly drunk corporal who had turned his attention to me before I went to bed.

"Old man," he told me, "it's better in here. Don't be in a hurry to leave."

"Why not," I asked him. "Is it so bad outside?"

"Yes, it's bad for those who get out. Their every move is watched. The slightest mistake and they'll make you come back. It's better not to let that happen."

"It's that bad?" I insisted . . .

He took out his dagger and showed me the blade. He scratched at something dry with his thumb nail.

"It's blood," he told me. "Those assholes used my belt last night and they haven't even washed it, see? They used it on two guys who came back. They take out their nails. Even though there isn't any authorization to do that . . . but no one's to blame for an accident . . . You do it like this. Give me your hand . . . Don't worry. I only want to show you."

He took one of my fingers and brought the point of the knife to it.

"You push a little to the front and you jerk up. The nail hangs loose, meat and all . . . If the bastard doesn't confess, there are still lots of nails . . . "

He smiled. Something told me that he himself was not a stranger to all that.

"Tonight there's extra work," he confided to me. "They have a few from Pudeto. The fellow who's a Congressman."

Seeing that I had laid back down, he left. Before he moved away he said.

"Sleep tight, old man . . . "

I stayed awake. I had almost completely covered my head with blankets to block the cold and the spotlight that shone on my bed. From behind, an order given in a normal voice caught my attention. It seemed to come from the second row towards the corner where the urinal was.

"O.K., get up! We're going . . . without your clothes you shit. Like you are . . . Just your coat and shoes . . . Walk now!"

"But sir . . . what have I done?"

"Shut up. You'll have enough time to talk . . . "

I couldn't, or shouldn't have turned around to see who they were taking away. Overall it was a bad sign. It could only mean one thing, torture. I remembered the corporal.

The night, like so many others, was gloomy. I saw some figures with hats move three bunks away, where the university professor slept. Lifting the blanket

I could see a little bit. Slowly, I lifted my hand and looked for my glasses under the coat that I was using as another blanket. I put them on. Something strange was happening.

The professor was still lying comfortably at the head of his bed and he was talking with the guards in a low voice. They were seated at his feet. You couldn't hear their voices, but their movements were very clear. The three of them seemed to be paying attention to something. The sergeant looked at his watch and he made a gesture with his hand to the professor as if to say that he should wait. A couple of minutes passed by. Then, the first scream was heard. It came from the side towards the rifle range. Now the dogs could be heard barking. I imagined the scene: the prisoner would run and the dogs would snap at his ankles. Nevertheless, it was the faces of those three men that bothered me now. Especially the compañero's.

The three men were still smiling and snickering. Between the shrieks they'd mimick what was happening. Like a nightmare the professor and the two guards were following the tortured man, laughing and nodding. The sergeant would fake shots from a machine gun toward the floor, and the corporal, who was now standing, would pretend to be punching the ribs and face. Later, the sergeant would lift his boot and point to the inner leg, suggesting a hard blow to the testicles. Meanwhile, the professor would strike his palm with his fist, he'd hold his stomach trying to contain his laughter. The three delighted in the pain of the condemned man. One time one of the guards took his cigarette out of his mouth and moved the lit end toward the professor's shoulder. He wanted to show the direction that the torture was taking. They laughed more.

It was strange to see this compañero participating in the delight of the guards. Especially since I thought I knew him well. The professor was a married man, he had two children and a compañera who was a militant. Outside, he alternated his university classes with cultural activities that he directed from inside the Party. He wasn't quite 30 yet. He was tall, thin and had a good build. Now that he was in prison, he was always called when the prisoners marched because he had served in the Air Force after finishing his military service. Even the sergeant would lend him a hat and he'd lead the line.

Upon hearing "Look to the ri--i--ght . . . !" he would remain stiff, serious, staring to the left in order to control the formation. The guards ranked his exercises as excellent. He excelled in soccer. In spite of being happy, he didn't like jokes. He usually reacted violently against them. He held a grudge against one compañero who had the bad idea to get in front of him and take away the ball, he chased him furiously trying to hit him. A lot of people would tease him for being allergic to water. They teased him and they nicknamed him "antiliquido." Some guards would infuriate him by sending him to the pump to wash parts of his body or to take a shower. Then he'd return cursing and he'd sulk for hours. He liked to talk with me. He'd open up. That's why I knew a few things about his life. I always saw him as a serious person, loyal and responsible to his principles, who suffered like everyone else at this terrible time. We talked a lot. One

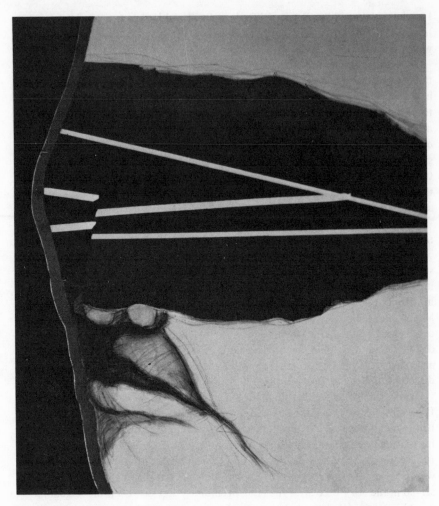

"A minute of light in the darkness will not blind us," acrylic on canvas by
René Castro.

time he told me: "The thing is that I can't stand them laughing at me and making me look ridiculous. You've seen how they tease me because I wash my face in the morning with my coat on. It's that I can't bear the frozen wind and that water so early. It makes me so mad that I'd kill a couple of those idiots that bug me." For the first time, I saw a lot of hate in him.

I asked, "And what about the guards, compañero? Those who tortured you in Dawson and who kept you naked and tied in a chair under the falling snow. Or those who made you walk blindfolded on the sides of the floodgate on the ferry. Is that o.k. at sea? Do you respect them?"

After a few minutes he gave me a thoughtful answer, "I would have strangled those lousy fuckers with my bare hands . . . But you know? Afterwards I thought about it. I've even come to forgive them. They didn't know anything about us. They were drugged, brainwashed in boot camp. And the truth is that there are pricks on this side too, right?"

I slept without forgetting his smiling face.

The next afternoon I got close to him and told him what I had seen. He made a resentful face.

"It's that motherfucker," he answered, "he's bothered me a lot. He always butts in to everything I do. He deserved it."

Later he abruptly asked me, "What would you say, old man, if tomorrow you see me in an Air Force uniform. They've told me that maybe I can return to the group . . . It'd be a way to get out of this hell. Don't you think?"

"Minus one and plus one," I answered.

"Come on," he said, "don't joke around. I'm interested in what you have to say."

"Minus one compañero . . . Plus one torturer" I said, suddenly feeling sad. Minus one, plus one."

Afterwards I moved away. I never talked to him again.

Visitors from Dawson City

There were twelve men. They arrived in the barracks at dawn on a frozen morning. They were sitting on the benches facing the clapboards behind the wire. They looked thin, with their faces burnt from the snow and the winds of the Magellan Strait. At that first breakfast, we were allowed to share our rations with them. The compañeros made sandwiches and with canned milk in their hands they stepped forward to serve them.

"Don't talk to them," the sergeant warned.

Almost all of them were members of the Party's Regional Committee. There were public officials, a geologist, a pharmacist, a pair of paramedics, and workers. There was joy in their eyes. They were returning from a long stay at Dawson Island. They were here in the barracks again, with their friends and comrades, on route to Punta Arenas. They'd see their relatives soon, and maybe, why not, freedom.

A little later they took some rocks of different colors and sizes out of their bags. They also had some metal utensils, can openers converted into small chisels or into iron clasps that screwed into the rocks. The guards became interested. Almost immediately those rocks got around. They were carved and they had reliefs of faces, silhouettes, zodiac signs, initials, and even a landscape, a poem, a wish and a message. Some of them had a small hole at the top so that they could be hung from a chain or a keyring.

The sergeant got jealous. Right away he ordered all the material confiscated until further notice.

"Prisoners aren't allowed to use instruments that cut," he said, "You know that; these are really sharp chisels."

Days passed and finally he let us use the tools under supervision and with the agreement to return them again. The carved rocks weren't returned to the prisoners.

Almost everyone got involved in this passionate labor. The truth was that something like this had already been tried, but the rocks around the regiment were too hard. On the other hand, the ones that the men from Dawson brought were soft, flat and had nice surfaces. Later we learned that the geologist had chosen them and that an artist would help to make the designs.

The rock fever began. The supplies quickly ran out and the geologist and another comrade were allowed to look for materials on the main road provided a guard went with them. True artists appeared.

But that's not all the comrades from Dawson brought. They came with a good deal of knowledge and a great enthusiasm for talking about art and other activities. In reality, they gave us a shot of optimism that "struck" our souls. They organized all kinds of contests. Professor Cachencho brought his cheerful spirit, his natural humor and his smile.

After a few days they let us put on a show.

Everyone liked Cachencho's presentation. He came up with two very good stories: one about a sex education class, with illustrations for the student's sake and one about the Flying Condor who had been given such a strong kick in the testicles that they were as swollen as ostrich eggs. The Condor couldn't forget the high cliffs and open spaces where he felt free and happy. He was in no condition to rise. He'd try to fly. On his flights he'd skim the branches of the high trees hurting his testicles and then he'd painfully cry, "u-ju-juy . . . u-ju-juy." The story had to do with events that had been censored. Jokes always underhandedly implied what was happening to us. Then, in response to a good story that someone else told, Cachencho told a joke about two gay comedians who were in a car wreck and furiously got out to see the damage and to insult each other. The most frantic one said, "Look at what you did to my car. I'm going to give you a hundred kicks in the ass." The other one, with a funny look answered, "Let's get this straight first. Is this going to be a fight or a romance?"

But Cachencho suffered from periods of sharp discouragement and anxiety. He often had suicidal tendencies due to the captivity and the powerlessness of not being able to find an answer to emotional and family problems. During those times all of our spirits sunk.

The prisoners from Dawson also brought sad songs, with nice melodies and short words that were repeated. Singing together broke the monotony. The compañero who was a pharmacist recited poems while accompanying himself on the guitar. Those were times of nostalgia.

Not much time passed before the men from Dawson were taken to "The Palace of Smiles." They left happily, thinking that this could be the last trip. They returned bruised and downhearted. The curtain had fallen. They had just learned the diabolical charges plotted in the torture offices of the Intelligence Headquarters. The prisoners were links in the chain of Plan Z. Now they knew that they were just beginning a monstrous process that could end with their lives. They learned that all of the investigations were meant to involve them in a big web that would take them to a Court Martial. Only two or three were able to get that precious five minute interview with the dear man, in the offices below, who came and went with his eyes shaded.

Until one morning, it happened.

I was writing a poem about the prisoners' quarters to read at a meeting that we were going to have, when they all returned from the rifle range. They came in silently, with their heads down, they were in line and guarded by army soldiers.

From the corner of my eye, I saw the geologist make his bed roll. I understood. Those expressions were not the ones of free men. I couldn't stop myself from getting closer.

"Compañero, what happened?"

"We're going back to the Island ... " he said, and he broke into sobs.

A soldier suddenly came over to separate us.

"Get away" he ordered, "they can't talk."

Some prisoners got together in the open space, some stayed in their bunks without moving. We saw them pack their things in a few minutes. They got into line, called out their names and, taking small steps, they went out. Many people had tears in their eyes.

I looked at one of the guards. He was looking down and his beard was trembling. I thought that he, too, was upset.

The Calafate Man

Reconstruction of a "treatment"

Even the soldiers, covered with thick capes and wearing fur-lined boots felt the intense cold of that frozen Magallanes night. September was dying with the last snow showers and this time, for many, Chile's agony in the midst of uniforms and demanding military voices was as painful a truth as it was incomprehensible.

In one area of the Marine regiment the lighting had been increased, especially in the part of the road, between the rifle range and the prisoners' quarters, where they secretly gathered more than fifty political prisoners or "prisoners of war."

In the prisoners' quarters they pushed one prisoner out of the miserable solitary confinement block. Many ears listened in suspense, straining to hear, and yet hoping not to hear, the compañero's fate. The threatening machine guns kept him from getting up and running towards the openings in the wooden fence.

Two guards posted themselves in strategic points close to the rifle range office to receive the enemy when he "landed" after the sergeant sent him off with a big punch.

Voices could be heard clearly from inside the office.

"Alright, motherfucker. Tell us now where you hid the weapons or you'll only get as far as here."

"But sir, I've already told you that in the University we didn't have any weapons."

"Then, are you going to go on denying that you're a communist and that you had a plan to kill us?"

"I served in the Young Communist League as a sympathizer. We got together to talk, have a good time and sing in the rallies."

"How about Plan Z, you son of a bitch? What were you going to do on September 18 and how were you going to kill us? With your bare hands?"

"We never talked about killing anyone, sir."

A strong blow came out of nowhere.

"Don't let them hit me! . . . "

"Here you're going to sing everything but *La Internacional*. What was the plan?"

"We organized some games in the country . . . "

"Oh, yeah? Likely story. So you were going to eat us up over there. Since you won't tell us the truth, get up you asshole and take off your clothes. Now you're going to learn what's good for you."

"But sir . . . "

"Obey, you shit!"

Sharp kicks made the prisoner obey the order. Since what little clothes he had on were falling off, the kicks were unnecessary. He was soon left naked. He was of medium build, about twenty years old.

"Stand at the door, you fag. That's right, in front of us."

The guards outside changed positions.

"Give the little boy a hand," one of them said. "Little ass, huh? Not even enough for a meatball. He's going to be missing a slice when we get through with him."

Now, one could hear the soft voice of the captain.

"I know your family. I don't want to treat you badly. But I'm here to get the truth and it makes me happy to punish Marxists. I'll give you one last chance. Answer me: where were the weapons that you had at the university and in the YCL? You'll be shot if you don't talk."

"Captain, you know perfectly well that there weren't any weapons. No one fired a shot. We've learned about Plan Z here in prison from what you've told us. Let me go back to the quarters! I beg you . . . "

The captain moved to one side. Already in position, the sergeant punched the prisoner's face, throwing him on to the wooden steps. He fell to the left. One of the soldiers grabbed him.

"Here, I won . . . I hit him first."

The other soldier was going to hit him when a sergeant, a corporal and some soldiers came out of the office. They had ropes.

"That's enough *jetones!*" the sergeant said. "Don't hit his face. You're going to waste him too soon."

Moaning, the boy rolled on to the frozen ground. They hooked his arms with the ropes and started to drag him faster and faster over the gravel road. The small rocks embedded in his skin, cutting him. Desperately moving from one side to the other, he exposed more skin to the gravel. Still in a way, he felt a certain sense of relief in struggling, turning and jumping.

While the soldiers shouted curses, the dogs were brought in. Several dogs jumped the prisoner at a curve in the road, they ran at his side biting his arms and legs. "Hey. Stop!" the sergeant yelled out of breath.

They had to pick him up and hold him straight. The soldiers called the dogs off. Small trickles of blood slid down the boy's body to his waist and then on to his feet and the cold earth. Now he opened his eyes wide; his teeth chattered. Every once in a while he'd scream:

"Mamita, they're killing me . . . !"

The sergeant bent over him.

"Let's have the brandy. Give him a shot of it. Why don't you start talking, you motherfucker? What did you know about the machine guns?"

"I never . . . "

They began to beat him with their ropes and made him run. He didn't remember the advice of his fellow prisoners; they tried to tell him that he shouldn't run. The soldiers let him advance. The night was full of voices commanding the dogs. Close to the prisoner, the guards and the sergeant kept up a rhythm hitting him with their ropes and the butts of their guns. They went into the field. More soldiers hid in the shadows. A boot entangled itself in the boy's feet and it knocked him on top of a frozen pond.

The soldiers smashed him against the ice with kicks and blows from the butts of their guns. When the ice broke, the boy fell half way into the water with little pieces of ice floating around him. He was trembling. All the same, he stopped feeling the thousands of stings in his skin and his numb mind soothed his fears.

"So, the son of a bitch doesn't want to sing, huh? Drink some water."

A boot flattened his face, sinking him into the water, while another tried to hit his testicles from above. For a few seconds, the dying boy's hoarse panting mixed with the yelling.

The sergeant motioned, "Enough, take him out . . . "

A soldier brought him back.

"It looks like the little boy froze, sir."

"Quick, walk him around and move his arms!" the sergeant said. "Bring the brandy, stupid."

They worked for a while until the prisoner began moving and breathing.

"There, don't let him freeze again. Stand him up. Hold him on this side stupid," the sergeant would say. And then, "Hey, kid, let's go. If you don't jump to it, you'll freeze to death. Walk."

The prisoner got up. He rubbed his bruised body and tried to walk. He took a gulp from the bottle that the soldiers stuck in his mouth.

The sergeant put his face next to his.

"Now what were you saying, *cabrito*? Talk or we'll start again."

But the answer was unintelligible.

The sergeant moved back.

"I don't want to talk to this shit. He's a tough one . . . ! Hang him."

Again the ropes. Now they took him to the nearby fence and leaning him against a fence post, they lifted him up. He was left with his legs tied back and his head fallen on top of one shoulder. So that he wouldn't slip, they supported his feet with a board. The figure stood out clearly against the sky, illuminated by the distant spotlights.

The sergeant looked at him.

"Look, the queer looks like Jesus Christ. We need to crown him. Bring calafate branches," he said.

A soldier came forward.

"Here are some, sir," he said obligingly. "They're the ones that we saved for the chosen one."

The sergeant smiled.

"How nice," he pointed. "Put them on . . . "

Then they stepped back.

"Now we have it," said the sergeant. "Turn your lights on him. He even looks pretty. All he needs is the little rag . . . it looks like he went to sleep again. Give him a few whips . . . "

The wounded boy slowly lifted his face. The soldiers laughed.

"Look. The son of a bitch is livening up. Do you think he's risen from the dead?" one asked.

The corporal moved close to him.

"Now. Talk or we'll shoot you. Don't want to, huh? . . . Then say goodbye . . . sing *Venceremos*.

"Good idea!" the sergeant said. "Bring the thermos and we'll have a little coffee with brandy to listen to him."

"Sing . . . sing, you shit . . . "

Sitting on boards, having sips of coffee, the guards threw rocks at the prisoner while aiming the beams of their lights on him. The thuds could be heard in the stockade. Others hit the prisoner without a sound.

"Sing, you shit."

A thread of a voice came out of the pounded flesh. "Ven . . . ce . . . re . . . mos. Ven . . . ce . . . remos . . . "

From behind, from the holes in the clapboards of the prisoner's quarters, the song came out:

> From the deep hearth of the country
> the voice of the people can be heard
> A new day is dawning
> All of Chile begins to sing . . .

It was the prisoners who accompanied the tormented man in the distance.

The sergeant got up. The rest of the soldiers followed.

"So you are being brave!" he roared. He cocked his gun.

"Attention!" he yelled. "Fire!"

Machine gun bursts thundered in the darkness. They were shot into the air. There was a long silence in the prisoners' quarters.

The soldiers untied the prisoner and made him drink again.

"This is only the appetizer . . . You have to resurrect . . . "

They dragged him toward the ditch of the privy.

A soldier grabbed a stick and sunk it into the excrement. Then he brought the stick up to the prisoner's mouth.

"You sang really bad, Sandro. Eat shit so that you're voice will get better and stop shaking."

The sergeant took advantage of his position to deliver a blow. He steadied the tip of his boot on the prisoner's lower thigh and he kicked back, with the spur, to the boy's genitals. A horrible yell pierced the night. The prisoner jumped up and remained seated.

"Stand him up now," the sergeant said.

The soldiers moved the ropes. The prisoner fell flat on his face. They dragged him again, this time towards the grove of calafates. They lifted him up there and they threw him in the middle of the bushes. The boy screamed. Thousands of stickers pierced into his flesh. He would shake, trying to free himself, but he'd fall again, sinking back into the stickers. The soldiers were laughing.

When they took him out, he didn't have any skin left. He was but a mass of blood. The dogs drew close and began to lick him. The stickers, still nailed in, made them give up.

In this way, in that night, in the southernmost city of the world in Punta Arenas, a new specimen in the times of terror was born: The Calafate Man.

The next day, when the prisoners lined up in the morning to sing the national anthem the flag did not wave with the strong breeze. Gathered on the mast, it looked anxious as if it were not sure whether to wave or slip alone into half mast.

That day there was a strong wind. It rained too. The water intermittently slid through the clapboards of the prisoners' quarters in the Marine regiment.

Visits and Surprises

For days the guards had been demanding that the barracks be extremely clean. They made us straighten out our belongings and they wouldn't let us hang our towels or wet things on the clothes lines. They took special care for appearance's sake. We realized that they were expecting visitors. This we gathered from the newspapers and a few extra bits of news: the International Red Cross Commission had returned.

One morning they ordered us to straighten ourselves up. They called off work, they took away our writing paper and pens and we were left waiting. At ten in the morning the Red Cross members arrived: a tall, well dressed, older woman who seemed uncomfortable in this prison environment, a large group of high ranking officers from the Armed Forces, a few civilians, and, as executive of the commission, a young, blond, medium sized man with a big smile. We were told to move closer to the fence. After an introduction made by an officer, the executive explained that he was Swiss, and that he represented the International Red Cross. He had come to see the conditions in which we lived and he assured us that he especially wanted to talk with us privately. He spoke fluent Spanish. As soon as he said that, he excused himself, crossed the wire and came over to join us, trying to get away from the official group. The people from the National Red Cross, including the distinguished woman, also got on our side of the wire, but they remained separate. The officers stayed behind, scowling, serious, looking on threateningly.

We took advantage of the opportunity. We surrounded the man, who was then totally hidden. We started to talk. The words came out by themselves. In a few minutes, one of the prisoners took everybody's name in order to tell about the conditions that we were in and the bad treatment that we received. The Swiss wrote down the information in a wide notebook in his own language. The conversation was frank and direct. He told us that he knew about this secret detention center, but that in an earlier visit they had denied it existed. Now the prisoners from Pudete had talked to him, insisting that he should "Go to Cochrane . . . It's a torture camp . . . there are more prisoners."

We described in detail the arrests, the forced confessions, the bad treatment, the interrogations at Intelligence Headquarters, the whole procedure.

The Swiss bowed his head.

"They're the same methods," he said "that were used in Korea, in Vietnam, and that are being used even now in Brazil." Then he looked at us, "Are there any recent cases of torture?"

Several men showed their scars: the wounded ankles and hands, deformed from blows, the whipped backs, burnt skin from cigarettes, broken bones. The Calafate Man lowered his pants and opened his shirt.

Someone told the Swiss, "In the corner bunk there's a compañero who was questioned by the Intelligence two days ago. He still can't move."

The Swiss nodded.

He continued speaking. A high ranking official had quietly gotten closer and stood close by.

"There," the Swiss finished in a loud voice. "I'll speak with the commander immediately to make sure that conditions get better, he respects people and grants pardons."

He was going to leave when he suddenly headed toward the corner bunk. He sat on the one in front and began to question the "sick man." Some of us moved over quickly and blocked off the area. For the second time, the official had to look on from a distance. The Swiss wrote more than two pages of notes on what he talked about with the compañero.

Afterwards he left.

"I promise not to give up until I reach the objectives of our mission in your case. For the time being I have the list of names that will protect you internationally. There are more than a hundred. Right? As of today you are registered as prisoners of war. Goodbye! I'll return soon."

"What did he say?" asked a man who had obviously stayed close to his bunk to avoid implicating himself.

"That we shouldn't worry," someone answered. "That he'll be back in March."

There were no reprisals. And for us, faith returned.

These were days of great speeches. On the 11th of December it had been three months since the coup. The grand General was talking that night. The guards brought a radio. Would there be an amnesty? Would the state of war end? They had said that many prisoners had been freed from the National Stadium.

In the afternoon someone made fun of an improbable speech. He said:

"The situation as you will remember could not be sustained. If we could have had seventy percent of the votes or more in the Congressional election, perhaps it would have been possible to go on. But the dialogue failed and the Christian Democrats sealed their unity with the rightists. Foreign pressure was very intense. The safest thing for us was to start a civil war. Then the Armed Forces stepped in and saved the country, even though they did it with a little blood bath. They had to adopt an anti-Marxist attitude to get U.S. approval and badly needed dollars. When all is said and done, through our captivity we have made a great contribution to the military Junta. Now you'll see how in a couple of days they'll happily let us go. It wouldn't surprise me if the General himself sees us through the door of the regiment with a strong handshake, "Thank you compañero, thank you!"

The President of the Junta spoke that night. He was very tough. Yelling and hitting the table with his fists, he warned that he wouldn't let up against the Marxists and other enemies of the country, that the members of the Court-Martial had to be ruthless in their sentences. Because if they're not ... . !

We lost every hope we had. Santa Claus was in other parts of the world. He wouldn't bring presents for us.

During those few days something unique happened. The Communist Party Secretary received a letter from his daughters in which they asked him to forgive them for not being able to send a package that Thursday, because of the prices and the hard times they were in. We quickly agreed to take up a collection for the compañero's family. It was during the very strict sergeant's watch. With his approval and accompanied by him, we took up the collection. Suddenly without losing his military posture or changing his scowl, the sergeant put his right hand in his coat, opened the top part and took out 1000 *escudos*. He gave it to the group and said, "Give me five hundred."

The 15th of December passed. One day the captain came. He had a serious, sorrowful look on his face. It was bad news.

"They have finished building special barracks for prisoners of war at Dawson Island, and you are going to break them in," he said. "You won't have reason to complain there. I'm sincerely sorry. I had gotten used to you and won't be able to go with you ... the first group leaves tonight ... the rest of you will leave at dawn. I'll read the list of those who will stay to be court-martialed. Those who have already been convicted won't be transferred."

He didn't surprise us. Nothing could surprise us any more except our inability to forsee the future. Yet, we should have understood that for us the real world, the yes and no world, the likely and the unlikely and even the absurd and the inconceivable, went only in a negative direction. We didn't get bitter. One chapter ended and another began. At a time when peace seemed near they moved us away from Punta Arenas, from our homes that were so close. But, they were moving us away from the "Palace of Smiles." And that was something.

Everyone began working feverishly. Especially those who had to leave in a couple of hours. They had to pack their clothes, take a few books, write a letter to their families.

"Only one sheet," the sergeant reminded them, "and you can tell them that you're leaving for the Island."

The rest of us from the second group spent our time helping the first travelers.

Barbed Wire Fence

Later I understood that I was not free. There was a fence that came out of the detention centers and around the city. You could see it in the streets around every house, surrounding the people, with its barbs ready. Those barbs had acquired many forms: they patrolled the streets in dark cars, they were in the threatening weapons of the soldiers and police, they were fixed in watchfulness, they had the sound of metal in the sly footsteps that hounded people, they were writers in lists and accusations, they became voices and actions in the events of every hour, by day and by night.

Yes. I was free. Free to see and hear and even to walk within the occupied city. But I could hardly speak. My movements had been restricted. I knew that I should stay far away from the street and people and be seen as little as possible. I had to avoid the risks of one discussion, the demands for one piece of identification, the fall back into prison.

I was now a branded, muted man.

I remained inside the house. That's all—nothing else. Looking at my wife who walked in her own house hardly making a sound, alert, looking fearfully out the window, worrying over the slightest knock on the door, talking in whispers. Later I learned to do the same. It was not impossible for them to install microphones when we left. Maybe the telephone was even tapped. Or maybe the mail was checked.

I returned to work.

They continued with the elimination of leftists and the dismantling of the social security services. They laid off hundreds of thousands of civil servants. Meanwhile, they thoroughly organized the Intelligence Service, doubling its figures. They created more torture centers and, with imported machines, one "house of electric chairs" in the capital. And this without counting those who worked in the actual public offices and in the trade centers. The number of paid informants grew in each block and office building.

Not much time passed until they told me, "So, you think you are going to be fired this month, huh? You were a prisoner and you'll head the next list."

I moved my head.

"I hope to go when it's my turn," I answered, "I've put in 35 years of service." The man who talked to me smiled.

Nevertheless, he had a reason to smile. Very few of us remained in the office where they had crowded us.

One woman who combed her gray hair, complained in front of the guards.

"A person can't work in peace," she'd say every day. "There are still too many Marxists here."

The insensitivity of the conquerors was impressive. They seemed to be insatiable, they kept pushing people into the prisons, to desperation and misery. They kept living without remorse and doing business, as if they were detached from that sinister world. They were like vampires, constantly after their quota of blood. It was a new cannibal species that satisfied itself with stripping its neighbor, its fellow worker its professional colleague; that took away the job, the desk, the waiting room, the living. They were a few more barbs, watchful, inciting, denouncing barbs.

One day, I managed to go to my comadre's house. She was still suffering from one month in prison. She had been the director of a Mother's Center. It was worse than what they told me. I had hardly knocked on the door and I heard loud screams. Her husband let me in. She had run to hide behind the bathroom door. I saw her later. She was curled up yelling: "I haven't done anything. I haven't done anything wrong, sergeant." Her eyes were wide open and she didn't recognize me.

Nightmares returned. I would wake up very late in the night hearing the bell from the street. But it was a sound that was only in my mind, in my fears. During the nights, I'd sail through my fears. The flash of machine guns, the chases and yells interrupted my rest. The insomnia came with the circling of military vehicles or of the Intelligence that would stop unexpectedly in front of a neighbor's house. Then you could hear the steps on the sidewalk, the noise on the grating, the pacing in the nearby garden, the pounding on the door. Later, the punished flesh, the confessions, the dragging of the bodies through the streets.

I remember the young university organizer who disappeared one afternoon from a house in the neighborhood. At about 4 p.m. a woman came and begged the young woman to go with her to a car that was around the corner. She told her that some compañeras from the University, who didn't dare visit her, were waiting. She went. She was trusting. There were two of her friends in the car, but there were also two men from the Intelligence who had detained them. She returned a few days later. She was strangely unfriendly and quiet. She only spoke one time.

"Mamita," she said, "I've been raped by 12 guards. They have had me down on the floor with rocks on my breasts. I've had a lot of filth in my vagina." She immediately looked for the darkest place in the house and she stayed there for a long time, staring at the empty door frames or the boards in the ceiling with her empty eyes.

Yes. They were barbs. Barbs and wire. We could feel them by just looking at the occupied city, crippled by so many missing people, by forgotten feelings, by lost shame. In the streets, it was common to see the new victims against the walls in humiliating searches; to see Intelligence agents detaining a transient, tying his hands behind his back, blindfolding him and pushing him to a van. The operations of war! The men of repression lurking on every corner, with berets and machine guns slung on one side, their eyes fixed on an apartment or on some office on the watch for a sure catch.

Barbs and wire. That was freedom. Misery. Misery from hunger. Misery that grew.

But there were signs of resistance. Sometimes from the top of buildings pamphlets would fall. Some would confront the military with weapons, and they'd die. A lot of military accomplices were beginning to weaken. Their personal lives were being touched. The barbs continued to toughen.

On my short walks I'd look for the face of a Christian or a free thinker. I wanted to see their eyes. I didn't find them. Their eyes were dodging, false. Waiting for a miracle some looked at the cross; others were still dreaming. Only the look of the compañero had a strange sparkle.

One night I knew.

I was hurrying home a few minutes before the curfew. A dog ran up to me and stayed by my side. It had its ears turned back and its tail between its legs. I didn't want anything to do with it until I put the key into the lock. Then the animal stuck to my legs and began to shake. I knew that feeling. It was fear. Fear of the unknown. Maybe that dog sensed that it wouldn't reach its refuge. The order was to shoot at anything that moved and didn't respond to "stop." He too, like me, couldn't speak. I let him in. He was my inmate until the next day. All the same, he gave me the message.

If it was impossible to talk, sooner or later I could write.

That's what I did.

Part II

War Chorale

By Fernando Alegría

Translated by Stephen Kessler

—Your wife will turn up—says the one in uniform—, don't worry about it. Almost all of them turn up, so why not yours. Tell me why she should be an exception. Because she's good-looking? She's cruel. You'll say she never hurt anyone. But obviously you don't know what she did to me. Much less what she did to you. How would you know? I always admired one thing. About you. I admired your jerk-ass face. You know what else? You talk so much and *so pretty*. That's why my colleagues can't stand you. You're a mouth-off. I'm telling you the truth so you better learn to live with it. If you want to get mad, get mad. It's pointless. I've always been peeved by the presence of people who just don't fit in the world they live in. They're too much, but not really too much because they don't count, they're unseen, unfelt. I swear I hardly saw you at all. Really saw you, I mean. Now is another story. But then, I never even noticed. Just like that. She was too big for you and me both! Man, so big! Her little body wouldn't even fit in my hands, not even her ass in my palm, her sweet little buns, so round and shifty, slippery, opening and closing, always tender and soft like two big lips calling my name. One time I saw you sizing her up and getting her ready and I decided to copy that position exactly, down to the last detail. That's why when she got here the first thing I did was to sit her straddled across a plank, wide-open, easy, face to face with me. Get it? Like on a see-saw. Right. She started to cry and, without looking at her, I figured my tool was doing okay. So I stuck it in. But then I was the sorry one because the idiots started laughing and, I swear, I felt ashamed for her, such a lady and so refined, so intelligent with her big rosy legs, her curly wet pussy, her long long back, her hair down to her ass. I told them to untie her hands. I thought it would be so sweet if she touched my face. Not that I thought she'd kiss me or stroke my head. No. I'm not that stupid. Just that she might touch my cheeks and with luck say a little word. For the love of God or out of pity. Either would have pleased me. For God or for pity. And if she'd repeated it over enough times I would've come right there and left her in peace. But she didn't do or say anything. Just those big thighs, so slippery firm and thick, like gold or a little dark, and the shadow wider open all the time. Seeing she was saying nothing, I wanted to slam it in good. The assholes broke out laughing and I shot my load. Have you ever seen a grown man, a family man, like me, not a piece of shit like you, spill his hot jism on the ground? Fluttering, mouth open, moaning like he was dying, twisting and turning and panting? And this distant woman gasping with her eyes shut. When a hairy-chested man jerks off by himself what falls to the ground is the world with its walls and doors and windows, and the puddle that forms at his feet is like the face of a hanged man. What good does it do to tell you these things? Today makes two weeks since I saw her. You say you haven't seen her for months. You're lying. Not months, no way. We picked her up right at the start of December. If you didn't see her before it's because she had you hoodwinked and, jerk that you are, you never put a stop to it. Did she tell you she went to Communist Youth meetings? You turkey. You're a blob with a prick. Those people are completely into fucking. No accusations or suspicions where you're concerned. Did you know that? Why do you think we let you go on hanging out with them? To follow you and then haul you in for questioning? Don't kid yourself. We could stick it in and out of you without taking your pants off. Get it? The strange thing is that they seem to understand life the same way we do. There'll always be people who take advantage, and thank you on top of that. Down at the station there was a major who fucked all the hookers before sending them to court. That is, he tried them out to see how good they were. Afterwards, he'd offer them immediate unconditional freedom. They'd turn down the offer. You know why? Love. Just like it sounds. They wanted one more. For tenderness, craving, or size and depth, who knows. He filled every one of them up to the eyebrows. They asked for more. People like you just go to bed with each other, it lacks humanity. You don't know what love is about. I bet you they measure you with your own stick and you don't even thank them. She was always too much for you. No question about that. But since you're not convinced, what do you want? And you still have the nerve to say you never saw me with her. Never? Look at me. Look at me good. Keep looking, con man. Take a gander at a real man. Though it could be you're telling the truth. It's hard to figure out people like you. I remember when we were living on La Paz and you had the habit of meeting her on the corner by the precinct. Then you'd walk off at a slow stroll and I'd come out behind. Sometimes I just watched you, other times I'd sneak up close to get a good look at her secret and put myself in your place, I got so close I could put my hair against her neck and a finger, first one finger, then two or three, inside her till she'd scream and give out a little blood. You took her by the waist and went into the Derby, you ordered your little beer and I my little glass of white. While you were eating I liked to get on all fours and crawl around under the tables till I got to yours and there I put my face in her lap and she let me have a nice long drink, and when I felt her getting tired I started licking her, non-stop. It was like getting up close to a starfish on the sand, and you ordered your little coffee, and then she kept staring at me and I gave her my best and boldest but she didn't even notice. Incredible. One night she came into the station. She'd locked herself out of her car with the motor running. Since I was on duty I went out with her and together we stooped to look through the window. That was when I recognized the smell, something you don't understand because it's something that comes and yet doesn't come from her clothes, it has something and nothing to do with her body, it comes out of all the years that I've loved her and it's not like anything else. It's in her hands and it isn't, but in her arms, along her sides and on her throat, it runs down her back, but it's neither sweat nor anything like it. I think there must be some ripe fruit that fills her. It hides in her breast, that's why I bent to kiss it and then I was studying her ears, I let my hand fall so she'd feel its weight, nothing more, then pressing my hardon against her cunt I gave a smooth shove and laid her out on the hillside. Another smell, then, of some grass I know and don't know, damp between the rocks, since it was hot and I laid her down, like I say, spreading her legs which had been stuck together. Never, you hear, not once did she say a thing to me. No little love-words, not even a squeak. You know why I turned her over to my colleagues? Because of that. It sounds bad to you, you think I'm a pervert. You can't understand a man, a real man. I love your wife more than life itself. She did us wrong. You, because you deserve it. It doesn't make sense you should live in the same century. That woman requires a man. She totally undid me, she killed certain things in me. Listen. When she was seventeen and I was about forty I thought of taking her off to a little lane in San Miguel. I dreamed of closing us up in a single room, putting in a brass bed, king size, since I've always slept crosswise and regular beds nowadays aren't made for horses like me, a couch and a wardrobe with a mirror, knick-knacks, you know, little nude figurines. Working late like I do, on the night shift, she'd often be left alone, too alone in four walls and a window giving on the neighborhood, the cordillera in the background. She might or might not get bored, but the table would always be set and I, very delicately, would take off my coat and my saber, leaving just my undershirt. The uniform's coarse, that's for sure, the boots are heavy and the straps get stained, so the whole thing is like a cloud of armpits and leather, besides the wine, in a bottle, of course, and the starched napkins. A dream, a beautiful dream, but never a word of love, not even acknowledgment. Remote, hard, though not cunning, she intimidated me, I'd never get her to sit on my lap. On our feet, sure, I could carry her over to the window. Like you, fuckhead. In the silence of my street, with the whole night in front of us, breathing hard, possessed by our parts, on my back, my mustache would blacken and grow till it nearly choked me, I'd beg her forgiveness, I'd throw myself at her feet and kiss them. I would've made it a house, if she didn't want a room, with a t.v. and refrigerator, if I could have, with a car in the garage, but that I couldn't do. Nor leave my old lady either. Nothing. Not a thing worked out. A pipedream. A man like me, strong, hairy and stubborn, with all my chest and my kidneys, I folded up like a stick on a riverbank and came apart crying alone, clinging to the wall, hugging a closed house. You know what I'm talking about. See how well we know each other already? We know the whole story, I yours and you mine. How I wanted to take her away to live with me! Living that way, really, she never did live with you.

—I don't recall exactly when it was I met my wife, sir—says the young husband—, I mean, the first time, because after years of not seeing her I met her again and then it was unfortunate for her. I know you don't believe me, but I must insist. And give you enough details. With your permission. I was living in a very small room that served as a sitting room, office and gymnasium. The only window gave on La Paz Avenue, facing the Ninth Precinct, yours, sir, and through the branches of an old almond tree I could make out San Cristóbal Hill, the dove-white image of the Virgin at night and in the background the cordillera. There was no bath in the pension. We gathered for our ablutions at the school swimming pool. Everyone. Men, women and children. There weren't any old people. The one who lived in the attic, barricaded with his relics from the War of the Pacific, had moved. To the cemetery. He was the only one. A handsome old guy. On May 21st he went out to march down the Alameda, loaded down with medals, like a bottle of wine, and he came back like a bottle too, soused to his toes. Then he went up to the roof to kill cats with his scimitar. As I was telling you, we watched each other through the keyhole. The tenants. Really. The woman who lived in the adjacent room knew exactly what time we took off our clothes. My wife and I. Before we were married. Later we lived, as you know, in an apartment without peepholes. Pressing her eye against the door she saw us embrace and fall on the sofa. But she didn't see much, maybe a leg in the air, an arm fluttering, some bouncing up and down, her hair spilling on the floor. Nothing really complete or rhythmical, no whole act, scarcely the sound of the river melting between us, stiff or loose, stuck together, one big navel returning her gaze like a sinking sun.

At that time I spent the days wrapped in an old fur overcoat that used to be my mother's, playing the accordion, spitting toward the window. My hands were covered with a kind of moss which went away leaving its frost. I wore burgundy pants and some little shoes, sort of Japanese. All the details are important, if not for you, for those who'll be studying this case some day. You ask, what could have attracted her? Let's take it slow, there's a long history between us.

First of all, I have to confess I was a lazy bum, totally irresponsible. A piece of shit. Dreaming about how great I was going to be. Here you're seeing me under constraint. It wasn't always like this. I had my lyrical fits and my April in Paris flirtations. To say I knew the reason for my flakiness would be exaggerating. I had some sense of the surprises that were coming because I was provoking them, but actually I just let myself be, stretched out, looking at the hill, full of a certain something that didn't quite get across to me.

I'd get up at noon and go out for a stroll on La Paz Avenue wrapped in white sunlight. Remember? A kind of milky emptiness that ran down the whitewashed walls and the little palm trees. Beside me the warlike noise of the jumble of buses and the iron hoofbeats of the carts on the way to the Central Market. For these walks I put on a blue shirt and bright yellow socks. Clashing, offensive. No one paid me the least attention, but I felt a collective consciousness (the palms, the buses, the carts, the horses) following my steps closely, examining the sense and direction I suggested, knowing it wouldn't be long before I agreed with those who were expecting some desperate act. A close friend of mine had done it already. A young anarchist, with a rosy face and blue eyes like a doll, whom I use to play billiards with at the Academy of the Franciscan Fathers and hung around the gyms where the professional boxers trained. He took on some plainclothesmen on Independencia, ducked into the Carmelite convent (they never show their faces), fired a few shots from the courtyard, they closed in on him, he kept shooting, they cornered him and he gave up, claiming they didn't understand him, that nobody cared about him and they were persecuting him out of revenge and resentment, since before they shot him in the Pen he'd managed to stab one of the resident big fish, a rich and influential character inside the walls of the indeterminate sentence.

This friend and I, just prior to his misfortunes, used to sit at a little table in The Escorial drinking vermouth on the rocks and he would say nothing, listening quietly while I spoke of my girl, and I really made an effort, getting inspired talking about the evenings in the Plaza Almagro, the sun setting like an old jar on the tin roofs of the barrio. Moved, he closed his eyes. The band struck up one of Troilo's tangos.

Nonsense? Probably, but the days passed and the nights wouldn't. That useless solitude of the open window that nothing went in or out of was hurting me. I tried to make friends with the cheapest streetwalkers, the ones who stroll along the river. A bottle of *pisco* would last us till dawn. I thought some heroism was rubbing off on me in touch with such pained soulfulness in those yearless nameless nights. My chest filled up with a peaceful sense of virtue, I felt myself chosen, partly on account of the Catholic flight still sticking to my wings, and partly because of a certain inclination to march in protest rallies and write on walls with chalk in the downtown streets. I won't deny it. Then something happened. The winter ended in Forestal Park.

Facing the entrance to the Palace of Fine Arts, on a bench half hidden by the branches of a maple, my father and mother were waiting, dressed in black. My father, with his mellow face and big yellow eyes and a blond mustache, seemed to have an invisible instrument in his hands, some kind of mandolin covered with glittering leaves, or maybe he was gesturing to say things which, in truth, he wasn't saying. My mother was just a sketch, shaded in like an old sepia photograph. My parents were living a disappearing act, as if posing for a photographer that hadn't yet got there but would show up any minute with his black cloth, his embalming box, his blank plate covered with nothing. I sat down beside them. It was cold. The people going into the Palace didn't seem to notice us. Something in our group made things erase themselves. A taxi went past, the wind stirred the branches of the trees, the street lamps didn't throw much light. Winter, all right. Old bronze bells ringing, one after another. Then, approaching from a distance, I saw this young woman bundled up in a chamois overcoat, a scarf at her throat, her dark hair pulled back tight and smooth, looking at us as if we were waiting for her. When she passed in front of the bench, instead of going up the stone stairs, she came up to us and said hello. She spoke with my parents. Without looking at her directly I began to recognize little by little a face from the past, as if it came out of the maple leaves in transparent perfection, and her hands which brought the darkness together. First memory, I saw her coming out of school. Blue uniforms and white collars. A single agitation lasting just a few seconds. The cannon went off on Santa Lucía. The bells of the Carrillón de la Merced clanged in the air. Sometimes I'd follow her, sometimes not. I think I was scared of her. She was a dovecote, a fluttering in the noonday sun. Nothing more.

Then we wanted to reminisce, it follows. That evening I took her to the Carrera bar and to her the whole thing seemed completely senseless. She told me so herself. It wasn't the right place for us to be, of course. But I was worked-up. The bar full of phantoms all acting crazy. As children, she and I formed part of a train of four couples who night after night went down the last blocks of La Paz Avenue for the sake of then turning into the white light of the little cemetery square. Passengers on a carrousel without music, a simple round following the cracks in the adobe walls. We only got worried when we heard the screams from Los Olivos madhouse. Then the first couple would stop and the rest of us too. We'd kiss like canaries and touch with trembling fingers, feeling around in one another's clothes. We got so excited that the cop on duty, under his thick black poncho, would blow his whistle and we'd separate.

You understand that meeting up again, after so many years, no one intended to start anything. She disappeared behind her screens and I went back to my room with its open window. But later, very late at night, I jumped out of bed, put on my fur coat, ran out and called her on the phone. Nothing special. Nothing, except I was left thinking and it occurred to me that, at best, tomorrow. It was like asking her for the time and agreeing that if it rained we'd meet at the Corregidor Inn, where couples drink hot wine in a kind of tunnel.

And we started seeing each other every day. In the morning I'd seek her out in the School of Education, in the midst of the jumble of coats and umbrellas in the Conversation Room, where the students were rubbing their chilblains over a gas jet. At nightfall I'd wait for her on the frosty sidewalks of República Avenue, passing in front of the French mausoleums abandoned by the rich. I walked back and forth like an orator without a public, a thick bundle of notes in my hand, spouting syllogisms that scared the dogs, provoking chaos among the garbage cans.

My ethics and philosophy professor was the first to notice the change. I went in to take an exam and he dismissed me with a twisted gesture of his long black whiskers. "Get out," he said. "What are you doing in here?" He seemed to smell me. The sacred scheme of Kantian categories had filled up with smoke, the luminous Platonic cave was spinning like some vulgar wheel of fortune crammed with old freeloaders. The professor smelled sulfur on my lapels, her smell on my shirt and my burgundy pants. He took a step backward and snapped, Get out, get out! He didn't want me contaminating the others, bringing traces of the bedroom into the seminary. "You've lost weight," he said, "you have bags under your eyes." Later I had nightmares where this maestro appeared dressed as a baker, whipping me with raw dough covered with flies and I moaning because I'd never amount to anything, much less become a doctor.

On the other hand, my conversations with her began to get serious. I'd say something totally trivial, for example, I couldn't live in a city like Talca, I know the plaza is lovely and all around it savings and loans are going up where there used to be dry goods stores but, year after year, so much hot air, so many Rotarian judges and Lions Club pharmacists, so many mournfully charitable ladies, lotteries and Catholic Masses, maybe a good earthquake every so often. We'd have to consider other cities. She'd ask for details and, since I'd never give any, she'd feel hurt. The subject that really interested me, the one she shied away from, kept buzzing in the air around our heads or hung like a water balloon right above us. I realized it was crazy to try to carry it any further, that it would torment her or at least ruin some plan she'd been preparing with care and skill for a long time. It probably sounds strange, but she wanted me to disappear, flash!—to the other side of the horizon, to go off and come back without my boyish carelessness. Mature, then, and responsible, she said, although I wouldn't put it in those terms. So, I was obliged to get lost for weeks at a time.

There's something, sir, which you ought to understand from the outset. Between that little nocturnal train which ran years ago along La Paz Avenue and the slow steps we took now around the Inn, no connection ever existed. All we had was a blind security, heavy and palpable, we gave it form in my bed, sometimes on the sofa or in the chair by my writing desk, with stormy violence, earth tremors, furniture banging. There were bonanzas of white nights too, long and empty. She'd arrive in the late afternoon. I'd make her a cup of tea. The neighbors would return to their posts at the various holes. Then, with the sun setting over the slopes of the coastal hills and the sad Cemetery-Pila del Ganso buses full of little lights and blue smoke, just like a tango, no children yelling or dogs barking, then, as I say, with the window open and the lights out, and the palm trees stirring, we undressed each other very deliberately, lingering over the details, until, at last, we'd climb into bed for a passionate infight, strong and violent, that would last till nightfall. The woman next door, with her face pressed to the keyhole, was breathing hard. Afterwards, we'd get dressed very slowly and she'd go out alone, the collar of her chamois coat turned up, hands in her pockets. And I began asking questions, more and more questions.

—Going up Merced Street, full of holes—she says not looking at us—, walking at times on the sidewalk and at times alongside the cars, I seemed to be moving inside a blue wind, heavy with earth. I never crossed where he said to, I never went into the passage, but I did go to a theater to see a work by Jorge Díaz about some strange elephants. One of the actors, sitting in the orchestra, started a conversation with me and when they addressed him from the stage he got distracted, or I took his seat and the spotlights hit me in the face. Anyway, I didn't say anything nor could I remember the names and addresses he asked me about after the piece. He started to take off his pants. I didn't see anyone else. I did hear the voices, though. I think he took one boot off first and then his belt, although I'm not sure, he didn't touch me at first and the rest were laughing. When we got to the antique store the whores were on the corner, but not the one with white pants and the iron hoops. They were smoking against the wall. The two men looked at me and let me pass, I don't know what they were saying, although it wasn't me they were watching but some door in the distance, now I think it was the door that you came out of, that's what they said when I opened the inner gate. There wasn't a soul in the park. Then he put me to bed and asked them to tie my arms to the cot. That's when they said you came out and that there was no problem because no car or motorcycle could be seen nearby. He unbuttoned me and I noticed he was sort of sad and his mustache was damp. The rest were laughing. The window was half-open and you set out for the pharmacy, maybe to deliver the envelope they gave you earlier. Who? What for? They asked me. For hours you took a few steps, got as far as the door and turned back, went out of the building again, stepped over the gutter, crossed the street and walked backwards a ways, I don't know how many times. Only you went on sticking stamps to the walls. He put his saber on a chair and his cartridge belt full of bullets on one of my legs. He clenched his teeth. My eyes were barely open but when I put out my tongue a black stain fell down my throat, as if he were standing facing the falls, and the wind were blowing his hair around, half closing his eyes he said to me baby and pawed my crotch where he'd put his saber now and the wires, I want you so bad baby, he said, and if you'll just behave yourself. They opened the car door on you and you turned back, the two plainclothesmen ran and grabbed you by the arms, and the bigger one, who'd gotten out of the car, hit you with a blackjack (so it wouldn't make much noise) and, when he raised his arm I saw a scar next to his right eye, his smiling green eyes and I remembered the name with his legs spread on top of me pushing into me till he started to pound the bed with his fist and his other boot fell, the others laughed hard and he stuck it in my face, between my eyes, in my ears. Hearing the order they spreadeagled you against the wall and one of them slammed his rifle into your shins. But then the jerk came, like a bucket of warm water. I was drowning. I looked right at him in order to understand how much he loved me and that he was going to leave his family and the force, but now with his saber off he pulled up his pants and there were lots of people standing beside the cot.

—Sir, there are other facts I could give you, so let me state them—says the young husband—. You, your wife and your son lived in the pension on the same floor as we did. There was a bell on your door and, above the bell, a Sacred Heart of Jesus. You, as we know, came up from the ranks and on the basis of your merits and intelligence were promoted from sergeant first class to lieutenant. The only officer of that kind we knew in the precinct. Maybe there were others, but we didn't know them by name. In those years you'd levelled off and were enjoying life by the mouthful, with your thick tongue, your six foot frame and your trim figure. You talked more than everyone and drank with such authority setting your right hand on your hip and taking long strides to hypnotize and command respect. You were admired, though I have to admit you inspired mistrust, perhaps on account of your rise to success, which the envious considered the result of some of your favors. Your manners were refined and elegant, your attitude never authoritarian, but it was imposing. You handled your leather gloves like a lady and you smiled from on high like some kind of beaten-up sun. As far as I know, you never cheated on your wife, and you were more than respectful with your son. You worshipped him. Other officers treated you without the least affection, more like a messenger boy in a high class casino. It was obvious they were reminding you of your humble origins: as if to say, you may have a saber and stripes but in your heart you'll never be a gentleman. Nothing bothered you ever, you passed among the troops like a thoroughbred, and among your superiors, like a green shadow, silent and obedient. With my hands tied to the chair you put me in, my back hurting, my legs cramped, one of my knees swollen up, my eyes blindfolded and you pulling my hair, one could deduce that you weren't really happy with your family, that your bosses treated you like scum, that your famous talk on alcoholism and discipline wasn't as successful as you'd hoped and that your final fall was the product of a combination of factors, not of a single individual. Not her, in any case. I don't know—or, better stated, I'm not sure. Falling in love is something that can happen to people like you, I mean, a he-man without vices, feared by his subordinates, a model of his profession, a flawless servant, the perfect family man. But to fall in love is one thing and to cry over a young woman who doesn't know you from your hat and who doesn't dare speak to you because she doesn't know if you can speak, is something else altogether. It's certain, as you say, that it pleased us that you might come to see us. I always treated you courteously, even warmly. I remember my father invited you over with a certain mixture of fear and respect and that you accepted a few big glasses of red wine which you drank slurping the strawberries through your mustache and laughing with your head thrown back as if expecting rain. You spoke passionately, sometimes shouting, sometimes in a whisper. The others might get impatient, get up from their chairs staggering, close in with their fists raised threateningly, or feet set to kick; but never, you who examined them distractedly at a distance, did you turn your back to them. The love welling up in you for my family I discovered suddenly. There was a block party, some chairs were out in the street. It was a summer night, the carts were going by toward the market loaded down with fruits and vegetables. The voices of the old men didn't bother me except for the nervous movements of the old freemason of the neighborhood with his cough, his bloodshot eyes, his tongue hanging out, his fly open. I walked toward the patio, looking for a side exit so as not to attract attention, I stepped off into a darkness of loose stones and low roof-tiles, and there was the couple, you muttering from above, like a weathercock, serious and pained, her in the shadows, her face hidden, hands in yours. That was all, nothing to be ashamed of, as they say, and afterwards—afterwards?—not a blow, not a shout, just a quick turning away, a face, mine, a kind of mystery. My father, as you know, had an untimely death, almost no one knew about it and, like in some popular song, he waited for his time at night, in summer, listening to some piano being pounded nearby. Another thing. Time passed and when they had you on the ropes, as they call retirement, and it was said you had a job as an informer, first, and as a bouncer, later, you sat watching me one night upset for a minute, suffering and nervous, but also annoyed, from your temporary post as a ticket-taker at the Municipal Theater when I entered with my wife, and it wasn't my fault if you saw in me something else, some other person. It's a sadly love-sick old man who sticks out his tongue to communicate and winds up flapping in the air like a chicken, its feathers fallen out on the damp ground. I can't even figure out what you see or don't see in this love which you insist on treating like your own death. Your dead son? Me? Surely not her who, I swear, never could be convinced of your sentiments until that day on the cot, or call it the grill, plugged into your electric prod which you showed off with a hero's pride, but upset with yourself because you couldn't stick it anywhere, since your love was so pure it wouldn't let you.

—It never occurred to me that he could lie—she says not looking at us—, he didn't give me time to think about it. His face above me was like a windowless house, dragging me down familiar corridors, rooms where I once slept and chairs that still held the weight of people I knew but couldn't see. What he kept repeating could never make sense. I mean the details made some sense but his insistence was absurd. He wanted to convince me that we once lived together in a lane called Picarte. His madness could have been more convincing than the prods. Sometimes, over my shoulder, I'd see him get up in his socks, throw some water on his face and hair and turn back toward me with the look of a sewer-rat, cooing through his whiskers and whistling between his teeth. Then he prepared some tea with milk, I helped him on with his boots which he pushed against my breasts. I imagined myself becoming that woman of his hallucinations. All this happened in the first weeks. I don't know how many. He galloped on top of me, swallowing air, suffocating, sweating. He surrounded me with a clumsy tenderness, craving, full of hard bumps which hurt my belly. Then there were no questions and nobody laughed. It's possible we were alone. A wire cot, the prods, he and I in our shorts, looking at the frozen walls and wet cement floor. The sounds of bones or irons or furniture and screams could be heard in other parts of the house. In a few days I lived whole summers and winters with him. The afternoons I spent alone I touched myself carefully, feeling blows from years ago, a permanent retching in my chest, something like dried blood, but most of all his face sniffing my ears, my mouth, my neck, and his teeth always restrained and proper, sucking what they could as if one part of my body were like an open box, smelling of death, whose pain was someone else's, maybe his, because I knew I couldn't doubt the future any more, his truth had become my truth and if his affection was real the dogs who kept leaving bones at my feet were also real. I understood how he felt about me one afternoon when he yelled out the window asking for clean clothes, shampoo and cologne, a platter of sweets and a bottle of white wine. We'd gone two days without eating. The swallow of water he gave me was a thread of mud I spat up on his coat. He wanted to conquer me with hunger, but not really conquer me or anyone, he was trying to change the world with an act of magic, he wanted people to love one another in the smell of his shut rooms, entwined with their prods crying for happiness and remorse, kissing his saber in order to believe securely in his powers. It was that he wanted and nothing less. The world must recognize him and it wasn't me who said so. It was said. By him and his thirty galloping horsemen, whipping my sides at times, or sometimes my legs but especially my face. His face. Together, bleeding, and in our ears the screams of those beginning to fall from the heights, my scream against theirs.

He spoke of our marriage with dates and a lot of details but no names, like that, lying next to me on a calm evening, a sort of break or recess between the screams and blows. He seemed like a young man in love with his shirt open at the chest, his legs relaxed, eyes tired, looking up at the skylight and the bars. He had untied me and spent a long time stroking my hair, pressing my hands, picking up pieces of my underthings left over from the last session. Now he started to move me and tried to cover me with his arms as if my body bothered him or would burn him if touched. He talked about our wedding in La Viñita church and what happened later at the party and how he himself received the prisoners and prepared the reports for the judge. He referred to your father and even said that of the whole hasty gathering he only regretted that the old man didn't come down to the precinct because he was ready to give him a good beating and after midnight drench him with buckets of ice water. I tried to explain a few things to him but he wouldn't accept the comparisons, he wanted details, he demanded faces, he asked why you and the orchestra musician, why the glasses first and not the furniture, and the gunshots in the cellar made him uneasy. Later he took my face in his hands and said none of this mattered, the important thing was to be saved now, he kept repeating, you can do it, all you have to do is see beyond those bars, go out with me and take my arm, which will never leave you, my darling. He climbed on top of me as always thinking he saw me in a tailored suit, with a permanent wave, high heels, or with an apron on in his kitchen, whispering to me with his bad breath about yesterday and the day before, all his same little wet my darlings, his balls and his curls, looking for wool stockings in his sloppy memory. It went on like this till nightfall and when he finally left me alone I knew he was in my power, even though this didn't make sense, was totally illogical to anyone, since it had nothing to do with a jail or torture or interrogations, but with a phenomenal rape, a rape for the faceless woman with an idiot on top of her sobbing and pledging eternal love.

—It isn't clear—the one in uniform repeated, opening his coat—why I handed her over to them. You say, or don't dare say, there were thirty. Exaggerations, lies. You lie as a matter of custom, as a discipline. It's more likely, and more logical, that there were twenty. More or less. Not being much of a man, you'll never know the suffering of someone like me who loves a woman seeing her crucified by fellows who, in truth, don't possess her, but who do their duty, uncommitted, creaming, believe me, in every one of her holes. Love, or let's say affection, can carry a man to all kinds of extremes. I'll repeat it till I die: I only asked for a sign of faith . . . Ah, one caress! They fucked her like thirty hyenas right in front of me, you should have seen the sperm squirting up my nostrils, splattering my whole humanity because its beastliness came running down my face mixed with my tears. Later, alone in my house, not totally alone, though, since my wife was with me watching television, I started crying again, without tears, you understand, upset, that's all, thinking how was it possible, for god's sake, the she couldn't understand how much I've loved her all these years, how I worshipped her little body, just like a sanctuary in my heart, her eyes that don't see me, cut off from me completely and her hair forever in my mouth, and me pressing myself against the wall so no one would see me watching her and showing her my teeth which she'd never understand either, not a word, not a look, hardly a glance of hate. I love her simply, the way one loves a poor room rich with memories! At a table and in bed, alone, seemingly in love, just the two of us, a little tea with milk in the evening and the nights smelling of leather. I could drink her like a shot of anisette, holding her between two fingers, never crushing her in bed because her body wouldn't fit anywhere and her face slips through my hands.

—Sir, what had changed?—says the young husband—. All right, I asked myself other things. Who, how many were there in those years I didn't see her? Do you realize? She had her adolescence, her boyfriend. Boyfriends? Well, no. I'll be frank with you. With all due respect. Your son, sir. In the first, and I'd dare to add, only place. Your family was highly esteemed in the neighborhood because you, who'd risen from below, were well-dressed and harmonious, I can't deny it, ceremonious too, though not exactly serious: while most of the cops made waves with the cream of the maids in the neighborhood, you circulated among the more affluent ladies, all admirers of your long legs, your hard smooth bust, your proud head. Your son, ah, your son was something else. In the first place, he graduated early from the billiard academies, the best ones, he hid himself away in the summer, grew pale, leaning across the green felt of the big tables, letting himself go. Prince of the Derby. That was your son. King of the gamblers. Black felt hat, pointed shoes, very stylish. He didn't say much. He coughed. The fairies watched him playing so they could imagine him in midnight positions. As if to punish them, he stretched himself out across the slate, his body straight as the table, one leg in the air, his tight pants hugging his hips, and he'd spend hours like that, studying the cushions and the angles until the cue would shoot through his fingers with the flash of a meteorite. Quite a guy! Just like a lady.

And you adored him silently and suffering. Because you couldn't understand him. In the tightness of your uniform, you wanted to turn him into a clerk. You couldn't grasp the suicidal elegance of the young man, couldn't sense the saintly smell he was creating night after night. When he abandoned his studies and moved his quarters to the Plaza Almagro you devoted yourself to giving him plainclothes escorts, retired colleagues, informers who owed you a favor. You wanted to deprive him of the only world he could breathe in as a hero.

About then, all of a sudden, your boy sang his swan song. And so, slowly, headlong, he fell into the delicate arms and insolent breast of our friend who came out to protect him with no particular intention, it's clear, but to take over so as to cut him off from his nightly rounds, opening windows and lifting him from the billiard table to wander again through open streets where he could be recognized. Still, it was too late. I'm sorry. He was dying.

And yet, he owed her nothing really. Nor me either, though he preferred me. For the neighborhood families the case of your son and her was an affair which, having lasted too long, turned into a dead issue. And nonetheless she, in those last months, described the patient in a way that worried me. I hadn't come to save anyone nor to interrupt anything. She became bored or desperate standing the night watch. Referring to the patient she said: "He's a femme fatale . . . " Yes, I thought, agreed, he has the pale elegance of an old-fashioned ladykiller, the cold eyes, the silky hair, the slender hands of a strangler. I've met plenty of such temptresses in the Turkish baths. "You're wrong," she'd answer, "or rather, you don't understand, you imagine some kind of hipster, and it's not like that, let's not forget that his father is an institution. Barracks. Respectable. There'll never be disorder in his house, the years will pass and there'll be nothing left of the deceased but the old family photos, a suit of clothes turned shiny, his felt hat hung from a hook, his blurred profile, a necktie on the floor."

76

Not withstanding, the visits continued. Your wife will leave them alone, I thought, she'll close the door, she'll withdraw discreetly, at best she'll go to bed, with expectations. You were always on duty. And the patient was agitated, even more beautiful on his white pillows, his eyes cruel, passionate. Perhaps he stretches his arms, kicks over a lamp, turns on his side, she supports him, he kisses her. What do I know? Maybe nothing. They look at each other, they hear each other breathe. Motionless. A tired bellows, loose and watery. At best they get supremely bored with such a long ceremony.

The last time I saw him—because I saw him more than you may think—he was in bed propped up on a big pillow. He seemed tired but not defenseless. On the contrary, his eyes were lit up with a frantic impatience. If he could just strangle me, I thought. But no. It had more to do with a rage against the things his mother had piled up around him like the footings of a catafalque. He offered me a glass of *pisco* and when I went to drink it he took the first one to his lips and said it's good like this, with ice, strong. I had my doubts; my repugnance was obvious. I raised it to my mouth, feeling the sticky wetness of his purple lips.

He watched me from the depths of a tangle of hair. For you he went on being a boy. To me, he was an explosive old man of twenty-seven. Hard, bony, enigmatic, with fingers like screwdrivers, long fingernails, diffident. He said something that sounded absurd to me. How could such a thing be? "Yes," he answered, "crazy about uniforms since adolescence." He put too much into the sentence and it wore him out. "Her mother watches out for her. If that old lady could cut off your balls with scissors, she'd do it and present them to our friend on a platter." I kept quiet, thinking. I didn't want to contradict him or make him mad.

That woman's a strict old lady with whiskers, agreed, I said. However, I find something a little too sweet about her way of convincing me. "There's nothing sweet about it," he snapped back, furious. "Just a bundle of black hair. A hairy chest. At night the corset comes loose and falls like a folding screen. Once I had my face between the kid's thighs, in the living room, with the lights on, and the old lady came down the hall and, seeing that I noticed her, lifted her skirt to the waist and showed me her pussy. Later she played innocent, as if it had been an accident. Some accident!" He started to laugh and ended up spitting. "She knew why she did it and so did I. Not the girl, because her eyes were closed and I think she was moaning. She couldn't see me the way she was squirming around, so slow and easy."

That's how your son spoke, breathing through a bad hoarseness, in a dry sweat, feverish inside, accusing me with his eyes. His arms were so long they hung outside the bed, like oars. Under the covers he hid things that worried me. He fell asleep talking. Then you came home. You stood there looking with your eyes squinted, then you came closer on tiptoe but your boots squeaked and your saber got tangled between your legs. The patient woke up and turned toward the wall. You stood there with your arm held out, you wanted to tuck him in, arrange his pillow, stroke his head. It's possible you'd heard everything, I mean, the part about the girl squirming. But, tall and stiff as ever, you frowned, took an about-face, walked out firmly.

A little later, in another room, perhaps the dining room, near the patio, glass could be heard breaking—a glass? several glasses?—and it kept on smashing, crunching, shattering. His mother came in with a syringe, uncovered his legs, turned him over, gave him a good pinch, feeling around, squeezing with her long fingers in search of some soft spot among so much hair and bones. I took a few short steps toward the door, politely taking leave, stepping out into the dark hall, walking backwards all the way.

By the time your dead son was really dead, she and I had long since established our routine. Or perhaps it would be better to speak of our excitement, since our confrontations had no particular boundaries: we fucked in the Miami Theater, in Forestal Park, in the Library, sometimes while reading the documents of Menéndez Pidal, underwater in the swimming pool, in my house, in her house, in the morning, in the afternoon and at night. One time we were fucking in my room when a firemen's funeral went by on La Paz. A beautiful company of blue, green and red uniforms, white pants, shiny Roman helmets, black horses, wreaths and flags. We got up from the sofa without separating and like that, stuck together like dogs, we moved toward the window to watch the parade and kept going at it furiously while the Police Force Marching Band marched right in front of us playing Semper Fidelis. The woman next door witnessed it all through the keyhole and, that night, the tenants downstairs found an anonymous note under the door accusing me of being an unpatriotic degenerate.

They were mistaken. Acting crazy may be the result of a youthful impulse, but, as you know, it can also be the sign of the foreordained. And so much, so much tenderness. We held each other up in our arms like a couple of lonesome little old people, lacking any other support, with no clear future and no sign of middle class morality. I wasn't making much, I earned a few bucks as a musician, a comedian and a reader for an old blind man, retired from the university.

Having lunch one day with her family in their house, her father, with his fine peasant voice, turned the conversation toward the future. There is none, I told him with my eyes. But he insisted. Yes, I answered him, I'll finish this year and I'll be one more veteran of wars never fought, another investigator of inflatable pensions, a holy bureaucrat in some office with no funds. Somebody changed the subject. Naturally, once we were married, our destiny lay in this same house. Instead of one mouth there'd be two and four arms fallen and four legs in the air.

I adored the blindness that let her burn herself at my stake, I mean, in a game, for the moment, with no conclusions. She burned with me, that's for sure, and she helped me stab her in the back with her own tenderness. She loved me like a son and that was our undoing.

Now the days were getting colder and one had to look for daily shelter by the heater in the School of Education. But one had to get there first, and the streets were hard, full of loose rocks and cobblestones and puddles all over the ground. The smoke from a few fires on the interminable journey from Mapocho wasn't enough. Those doors off their hinges, the glassless windows, the vestiges of screens, looked more and more like other things as I approached the Alameda. And this made me anxious. Some could have been apartment houses, the doorbells covered with marble plaques, but they were nothing more than garages, really. You know those old doors I'm talking about because for a while you thought they concealed communist cells when in fact they were nothing more than run-down rich people's places. That pink corner where you stuck your ears and informers got overgrown with weeds. Why didn't you go inside and see for yourself? Peeling plaster moldings, empty rooms, high ceilings, unforeseen offices, secretaries with yellowish beards, bald and bent over, jumping from shelf to shelf in search of books that no longer existed. They were going blind.

I said we didn't want to mention the future. But quietly, yes, we were making our plans. I believe she loved me without any foresight, she imagined I'd be a tame companion, that I'd last her a hundred years, warm, with plenty of cash. She could be maternally lusty, with a clear mind and spontaneous actions that made sense. Don't try to learn from books, she said, you've read enough already, but learn not to hide or be intimidated, take off your shades, when we write on the walls we must write on ourselves. Yes, love, I answered. But I was talking through my stomach.

Our energies carried us into a university theater group where we took small parts in a kind of red opera, a protest against the abuses of some government. Opening night took place in a theater in San Miguel one evening in October. At curtain time, with the house full, the police force appeared, with you leading the way like a wooden soldier, with a court order in your hand. Although there was no reason to take drastic measures, since the people filed out along the sidewalk heading home, you had to flex your muscles and take a few prisoners. It was the first time you arrested us. I was set free in a few hours. She was held till the next morning.

One day, a few weeks after this episode, she didn't come back to our retreat. She was gone for several days. Worried, I asked about her everywhere. I got the runaround. I tried to follow her and track her down, but not a clue. However, I did manage to speak with her on the telephone and I had the impression she was dancing with someone else. Someone else! I figured it was you, hard and old. You who swallowed a sword at an early age and move through the world's high places putting down disappeared persons like me, in pursuit of a ripe little body for your hands to squeeze.

I always imagined you as a man with a steady hand and a sweet smile in the moments the girl broke open in all her summer juices. Surely in some pension in Ventanas de Quintero. She, a pigeon. You in a white frock coat. When she came back she said to me: "You're wrong if you're drawing t.v. movie conclusions. Don't get upset." Secret weapons that fire themselves and pointless resistance, I yelled. "There's nothing going on," she had the last word.

But I said to myself: it's like the summer of an underhanded neighbor, with a wide bed, celebrated by little colored angels, a thick invincible shadow, naked as a tree, and on his feet, worn out boots, green wool socks, long underwear, his face and dark hair over her mouth, a calm look resting on her belly with the weight of a life that doesn't have to be lived to gather its fruits. "Nothing ever happened," she insisted. "It's all spelled out. I'm telling you. And you're still mad?" You'll pay. In a thunderous voice. We'll pay. Nothing happened? I wanted to smile but then I just disappeared.

I grew sick from solitude brutally lost in the four miserable streets and the sad square. All of a sudden I got the mange, my voice changed, my eyes got weak. This woman went off in a world that fit between two corners. Dead, shaded out. The bad feeling rankled inside me. It gnawed at me in the dark, there was no way out.

And nevertheless, sir, we started over at a blue dance under pale yellow bulbs. A dry cloudy night in the Palace of Fine Arts. Dancing the way I like between plaster statues and couples with white smocks. We seemed like patients in a psychiatric hospital looking for exits that led nowhere but into dark corners or into workshops full of clay and wires. We went from one studio to another carrying *pisco* in our smugglers' overcoats, without losing hope, watching for the decisive word, the sacred one, the sign we could leap through into the cold wind of the park and its stars. Later we walked along the footpaths which led to Merced Street and from there to the love nest, going upstairs saying nothing, maybe trembling a little because the cold filtered in through the broken windows; our hands were outstretched at first, because of the darkness, and then squeezed tightly together.

You, of course, kept your resentment under control, sitting on your big brass bed, in your undershirt, staring at your huge bare feet. Pardon me for saying so, but I hope it did you some good. We needed nothing but the same old sofa, its cat-smell, its wrecked and betrayed springs, that void where we opened our arms to each other and fell like acrobatic parachutists, mixing ourselves in the deluded air, dropping like stars over the unseen earth.

And how long did it last, this game of blind man's bluff? Good question. I don't know exactly. I do remember that once we'd gotten back together things had changed. You hadn't yet managed to come between us, you were still watching from a distance, a visitor from beyond who came sometimes to see the glass birdcage where we lived after getting married in La Viñita; you left little gifts for your goddaughter, as you said, knowing it made us feel sorry for you, while you checked out the ashtrays noting any signs of weed, or the covers of the red magazines or the names of the newspapers, and you stood there quietly listening to the "Prayer for a Worker," wetting your lips with the sweet wine you'd brought yourself. Neither she nor I needed to explain your presence. You just dropped by like other people's priestly uncles did. You observed and disappeared. That your gaze was like an ox's didn't bother me, in fact it was proof that you were storing up your desire and that the bull in you would turn up later at home.

That's how we lived for a few solid months. We were changing, as I said; I focused on my job as a scribe. We were getting more militant.

And suddenly she left me again. But this time everything was different.

Since she didn't come back and, in truth, it amounted to more than a week since she'd disappeared, I went down to the local precinct, I kneeled in the confessional, you pulled back the curtain, and we spoke.

And so—says the young husband—, like old friends rotting together, you a little older with your hair cropped, I still scared but not as much as before, always on the edge of my chair, covered with sores, pricked and poked and sewn (I haven't forgotten those subtle stitches you put in my neck and my shoulder), my hands untied, both of us sitting on wicker chairs, you sipping your warm beer and I my coke, seeing you sweat, too tired and worn-out to persuade or even to go on asking questions, I've given you these details to get some details, and there weren't any soldiers outside now, the summer passed wide and loose over the melted asphalt and the trees swayed covered with dust and birds. The students came out of the Law School again, took a few steps near the river, and disappeared among the many-colored lights erased by the weight of the hill and the smoke coming down from the sky.

—Your father—said the one in uniform—was respected in the neighborhood but not really liked—and saying this he wiped his face with a handkerchief—. He exuded goodness, but a stupid, mistaken sort of goodness. A weak man. Soft, even. With other people, not with himself. It's clear that some people are born to be duped and, duped, they're respected. Nobody criticizes them publicly, nobody says a thing against them, instead they just fuck them over. The kind of people who screw the rest with kindness. When they screwed your father and stole his shirt it was like safecrackers' work, those strongbox clockmakers with gifted fingerprints, mixed up maybe with a circus magician and his hypnotized assistant. Those of us who knew never doubted it for a minute. They broke him, they squeezed the wound till everything came out. But what he lost wasn't money so much as his self-respect, his presence. You lift up an empty sack and let it drop and it hardly wrinkles. All that's left is a sad lump on the ground. His form is what he lost. Seems like he never did have any content. But it's possible it was the other way around, that there was a richness deep down that nobody understood. Not even you or your family. And the wrinkles weren't random like a sack's, you put them there yourselves, some artfully and some not. Those who knew—ah, those who knew! The tough guys from Maruri and Las Hornillas came by in slow-moving gangs, shady and fat, with carnations in their buttonholes and their hats tilted, big men strutting the avenue from one side to the other, and over their heads a neon dragon flashing on and off in the August rain. They put the mark on your father the same way they brand the first arrivals at the slaughterhouse. He didn't realize he was being ruined, he let himself be venerated, and in our neighborhood to venerate is to love, as you know, and women only love a saint who knows how to sin and, without batting an eye, he had to fuck more than he could handle. Whoever leaves himself half-open gets jumped. The neigh-

"Wanted," drawing by Juan Bernal Ponce.

borhood was crawling with beauty queens and your father went around crowning them till he'd filled his quota. Not too many but not too few. They all counted. They didn't forgive him. This innocent-looking gentleman with his smooth unconsciousness cost me the saber I earned on pure merit. He'd been told that I put the thugs up to it, that I masterminded the operation, provided photos of the house and office, and the combination to the safe besides, and all out of hatred, not for profit but for revenge. Or jealousy. What's the difference between him and you and me? The few years disappeared soon enough. Your wife would know why she climbed on the float and got all involved in spring fiestas while you were learning to fill yourself up with mushrooms and cobwebs. What do you think your sweet little piece of ass was missing? I calmly followed the family tradition. From mourning I went straight to the sweetheart of the regiment. The little virgin of my beloved son. Nobody in the history of our neighborhood—and it's about time you learned the history of our neighborhood and forgot your uppity pretensions—awakened the patriotic soul of our young studs like this girl. Really, don't you agree? In other times they would have fought over her like men, with knives, at night and out in the open. Today, they say things as they go by, they dream about her mounted on sad stallions at a slow trot. I dared to win her for myself and you were never an obstacle. They chose you for the ceremony. Some heat the water, others bathe in it, eh? Every time you played your part, I was waiting my turn behind the trees, you sitting screwing on a bench in the plaza, and I biding my time with an even pulse, handling my saber, sinking into the milky ferns on the hill. You fucked like a little dove, fluttering your wings in a swoon, and I gave myself years learning to hold my horses, because taste, like love, is created out of rage, but there's no anguish involved, and the one who knows how to choose his defeats wisely is the one who wins. I lived to learn it for myself. She knows it now. The years go on polishing the delay, they don't spoil it, in fact it gets even more beautiful and, sometimes, when it's all over, we end up missing it. I'm telling you, without going into the days and nights I took her in my arms just to tear her away from the cavalry. Let's think about La Viñita. Okay? The apprentice punks, dedicated to sipping fine liquors, the ones who live on celery brandy, lost control early and locked themselves up in a well-stocked storeroom they stumbled into by accident. Outside, the barber's orchestra was playing its tangos. Inside, the wedding cake. Suddenly the barber was hit with an inspiration from heaven and started playing "Fascination." I made a distant and elegant appearance. I flew around like a plainclothes dracula with my arms open and a flower on my prick. You were laughing like an idiot sticking your tongue in your champagne glass. Then gunshots started going off in the cellar. But they weren't gunshots, as you know, they were glasses against heads, bottles against chests, hands in the air, full scale destruction of the whole wine cellar. I carried her over the carpet from one window to another, my leg steady between hers and my saber hard against her blue and white veins. Swaying, flying, from one end of the room to the other, back and forth, up and down, from the windows to the paintings, from the family to my chest, wide as a bed, until you couldn't take it any more and stopped the orchestra. Blood ran out of the wine cellar and as night fell there was a meeting of the older folks, but you two had already headed for Valparaíso and, against my will, I didn't follow you. You surprised me. The orchestra kept on playing forever and the ladies received artificial respiration all night long.

—He took me to this house painted dark red—she says not looking at us—, with a thick flat door, a coach house lamp, in the backstreets behind San Francisco Church. Only dim lights from the hall to the infirmary. I was taken quickly from one room to another and I didn't see anyone. Once I was in the bedroom, he didn't ask me a thing. He took off his hat and his belt. He sat me down on the cot and kneeled beside me. I didn't understand what he was trying to tell me. He started taking off my stockings and without even thinking I kneed him in the throat. He fell backward and passed his hand over his face. He seemed to be smiling, but he was crying. He started talking about his dead son, he showed me a photo of us together. He kissed it and went over the details of his sickness, the months in bed, the beard, the end, the funeral. Then he put it back in his wallet, took a deep breath, got up and began a strange dance of some kind, like peacocks do, ringing his spurs against the floor and raising his arms over his head. He came at me and backed away. He stood there fluttering slowly, as if measuring off the distance to pounce on me, but he didn't budge. At times it seemed like he was going to keel over on the chair or against the door. I don't think he saw me. He was blind, deaf, a big sack of feathers in search of a spot to drop his load. He kneeled down again. What do you want? I asked him. Why me? Why? He muttered something about this death that was tearing him up and he tried to console me. Remember, my darling? He said. You've suffered so much, but now we'll face it together. You didn't realize it, maybe, but when my son died and you were left without a sweetheart—because your bum of a husband will never count for anything—you and I looked for each other so that his death would hurt less, and in you I saw more than my son and in me you loved what the poor kid never managed to give you, you and I flew in the circles marked off by the dead one, a little closer all the time, you taking my hands, I with my arm around your waist.

What was the old shit talking about? Because I heard him saying his rosary a few times and maybe I dried his tears, because we both had memories of nights on the town, one in Las Brujas, others in the Nuria, and cynical as he was he even danced with me, trying to put his hands all over me—I mean, what did he think he was doing?

The second day he left me alone. He came in very late and told me he had been keeping the photo in a drawer so the old lady wouldn't see it but now he was carrying it in his coat pocket. We were alone in the room. He shoved me on to the cot and sat down a few feet away. He didn't say a thing, didn't make a sound. We stayed that way awhile. His head was lowered, I think he was crying. He had his hand between his legs and his pants looked like they were unbuttoned.

A little later he started to roar, to howl. He came closer trying to lift my skirt a little from behind and he was moaning. He must have been suffering terribly because he was sobbing, drowning. Finally he quieted down, buttoned himself up, put on his coat and left the room. This happened again several times during the night. Way past midnight he came back drunk. He pulled my hair and stuck his thing in my face. He wanted my mouth. He hit me in back of the neck and dragged me across the floor. I was bleeding and so was he. He threw himself on top of me screaming, begging forgiveness, pressing or falling into me.

—Between her and me—the one in uniform muttered—the proper distance had to be acknowledged. She didn't understand that my intentions were honorable and that her presence in that house wasn't due to any crime, that our conversations were, in fact, unnecessary. Logically enough, I brought her there to save her and so that she'd appreciate once and for all how I felt about her. It wasn't a matter of struggle, much less of insulting or hurting her. I'm a decent man and these kinds of things happen all the time. It's perfectly normal and Christian. The problem, you'll say, is that thirty men had her. Ahead of me. Nevertheless, I feel obliged to state that you don't understand compassion, much less love, because you see only some brutal ritual in that jumble of human bodies and you fail to understand that they were tearing *me* apart through her, that their fingers, their teeth, their paws were carving *me* up, and her suffering was never really hers. It was mine and mine alone. She learned my love with blood. All that human beastliness crawling over her, biting her, slobbering and squirting on her, made her all the more noble and beautiful. I think a few took a second helping. That's why there were probably more than thirty altogether. And some weren't satisfied with twice, they wanted three. So we could speak of forty, then.

—Afterwards—she says not looking at us—he stopped in the doorway and stood there with his arms wide open and his back to me. What did he see? What was coming to an end for him? What was he trying to see? I don't know what was outside that door because he never let me get near it. A hallway? A patio? An entrance? An exit? If the International Red Cross was coming, as they said that morning when they woke us up, maybe they would set up sewing machines and hair driers. The problem would be to wash the floors, since dried blood always looks like shit; besides, his tracks weren't like ordinary paw prints but more like goose steps. That morning, bound to the bedstead, stroking my hair, he kept asking me to stick out my tongue and wiggle it. Seeing it like that, he cried a little, but all of a sudden his tears stopped and he pressed his tongue on mine with a winglike slap and hugged me, scraping the back of my neck with his big bronze ring. "Baby, if you ever get out of here," he said to me, "I want you to take with you the memory of this back, you knew how to sink your nails in, not a piece of my shirt, not a lock of hair, nothing but this back where some time you lay down like in a sacred grotto to wash the stains off your belly and mine both. Till death, my darling." Then, as I say, he tightened his belt and installed himself on the threshold making like a vulture or something, without my understanding the strangeness of his gestures. But I did notice the hole under his arm. That, I told myself, is what he's trying to get across to me. I could get out through his side, like Adam's rib. He couldn't fail to notice it, and even must have been getting uncomfortable, but he stood still, looking the other way, letting me escape. He'd forgotten his saber on the table, but maybe he hadn't forgotten it. He put it there to tempt me or teach me something. I stretched out my hand. He didn't move. I realized I could not only reach out my arm but I could take the sword, slip it out of its sheath, pick it up. Those days and nights of exercise had hardened my muscles. I stood up, took a few steps, felt my warm wet thighs again, I looked at my feet which he had washed for me and again the nails were white and firm. With his arms still up he was now humming his farewell. From outside I heard women's voices, the sounds of scissors, pans banging. I tried to remember the course from the street door to my room. All I could recall was a little bed and a vase with flowers. A kind of steam was coming off his back and his hands were beginning to drop. My legs failed. Off my feet, with my bones every which way, my hips out of focus, I felt him opening me in the middle and forcing both his hands up inside me. Then he looked at me with a scared expression. "No, my dear," he said, "one doesn't express affection like that, nor gratitude. You'll only fall in the trap again with such maneuvers. Never forget what the old man taught you." He started to slip off his belt and stopped. Several persons went running past. No shouts, no orders. All you could hear were the drops of water dripping on the prod. He took me in his arms and kissed me, slobbering on my face. Then he pulled my knees apart and stood there staring, breathing hard. He turned me around and lifted me on to the chair. "One more time," he said, "could be the last." He undressed and sat on me, looking at the door all the while. He stayed like that awhile until he decided to stretch out like a snake and slide away whistling. "With love," he said, and smiled not finishing the sentence. Then he closed his eyes and, on his back on the bed, began moving his hands. In the doorway I stopped too and turned to look at him. He'd put his green shorts over his face. I don't know. I'm not sure. Maybe he was hoping I'd stay.

—Sir, what's hard to reconcile—says the young husband—is your eagerness to get the facts straight and your pleasure in getting everything mixed up. For example, my wife has always been slender, tall and aloof, with long straight hair, dark brown, almost black, she has a superior air which she conceals with a half smile but she ends up imposing it by looking at one ironically. She was wearing jeans, a leather jacket and sandals when they picked her up. And you tell me of an older woman, with curly hair and high heel shoes. Or didn't I hear you right? I wouldn't contradict you, but you say that on her arrival you took off "her rings," her watch and her necklace which you kept in an envelope which you later put in the drawer with the photograph. Rings? You must be crazy. Excuse me for saying so. You see her as fat and you put skirts on her, you make her lips bigger and, to take your descriptions seriously, she has hips like an infantry sergeant. But that's not even consistent because the next thing you say is that they cut off "her blond braids" and you claim that the prod didn't damage her breasts much, since "they were hardly noticeable" anyway. And what kind of scars are you talking about when you say she was missing a lung, that she was drowning, but that it wasn't a total collapse, and her face kept going purple until a fixed grimace stayed on her face "like a wart?"

No, surely you're joking, you're trying to confuse me with persons, dates and places that just don't fit. Permit me to indicate a few details that will be the last word on this. Because, as you yourself warned me, there's no time left for more. In those spring days we were making plans, like everyone, to move to the beach. We'd bought a little lot in a development for white collar workers. Big enough to set up a camping tent and have friends over. You know who I'm talking about. In winter, with the tide up, our property disappeared. A bit of a nightmare. Nobody drowned but we thought it might not surface again and would stay at the sea bottom with the rest of the summer ruins, the underwater deposit of tents, parasols, canvas chairs, straw hats, shovels and little colored buckets. No printed propaganda, as you state. Even so, we often went in winter and stopped the car on the dirt road imagining where we would put our house, impressed by the crashing of the waves, breathing deep the smell of iodine, salt and wet sand.

Things were going along smoothly, but I wouldn't call them normal. She finished her last year of Economics. I taught my little classes and once a week delivered my red pills of wisdom to one of the afternoon papers. The apartment house on Lastarria Street was good and secure. Whoever made their nest on the upper floors of those ruins shared a security that was strictly surprise-proof. I imagine it had to do with the paneless windows and the loose door-frames. Some police raid after midnight, which in other parts of the city wouldn't even wake up anyone, in our building sounded like bombs going off and kept echoing for hours. I'm talking about a community of books, paintings, wines, fat cigars. There was talk of a new life. It seemed like everybody was running around with paintings or poems or music—and forums, lots of forums. In practice, we did whole days of volunteer work that filled us with pride. A good life, nothing special, but a lot of commitment.

The two of us ate in a diner that was nothing more than a big room with rattan chairs and tables with red and white checked cloths. Our lives were cheered up by a few little pitchers of white wine, smooth and fragrant, that burned a bit going down and then turned cool and mysterious. We knew that maybe we weren't headed anywhere permanent, because the explosions, as you know, were happening more often and bigger all the time, but the awareness of running the road together fired us up. We discovered powers we didn't know we had. I always wanted to hear her speak, but she rarely gave me the pleasure. She had a tender smile that served to keep me in the dark. The noodles gleamed in our plates with oil, tomato and basil, we raised our glasses and I hoped her statements would match my plans for big things to come. Nothing. It's possible we had a premonition of a break, a sudden fall like when we stumble in dreams. But she didn't leave me yet, she was stirred up, that's all, with her head on my shoulder, far and near at the same time, united somehow for hours, whole nights, moving together and apart by turns.

They were difficult days. Our city had changed. People preferred to look the other way. 1975 ended in the midst of rumors which instead of inspiring us, crushed us. Our friends took off. The ones who didn't leave figured out ways to avoid being seen. A willingness to disappear contaminated us all. And we had to resist, not frighten the rest with the real face of fear and paranoia. If we sought each other out it was to convince one another that we were all right, okay, surviving hard times, but not that bad, it was still possible to do important things, the blackout couldn't be fatal, one could even get used to the horror and comprehend it, that is, swallow it and keep it down. Who in those months could speak without terror and shame? Some did and disappeared. We called each other to tell of daring, subversive actions, strikes and protests, but everything came to us like news from another country, a world separated from ours by secret walls. We wanted to impose on ourselves the obligation of sharing a seriously frightened city. The ones who lost their heads convinced themselves that turning themselves over to the dictatorship was justifiable if they did it shamelessly and with a cynical optimism. To flatter the dictator with their blessings amounted to blessing themselves.

We followed the only course possible. We'd learned to speak a language of signs which functioned only among intimates. All those smiling people who were lying out loud saying no one was dying, no one was disappearing, everything was fine and in perfect order, formed a giant fly-trap in the face of which one kept one's eyes and mouth shut. Some, as is well known, accommodated themselves to everything, others reserved the right to revenge. And don't look at me like that because I'm not telling you anything new.

The day you picked her up we had lunch with a doctor who was leaving. He seemed a little distracted. I had the impression that his head had suddenly grown. Or it could have been his hair standing up, or his eyes plucked out behind his glasses, or his mouth definitively open. This was his second attempt to leave. The first time he got as far as the airport, passed through the security checks, said goodbye to his friends and boarded the plane. Two plainclothes agents took him out of his seat. Not dragging him by the hair, like they do others. The fingers gripping his arms like pincers were enough. Now he wanted to convince himself that everything was running smoothly. "They interrogated me that time," he said, "because some idiot neighbor slandered me. They said I was carrying messages for the resistance. But, I have to admit, they were very proper. Even polite." We weren't convinced. He wanted to believe that they could even be polite, that taking a person out of an airplane is bad, but not so bad, that it could be tolerated and even understood. We let him talk. The wine was showing me a different face behind his wrinkled features, his thick glasses, his big mustache. I looked him over as if they'd already skinned him and his gestures turned into the twitching of freshly inflicted wounds. His words came out wrapped in unspoken excuses. They changed in transit between his tongue and his lips. His eyes concealed nothing, we could see his uncertainty in them, but also affection and a kind of panic at the possibility we might be taking his words at face value. It seemed to me he was having a hard time swallowing his cold meal. Maybe we drank to show the rest that we had faith in the country and that the meals of that summer would be followed by siestas like in the past and that new lovers and refreshed travelers would get up from these siestas. We said goodbye to him with an embrace, not looking one another in the eyes.

Afterwards, we went to a movie. The film portrayed a moral problem with no solution. A priest, complying with the dogma of his religion, sacrificed his sister's life in order to save her child being born. It was a vicious circle and he did the only thing he could, suffering but without hesitation. To save or to condemn had in our world been transformed into actions which were taken but never confronted nor discussed, not even mentioned to third parties. So the man was lost from the outset and his duty consisted in covering his defeat with an imitation of respectable efficiency. No one respected him. Nevertheless, when you think about it, his heroism consisted in crushing all doubt in order to maintain an awareness of his failure. More power to him. She asked me what I thought and I told her the truth. We'd come to a point where what interested me was not the morality of those persons who stepped on and off trains, boats and taxis, who danced and ate or jumped out of windows, received honors or dishonors, but the concrete *things* which led them from their beginning to their end. The film fascinated me with the smoke of a locomotive advancing through the snow, the luxurious emptiness of a Boston cathedral, the bicycles in a park in Vienna, the deathbed of a village priest, the little kitchen where his servant built a woodfire, the splendid avenues roamed by bands of Nazis armed with flags and axes. Maybe the day would come when we'd go back to concerning ourselves with men and women, and things would leave us indifferent. Now, the important thing was our little car. For others, it was passage on an airplane, that is, an airplane that might land eventually.

She went home. I, to the newspaper.

I came back late. She wasn't there. The apartment had been searched. The next day she didn't come back. I started looking for her. It was a job at which I had plenty of experience. I'd go on looking for a long time.

—Your wife will turn up, don't worry—says the one in uniform closing the folder—. How many times have you come here? I guess we could say you've lost count. But tell me, confidentially, do you really want to know? Are you really interested? What for? Man to man. Because you know what happened to her. Some of it, anyway; not all.

What kind of person is it you're running around in search of? The same one you left in your apartment one afternoon? You and your lawyer allege that a woman named so-and-so was taken prisoner in her home and transported, like a piece of furniture, to a place of detention. According to the witnesses it happened in the late afternoon, in a pretty strange light. We all know what happens in our city when the sun goes down. Between the Andes and the coastal hills reflections are generated which cause the citizens to see things. They say these plainclothes persons took her away and put her in a blue Fiat. The lady never made the slightest protest; on the contrary, she was seen to be calm, like someone going out for a ride who expects to return soon. Traffic was heavy and though the street you live on isn't ordinarily very busy, that afternoon there was some congestion due to a performance by the Noisvander Mime Troupe.

Who took her away? You're wasting your time. I'm telling you as an old member of the family. You imagine that I know more than I'm admitting. But you're mistaken. It's the truth. I swear. Nothing but the truth. Rest assured. You'll walk out of here like a new man, with a clear mind, a light heart, blameless. To live, my friend, to forget—and you can. I'll never be able to forget and I'll go on suffering because you and I are different. I loved and love that woman as she deserves to be loved. You deserve to forget her. If only she'd understood her dilemma you and I wouldn't be talking now. You're not a prisoner. You're the one who insists on coming in here. And if you were roughed-up a little it's for your own good. Wise up for once. Learn your lesson, since I haven't yet learned mine. You say you want to find her. Look for her. She's yours if you do. And why haven't you found her? It's such a small world. She'll turn up at home one day. The same leather jacket, the same little blue jeans and sandals. A little girl. Be careful, though. She won't be a girl. You'll notice it in her eyes, or better, around her eyes, you'll see a little weariness that's not really weariness but wisdom, because she learned a lot with us, and you'll note on her mouth the years she lived this year. Take a good look at her tongue. You'll see how bitten it is. Her neck will have sunk and you won't be able to see it from the front. It's not a matter of sweaters or pants. Observe and examine the inside. What you, even before my son died, banged around your room like a drum, what was a circle of honey, as you know, and golden like a sun and which guided the night's hours and the day's eagerness, you'll find that larger than it was. Although another word might do: more mysterious, frightened and, perhaps, a little flooded. Because from me she inherited all the love she denied the rest. I want to tell you the whole amount. Roughly. As it should be. I inherited her from my son. It's natural, fine. We understand each other, isn't that so? You just butted in, an intrusion. You had nothing to do with it. When my boy died she and I kept alive not just his memory but also what he wanted to do with her but didn't have time to. Why do you think I brought her here? You people don't think, you believe you're part of a defeated army and you act like prisoners of war. You're cracked.

You lack imagination. I brought her here to wipe out all the sins of an unfaithful persecuted woman and teach her a lesson tenderly, guiding her step by step toward a new life. I mean a life with me because I deserve her, I won her. But I lost her. If only she'd learned a few things! To love her or beat her, to caress or torture her—those aren't things you invent in your cowardly accusations. I never beat you, right? You know why I never beat you? You don't deserve it, shithead. Beating you would be beating a wall. Even less. Because a wall won't cry but you will, you faggot. She'll show up. But you won't. Funny, eh? No, shithead. You'll both show up. The problem is where. And I'm going to help you solve this problem. Listen. The sad thing is my old lady doesn't even understand. She never has. She says the girl is a whore. Funny, but in a certain sense she's sort of right because it's logical and natural that, even if she accepted me some day, I'm not going to leave my home and live with her. I'd set her up in a furnished apartment, I'd give her an allowance and sometimes—sometimes!—we'd go to Valparaíso, to an out-of-the-way but respectable pension, to take in the salt air, me full of a sailor's juices, she full of me. A man like me is indebted to his profession and his institution. Your kind exist by virtue of our work, our duty as officers. How can an innocent child sleep when there are maniacs loose on the streets wielding clubs and throwing knives? The answer: because there are creatures like us willing to sacrifice our happiness on the altars of the institution and the home. I already know what you're thinking. That happiness never existed. I understand that there must be an area in which you, she and I don't connect, some part of the days we live where we go along side by side and don't see each other, we even speak to each other and say things like the deaf do, meaningless. You don't have to be too bright to be aware of this. Particularly in my case. Sometimes I think I'm just making up the whole thing, that this woman doesn't even exist, or that she's some person I got the hots for on the street and I brought her in here to run her through the gauntlet and, that done, return her to her regular rounds, her routine unbroken. Obviously, you know it's not like that. I, personally, with tears in my eyes, delivered her with her hands tied and her legs spread to the whole regiment. It is, then, a passion with a long history whose details should be collected so that, some day, your questions can be answered.

You want to know, in the first place, where is your wife. It no longer matters to you whether her detention was legal or illegal, or if the letters delivered by your lawyer are still in the toilet or are now on file in the sewer. In the second place, you want to know if she's been set free, if she's taken refuge in an embassy or was put on an airplane and, if not, when she'll be leaving and if she'll be able to return home or will have to expatriate. All very reasonable possibilities. In the third place, you fail to ask the most serious question of all: if your little woman was here, if abuses were committed against her, as you claim, if she was turned over to the personnel on duty and they fucked her one on top of the other, if she heard from me day after day, night after night, the expressions of a hopeless passion, but—and the but is important—heard them flooded by my love and my caresses, if she survived a chain of historical events that could be called

91

traumatic, is it possible that she, once free, will recognize and accept you, as if nothing had happened—you who've done nothing, besides, but whine and beg for mercy? Will she want to accept you, having tested my powers, my faithfulness and integrity standing up to all your complaints and abuses and insults? Or let's turn the question around. A young fellow, whose brief marriage, since we have to recognize it's been interrupted on account of the irregular circumstances we're all living in, seems shaky, if not broken—and I repeat I'm not talking about any personal blame—knowing that his mate has been in trouble with the law and the authorities, as a result of which she herself has had to experience the glories and reverses of the regiment—will such a young fellow be able to forget, pretend to forget, resign himself or understand, and resume his domestic activities—not to mention the political ones—as if everything had been cleansed and purified? I think the voice of experience has the obvious answer. You don't have to be a drum major to understand the nature of the damage done her and the consequences due. Right? Let's be frank. During our chats you've seen tears run down my cheeks. Right now I should sign this paper setting you free and I'm already smearing the ink, an emotion that won't calm down, my boy, that a hairy-chested he-man can't, doesn't know how to, control. So you see, we've come to know each other and I believe we've even come to understand each other a little. We won't be seeing her again. Listen to this and don't chuck it out because it's neither advice nor opinion. It's not an oracle talking to you, boy, it's her talking to you through my mouth. You'll run into her on the streets of a city you're not going to recognize, you'll see her sitting on a bench in the square you like so much and she won't signal to you and in the square the people will all be walking backwards. Believe me. You had your days and nights of glory. I had mine. They cost me more and I enjoyed them more. She is a person who will never turn back. What she learned will make it so she won't need you anymore, and so she'll never be afraid of me again. Where have her blessings and curses taken her? That's her business and nobody else's. As for you, why don't you get out of here and go back to the den where your terrorists are waiting—bored, no doubt. If you want to try to measure up to me in the future, you won't find me. You'll have forty judges. Maybe a few more. Some went back for seconds. Not me. I'll keep waiting. A little show of appreciation. That's all.

And now, get lost. Your wife—yours, hear?—will turn up. Don't worry. If you like to worry, okay, give her up for dead, you asshole.

Chorus

The officer showed me his know-how consisted in wasting away on the outside and letting his beard grow inward. His eyes had learned to shine with rage, humor and catlike disdain. He often sat naked on a sunlit bench observing the skin on his long arms, the bones of his hands, the shine of his shins and his big see-through feet. At noon, when the channel is a single red light and the hills' clay hardens its quartz rings and lights its jet-black bangles, the officer went down to the beach and stretched himself out on his back on the sharp stones. The water came up to him in cold ripples and retreated burning with the blue fire of the stones.

The man felt a great respect for my wife, but the kind of respect some people have for floods or landslides. Maybe some special bond united them, like breath, for example, or the trouble they had expressing themselves. The fact is, when youth was mentioned, he thought of her.

The happiest days of a man's life are spent watching his little children playing on the beach, he said, and though this thought was spoken lightly the seriousness of his words and the silence that followed gave them a motion like water and a sound like the wind swiftly and softly rustling the pine grove and the pier on a summer afternoon.

I place my diplomas on the floor, I await the delayed lady traveler, I arrange furniture and curtains and I straighten all the paintings.

A thin trail of wine runs from my door to that hand in the air waving goodbye.

The pictures they take of me don't come out; before they came out blurred. I consoled myself thinking that my face had time before defining itself completely, that some feature would change or I'd get refined, get deeper. I had to be disillusioned. My eyes gave back the executioner's look. An eye for an eye, said the executioner, as he put the hood over my head and the tape on my lips.

He's fighting for his life, said the onlookers, while I put the finishing touches to one more self-portrait. I painted and rubbed out and went on painting till all the colors were gone; then I went back to the palette-knife and kept scraping. I recalled the plump little gentleman, respectably bought-off, whom they buried alive in the Public Cemetery and who left tracks of his rude awakening and sudden disenchantment on the polished wood of his coffin.

With the palette-knife it's possible to penetrate, layer by layer, the empty shell of a model. I mean, till the knife hits bottom and blood pours from the portrait.

But if the world resists palette-knives and brushes too and doesn't bear fruit, where do we put roots?

Birds fly determined toward the grave passing swiftly among dry branches in a cloudless twilight. Obviously the tree grows upside down. Earth and sky change places. We have no way of knowing who gets saved or who has hope or who goes out in a rage slamming the door.

One thing is clear: it's possible, quite possible, that all may be saved. And this I can not understand.

For the moment, I accept no other form than that of the trapeze: reason and the void of the mortal leap are hidden there.

I come and go in a closed space, pushing my way through the crowd that covers the walks and blocks the exits.

Down on their knees, the young learn to protect themselves from night. They've traded the rugs for skins and the tigers for paper flowers. They look in each other's eyes and what they see gives them a tenderness.

You said to me: repeat this word to yourself, repeat it with your eyes shut till it fills you from head to foot, till it goes inside you ringing like a bell and the whole world disappears in it; trace the circles of the universe with your fingers and extend them the length of your arms, your shoulders, your neck and your head, in such a way that the universe embraces you and you the universe.

So I chose the word *band* and was filled with soldiers coming and going inside me, marching around and playing brass horns the whole length of my silence.

Then I chose the word *evening,* the sweetest and most serene, and I was filled with the world that's paused to look at the trees, the stars, and a few twinkling airplanes.

I'm on the way back, alone, thinking about the houses I've lived in, recalling a few images for windows.

I remember a tiled hall in a sparkling clean house, cool on a summer afternoon. The light: green, alive reflecting the trees and indoor plants.

Later, a narrow room, nothing more than a door, a sofa, and the bulbs kept going out in the lemony floodlights. Sitting with my legs together, wrapped in my mother's fur coat, I'm playing the accordion and I squeeze the box so violently I rip my pants. A thick-lipped black-eyed friend cries at my side.

The lights went out; I'm reading surrounded by candles in a house with a high ceiling and no furniture. The street is called Maruri. Today I'm thinking of Neruda. Then I was thinking of the late Matías Pascal and, opening the blinds, I saw the sun going down in the coastal hills, pausing awhile like a brazier on the low roofs of the brick houses. The people withdrew without noticing me and I lay down in the air reading *The Spiritual Canticle.*

In an attic, something like an aviary, plaster busts were kept, and in the morning I took them out into the sunlight. From the balcony I could clearly see the mist and the ocean. A young man with wavy hair and a black beard was watching me seriously. I opened my eyes and he was gone. Later, a black cat with white whiskers took his place. I have a big window that faces the hills. A gust of wind blows the frames open suddenly and all the green curtains start billowing furiously, I don't know what to do or say and the curtains flap still harder. The carpet is red.

I live in a house of stairways and go up and down along the walls in search of the dining room. I'm sitting at the table and at my side is a purple bottle, an empty glass; looking steadily into the glass I see that I'm terribly hairy and my skin is a violent yellow. There was someone next to me.

Neruda now finds himself facing the same window in the dusky darkness. Suddenly a big dog jumps up behind him barking and Neruda turns away, whistling sadly.

I don't remember clearly enough those houses with stairways going nowhere. I do remember the eternally lit-up walkways and the plastic carpets over which a lady prisoner passed carrying a heavy gold-framed mirror on her shoulder. I remember also that she never could find her door. And, on the other hand, I was buried in that house.
I never got any rest, nor will I ever.

I sleep in a brass bed covered with piles of quilts and blankets; a palm tree commands the patio, and at the foot of the palm a dog is scratching. Surrounded by stars, the belfry has no bells.
The neighbors are calmly shooting at each other. A helicopter patiently cruises the rooftops.
I get up early, asking if anyone's been killed during the night, I'm told yes, one near the metal door of the bakery.

The finest house was built by this mastermind in a treetop, encircled by hoot-owls, stool pigeons and chicken-hawks. Perched on his terrace he watches the eucalyptus growing and tosses seeds into the air. The ground breathes. A brilliant drizzle falls on the fields. By morning the house has vanished.
Everything's covered with violent poppies.

The grapevines start climbing my legs and soon they cover my belly and chest.
The world has turned familiar and also begins to give way at the edges: we go on growing and aging together in my trees' bark. I'm turning the earth with this soot-covered shovel I inherited. All depth encloses its dampness and its wealth of shadows moving quickly from root to root. My garden grows fast and bears fruit underground among the silent ones who keep me company. They grow and I understand them. To grow is to reach out to the shoots already climbing the crest of the hills.
In the morning a cow appears, like a tourist, in a clearing of the countryside; the cow moos and the town answers. I am a shepherd, the bell is trembling in my hand, but I breathe deep and inside me pine boughs stir and peppers bloom and a tomato splits open bleeding in the beak of a quick bird.
What destiny does this summer offer us? And why ask for a destiny at all? Perhaps the problem itself has not been clarified! Didn't we say I'm planted in the grove and respond to the ground's urging?

We're holding out for a downpour; thunder and lightning over open country with girls on bicycles coming down the road. There are legs more powerful than the best-equipped armies. Their sweat smells like gardenias.

Suddenly I notice a change in the landscape: one sees clearly who's fighting for life and who's hoarding it, withdrawing like an empty net.

I'm in a glass house and the strait at my feet disappears. The sky starts crackling. I hear the ferment of the dwarf apple inside its red and green knots exploding on the sand. Everything in that expectant world breathes with the rain's rhythm which at times turns into something else sticking to the trunks and the limbs like the memory of other rains and other woods and other ferns going the way of the dawn train.

To fight for life, at times like this, is to understand I've wasted years refusing man my surrender and woman her pregnancy, haggling like some shady trader over the courage and tenderness I should have left free and clear, believing myself the plastic clerk that everyone touches and no one cracks.

What did I gain? A face of fixed features in my portraits, a dance step that let me come and go on stage without applause, a document written on velvet that says:

Cast the first stone

Everywhere cups with my name, mirrors and backs, gestures scarcely suggested then erased, young men who eye me strangely and turn to look which way the sun is shining on the walls.

The earth has begun to sing: first it's that rain I feel falling softly over the world, then the flight of the blue birds in the dimness of the house, a slow breathing among the trees, the movements of water from one century to another, deserted airports and the footsteps of armies retreating to their barracks.

It's the familiar life once more timidly trying its tune, friends and family meeting at sundown, a little older, learning an idiom of signs and gestures brought on by the need to communicate in exile, and it's the children who gather round me and write their names in my breast and speak of my house abandoned in the land of flutes and cousins.

What happened?

A change in the landscape: I'm coming to understand you now that everything's said and just a few lives are left ahead. Can years be recalled which we never lived and we went on arranging like a border of stones around the bedstead? I think so because they're full of your images I summon at will. But this will has nothing to do with me, you did it. You go on walking around the day surprising me with the flowers sprouting from your fingertips and the plants you hang from the lamps in the house: it will be said you pass with the last breeze moving the tops of the vines and you stay there afterwards slowly smothering me, smoothing the ashes, conducting the smoke out the windows.

I don't know how many times you've been born in me, but this is for real. You begin to distribute the shine of the silverware surrounded by children and animals, confusing friends and family with your air of a wicker chair or a little queen grayed by country labor, a weaver of threads which attract both bees and angels. You drink like a fish in the afternoon when the churchbells ring alarm and ice jumps out of the glasses and I, on my back, smile seeing you stroll this way again and everything discovered in your absence turns to a good word, a rose on my plate, cool sheets flapping on the balcony.

So I love you and I smile again and that's how we'll spend the summer, you returning and I learning, happy and filled with memories I thought lost, surrounded by photos and paintings, and children who come down out of their picture-frames and are the home we're to live in renewed.

The world I know is in bloom, as I say, and it's a single plural motion of snow suspended among dark pine trunks, floating on the limbs which celebrate their load, a lithe and varied nightfall which doesn't quite fall and even rises infinitely feathered, the forest dances half-way up and in the rhythm of snow and silence everything shakes and responds, without distance but with depth, and the light being born over the lake blinds us gladly, palm of your hand I caress shining, since nothing separates us and the sudden ashen sun comes flying out of the chimney one more time.

I've come to make a pact with earth: I need its silence, it needs my transience. People appear and disappear around me.

Today my house was full of brown gardeners with yellow hats. Now they're all shaded out. The willow murmurs like a boat among waves and the leaves come and the leaves go. Nothing makes sense but the whispering evening which stirs and advances toward the soft hills where the dew-gardeners wait.

I'm patient and I know how these things I considered part of my life will be the life of some other public employee in future centuries and I'll go on resisting, or sitting or thinking or watching among pieces of furniture that denounce me. They'll come back to see me. But that other one won't see a thing. He'll know that someone called at dawn but won't know where the unknown whistler is.

You'll carry me like the shadows that suddenly appeared on the young mother's face.

Maybe we're born over again and you already bear me in your womb. Perhaps you don't have time to bring me to light, perhaps that light is reserved for another who loved you and wanted you and waits impatiently to jump you from behind.

I exist in whoever understood my strength, but didn't let on; in whoever preferred to smile inside and got away with no time to consume me.

Everyone who destroyed me gave me a bit of his strength and his beauty. I live and survive in whoever is ashamed of their thanklessness and would rather not think about me; or think of me when they turn out the floodlight and fake sleep. I have more friends among the persecuted than among the blessed.

A woman dries my face once a week and no trace of my looks is left on the cloth. I've told her piously I don't deserve her sacrifice, that she should look for another more worthy, another who, finally, may leave some impression of the blood, the sorrow, the hope and the love she deserves.

We are a round couple turning like rosary beads
we are a motionless sun breathing out of the swamps
a dry flower flying among the stopped sailboats
a day hidden behind the blinds
we are two hunters waiting to shoot the sun
quick lightning, breaking up, throwing out spears, taking prisoners
in the air
a tongue hanging out
some world of water and clouds trying to dawn, in your face so open,
in your hands so closed
a deer covered with snakes
a bird eating breakfast and the squirrel sewing its pillow
we are the edge of the mountain and all the sky's mistaken rays
of dawn
a second of doubt, a whole life burning
a great red melted bell
the shadow of the last airplane, the hurricane wind that set off
a shooting star
we are a chapel of dry pines breathing the first smoke
a long whistle on the lagoon, a strong breeze
a deafening explosion one morning and the shape of the crater
becoming a hammer
two acrobats in the sky throwing flames
we understand one another like two tongues pulled out
by the roots.
    Resistance is the word that defines us: the uniforms hang drying
in the noon sun.
    Homeland is a mysterious cipher where the lost winds of the
calendars are fused
it's a wake, a gravestone, sometimes water, sometimes foam
and sometimes snow
it's a forest of brass trees, a flock of birds burning on the
immensity of the emerald.

    I breathe deep, I'm paying attention: on the pier an anxious
young woman is signalling to me.
    It's time to shove off, the red sails are up in the East.
    Who separated the sea from its violence?
    Why do the nights come on like exhausted armies?
    Who's in control of the last fires?
    They are fighting at the gates of our city.

Part III

Like the Hyena

By Poli Délano

Translated by Marilyn Mcgee

There are some days, especially mornings, when I feel a kind of happiness that's
really indescribable. Maybe it's something similar to what the hyena must feel;
an ugly creature that feeds on excrement, fornicates once a year and can still laugh.
It's very likely—I'm not the one to deny it—that somewhere, in all of our sorrows,
in all of the darkness that surrounds us, there's always room for a little laughter.
And, like the phrase "one man's famine is another man's feast" that I keep repeating to myself every time reality tries to pry a little consciousness into my head,
and like the thousand year old poet used to say, "Nothing is ever so bad that it
can't get worse," you have to realize that all of this blackness doesn't even begin
to touch the shadow of the other guy's darker misfortune. And so, I guess I'll just
stop complaining.

Today, for instance, is one of those days when I can walk down the streets feeling as though they were really mine, the trees, the branches of the trees, the leaves
of the branches of the trees, the insects on the leaves of the branches of the trees,
all alive, sucking in drafts of the same poisoned air that's eating away at this city,
this place we always come back to in spite of ourselves; but, instead of being mere

puppets on a string, it's as though the world actually did belong to us like before, without drugs, yet curiously enough with a carefree, floating sensation like you might have after smoking pot.

I left the house early and headed off in a different direction than I usually go every morning. Perhaps one of the motivating forces behind this decision was: I had had enough of the office, because, I must admit it, the fellow who's speaking to you is a bureaucrat, and I've had enough of accounts and good morning, sir, and sweating my ass off in a chair covered with sickening plastic, and admiring—almost green with envy—those toothpaste smiles the secretaries flash at their bosses, and enough of Charlie the office boy who always says "Coffee, engineer?" when he knows damn well I'm not an engineer, that I'm just a poor insignificant s.o.b. And maybe the other reason was the park, the birds singing, a few couples already embracing, the clean grass still wet from last night's shower, a light caressing breeze that wasn't at all like the sun's violent rays pouring through the curtainless windows behind my desk, flailing me relentlessly every day between ten and eleven, and this walking without hurrying, almost like wandering, just the way it was back in those happier times, ready for anything, almost as if I weren't living 'right now' and almost as if I weren't ill. Because, as you should know, I'm sick.

After crossing the park and walking down three or four blocks of a very stylish avenue ("popoff" as they call them here in Mexico City) I arrived at the Consulate. They attended to me quickly, efficiently, cordially—as the Swedes usually do—though I had few hopes since my "Swedish passport"—one for foreigners, I don't want you thinking I'm Scandanavian—had already expired and my papers still hadn't been settled by the State Department. I had, for all practical purposes, been reduced to the status of an outcast. They told me my case would be investigated and that I should return in ten days.

I left there before eleven and smiling to myself, made up my mind to avoid the office for the entire morning. Or rather, what was left of it. I began walking, dominated by that same incomprehensible, almost euphoric mood, intensely enjoying the smallest detail because today the world was mine and I was king, and even if the bees weren't buzzing around happily because of me, I soon found myself face to face with the large door of a seafood restaurant that tortured me again with those useless memories of the clams in my country.

I can't say that I hesitated: without giving it a second thought, willing to spend all my medicine money, I entered. (Not that seafood is all that expensive, but what was jangling in my pockets really didn't amount to very much). It was still early, I was the first and, up to the moment, only customer of the day. I examined the counter, then the tables and decided to behave like a gentleman, that is, I sat at a table. Then the old woman came over to me. What's on the menu? The only thing she could offer at this early hour was an order of oysters on a half shell, with a lot of lemon and two cold beers. Later a chubby, spirited young girl with a white shock of hair brushed over her forehead like Tongolele, came over—smiling brightly like my soul—to set the table.

"How much does it cost to hear a record?" I asked.

"Just a dime, señor."

"Do you know if there's one about 'I know how to lose and come back' or something like that?"

"I'll go have a look right now, señor."

And like a lord in his castle, without having to go over to the juke box, I was listening to the song that a blind man had sung on the *micro* (that's what they call buses in Chile), the same song that had surprised me another night in Garibaldi Square as I wandered among the *mariachis,* secretly hoping for the impossible, to meet someone I knew and share a bottle of tequila, because I've never liked to drink alone. "Oh to be back, be back in your arms once again" and then a line I don't remember very well but it's something like "lalara-lara-lara, I know how to lose, I know how to lose, won't you take me back, take me back, take me back." There was something in the song that moved me: the urgency, the hurried and imperative tone which said, "I want to go back, go back, go back." Because I wanted to go back, too. Not to a woman's arms, but to those of a long country, stretching from the mountains to the ocean, from the desert to the Anarctic ice floes.

I nearly cried when the music ended but I controlled myself and when Tongolele came over to ask me if I wanted to hear something else I told her, like a true connoisseur, to look for a song by Angelica Maria and, I said, hopefully it will be the one about 'how does our love stand.' She told me it was there and headed straight for the machine. But, you know, I'm not trying to fool anyone: the first song, like I said, I had heard on the bus during one of those interminable rides down Insurgentes that take more than an hour, and the other one was the sound track for a t.v. soap opera about a young Italian girl who was going to be married, that I had first watched from my bed when I was ill with the flu for three or four days in Santiago, and then later, when I returned to take in the images of this city after a long absence: the Angel of Independence flying over Reforma Boulevard, Diana aiming her bow over the trees in Chapúltepec Park, those monstrous buildings around where I work, etc. Returned, I say, because I had visited Mexico before as a child when it was still a provincial city and I had travelled through the country from north to south, from the plains to the jungle, from the Gulf Coast to the Pacific. I had seen the mountains and those green undulating valleys all filled with scorpions and snakes, opals and amethysts.

Before Angelica Maria had finished singing—and it wasn't too clear what she had sung about—they served me a beautifully round platter of oysters. I was taken aback since they looked so much like the oysters from home though they were somewhat larger, even more so than those gorgeous oysters 'For Exportation Only' I had had the good fortune to devour once in Angelmó, snatching them from the pile where they were being weighed, in plain sight of everybody, with my friend Horacio; Horacio—ever since I read a copy of *El Mercurio* about how in the line of duty a young soldier shot him down when he tried to escape as they searched through his modest home in Rancagua—his name sticks in my soul like a fish bone caught in the throat.

And just as I was sprinkling a few drops of lemon on the first oyster of my cursed life, the old lady came over from the cash register and said, "Where are you from, Argentina?"

"Chile," I said.

"Ah, everyone from Chile speaks so beautifully."

And then the second customer of the day entered the restaurant, a tall, very pale looking man with blond hair, who was probably a Swede since the Consulate was nearby.

It's not that I wanted to be sociable, or ease my loneliness or anything, but with the owner standing in front of my table and the Swede greeting her, and me still unable to down the first oyster and she telling him I'm from Chile and he euphorically saying he knew Valparaiso like the palm of his hand, things worked out in such a way that we ended up sitting face to face at the same table and while I still didn't eat out of politeness and he waited for an order like mine and another couple of beers, I wasn't sure what song to tell Tongolele to play now, first, because I didn't know any more songs and secondly, because my limited imagination (as far as musical aspirations go) only carried me as far as the tango, a type of music I had wanted to believe couldn't fit inside of that machine painted in such loud colors, even though I have to admit I was mistaken.

You know I've always been curious about masks. For instance, the secretaries in my office knew nothing at all about me, a punctual employee who industriously worked his eight hour shift. And maybe for Tongolele that same person was a man who dressed well, suit and tie, carried an expensive black leather portfolio and knew just exactly what music he wanted to hear. For the old woman, the thing that surely stood out the most as a symbol of distinction, was an accent that, though I could be proud of it, was completely unassumed. Now, who would I be for the Swede, I asked myself. In any case, I knew very well who I was: a hyena in the jungle who can't understand why he's laughing, or what the reason might be for his momentary happiness.

"You know," said the Swede, surprising me with a perfect Mexican accent. "I can see in your eyes that we'll become good friends. And you know, I never make a mistake."

I wanted to ask him where he was from and especially, how old he was because I had no idea whatsoever. Nevertheless—well, I've already said it was a strange day for me—the only thing I asked was if he liked tangos, maybe because I sensed the potential threat of another approach by Tongolele.

"Tango? Are you asking me if I like tangos? Just listen." And he began to sing in a low voice, without being theatrical, the one about 'how well she dances around the solid earth' with a rhythm and intonation which struck me as perfect. I stared at him and he was Manuel, he wasn't the Swede, he was really Manuel and we weren't in the restaurant any more but were ambling down the harbor streets in old Medellin—after drinking three bottles of wine in a joyful uproar and after losing our last dime in the Casino de Viña, where none of us had ever been before—drunk, broke and very happy, singing, all three of us, at the top of our lungs as we walked down Brazil Avenue, "Come on, woman, I don't want you to be sad, the night's just begun, why are you feeling so bad?" Of course this was a long time ago, but the Swede was Manuel, with the same prominent eyes, his loud laughter; Manuel, another fishbone ever since the day his third child was born—a girl this time—and they wrote to tell me how he had been fired from his position as professor for being a "Marxist" and how he had to make his living selling marmalade and sewing needles on the buses in Santiago.

The Swede finished the tango and looked at me as though waiting for me to equal his effort with another. But, I'm one of those wretched people who can't carry a tune, or even memorize the words, except for the national anthem they taught me as a child in grammar school, and so, valiantly, I diverted his attention with a question that was like a slap in the face:

"What do you do?"

"Me? I'm a grave digger," the Swede told me. "I work in the French Cemetery. Have you ever been there?"

I answered that I hadn't.

"One day you should stop by, it's a very beautiful place."

You might think it's absurd to consider cemeteries as beautiful places, but suddenly, carried by a flood of memory, I revisited those afternoons when, with convalescing steps, I used to wander about the secluded older section of General Cemetery, in Santiago, that faced the hospital where I had been bedridden for more than two months. I don't think I'd ever thought about it before . . . But now, as I look back with more perspective, I was sure it was a beautiful place, a small city of mausoleums resembling houses, castles, palaces and Rapunzel-like towers, everything in miniature, as though plotting out the best location for dramatizing fairy tales; those huge and ancient trees, the deep shadows pierced here and there by the sun, those dried and withered flowers—the essence of flowers and sulphides—the distressed young people looking, perhaps, for a quiet place, women dressed in stubborn black and transparent veils, surreptitious cats and a heavy perfume that now, amidst beer and oysters, I try in vain to invoke. And at once I was seized by the almost mad desire to visit the French Cemetery and the unavoidable certainty that I would.

"Cemeteries are very beautiful places," continued the Swede. "They are places filled with life."

"Filled with life?" His tone, his enthusiasm and a kind of urgency that couldn't be concealed by his words stimulated and further provoked the paradoxical happiness that had overwhelmed me this morning.

"Of course they're filled with life!"

And then he looked me straight in the eyes and it seems we shared our souls for a moment and suddenly, something became very clear, because I, too, had felt once that love could be much stronger than death. Then he told me very simply, with just a slight trembling in his voice and without the smallest tear washing over his dilated pupils, he told me that Sybila was buried there and that he hadn't been able to rest until they had given him a job as grave digger.

Disconcerted, and like a good bureaucrat, I looked at my watch. I couldn't miss the afternoon shift, besides, I had no excuse.

"And every day I talk to her," said the Swede, "I tell her the little things, or rather, I laugh or I cry or I howl" . . .

Then you exist, I thought to myself remembering how a couple of Sundays before as I wandered through Chapúltepec Park I had caught the words of a speaker as he recited to his audience in front of the Lake House and the lines went like this: "I cry, I howl, I curse, thus I exist." So—I said to myself—this damn Swede *exists,* and I wondered if I, who didn't cry, didn't howl and didn't curse, could possibly exist; if all this were true, then what was happening to me was existence. And then I had a bright idea, very much opposed to what I should have done.

"Hey," I said, almost laughing as the happiness sailed around my tongue. "Let's have some more oysters!"

"And a couple more beers!" said the Swede.

"But don't be offended by what I'm going to tell you; don't talk to me about Sybila. Don't say anything more about her. One day I'll come visit you in the French Cemetery and I'll meet her. Right now, let's eat, drink and sing another tango."

And just when Tongolele arrived at our table to take our order, a grey haired couple (he, wearing shorts that exposed to the public eye the greenish veins on his legs and she, sporting a huge straw hat that didn't quite cast enough of a shadow to hide her wrinkles) occupied the next table and threatened to shatter the luminous atmosphere which until now had blocked out all the immediate reality that had nothing in common with the taste of oysters or the fluid freshness of beer running down the throat. After writing down our order, Tongolele handed them the menu.

"Do you have any fresh juice?" asked the woman.

They have to be North American, I thought; the unmistakable picture of those tourists who move about from one continent to another searching for the fountain of life, which certainly had been denied to them by the gods. Here they were, in this little corner of Mexico, assaulting everyone with the few words they might know of the language.

I looked at the Swede. We were eating together, that was real. Even though half an hour earlier I didn't even know who he was. And when the decrepit *gringa* smiled at me, I still didn't even know his name, but what did it matter? If he was Swedish, then most certainly his name was Johanson, so I never even bothered to ask him.

"Hey, Johanson," I said, "what were you doing in Valparaíso?"

The truth is, that in spite of the oysters, I was getting a little high from the beer: it didn't really matter what Johanson had been doing in Valparaíso; what did matter, I knew I would never ask him because I didn't want to listen to him about it, but I knew it had nothing to do with Valparaíso. It was about Sybila. How, where and why he had known her. How, where and why she had died.

"Do you have canaries, Johanson?" I asked him.

"How did you know?"

"Because several years ago in a bar in Santiago, I met a poet. He was an alcoholic and besides that, a loner. He had to drink a bottle of *pisco* between six and nine every morning in order to be able to work and get through the day in a more or less reasonable condition until four. And he was a loner because everyone had abandoned him: his wife, his kids, the few friends he had, even his dog. So, Johanson, this guy ran from bar to bar looking for someone who would listen to his poems or to the few stories he had written. "I don't have anyone, but I have my poetry" he'd say with shining eyes. One day, I couldn't resist listening to one of his stories during lunch; it was a very careful and well modulated reading, full of inner tension. Listen to this, she was called Sybila and he, Virgil.

"How interesting."

"They were a married couple who had no children."

"How interesting."

"But they did have a pair of canaries who became the object of all their tenderness or all of their frustrations."

"How interesting."

"And the end of the story almost knocked me out because Virgil and Sybila, Sybila and Virgil weren't the married couple, they were the canaries, like the story ends right when the two old people begin to dance around the cage singing (probably with high pitched and trembling voices): "Virgil and Sybila, Sybila and Virgil are two good children who will never die, Virgil and Sybila, Virgil and Sybila, Sybila and Virgil."

"How interesting."

"Why do you keep saying, 'how interesting', to everything I say, Johanson? You're beginning to sound a little crazy."

Tongolele was trying to explain to the large and dried out *gringa* (whose make-up was washing away with the heat) that the juice was fresh but not made with electrically purified water, so she'd be better off drinking Tehuacán, a bubbly mineral water. The *gringa,* her face revealing little comprehension of what she was being told, ended up ordering a beer.

"The reason is, my name is Virgil," said Johanson. "And I have a pair of canaries. Before she died, Sybila begged me to take care of them like they were our children, and, you know? I have taken care of them like they were our children. And I always tell Sybila how they are, what they do, what they sing, because they really are singers."

"Speak English?" The *gringo* asked us.

Personally I played the fool. I speak a little English but I wasn't about to fall into it here. On the other hand, Virgil Johanson said he did and so he told them what they wanted to know: what the *enchiladas suizas* were made of, the *quesa-dillas,* the rice with *mole,* and if the oysters in the cocktail were sufficiently fresh. A short while later after running out of things to ask, the man tried to start up a conversation:

"The city has changed a lot," he assured us with great originality. "Very, very much. I was here about 20 years ago and it was *another* city entirely. It really was."

Yes. Of course I wasn't going to tell him that I had been here thirty years ago and since then it had changed a lot, a lot more, because I had been only ten years old and that in itself explains why the city was different.

Tongolele, passing rapidly, stops at our table for a moment and tells me:
"Señor, I'm going to play the song you like again."

The *gringa's* husband asks, "Kei dihou?" and then repeats in English, "What did she say" when he sees his question has fallen on deaf ears. I seriously thought to tell him to get the hell out of there, like little Juan used to say when he was only two years old; just leave us alone; go out into the goddamn street and both-er someone else if he wanted, but just leave us out of it, Virgil Johanson and my-self, we had some more talking to do. Nevertheless, the love I was feeling didn't subside; was it really love? And I wondered if maybe these two tourists carried their share of the guilt for the tragedy punishing my country for the sin that . . . Yes, I was beginning to comprehend, and suddenly, like a flash of light, I knew what I was going to tell them, later. But before that happened, Johanson told me about the lobsters in Tehuántepec, the giant escargot cocktails, the horse-neck clams and he listened with a kind of passion to my eulogies to the green sea urchin, the clams of Talcahuano, all the gold, the ivory, the mahagony brought to us by today's poisoned sea, and we drank some more beer and we laughed a lot, and he wasn't going back to work either; even though Sybila might miss him, she had to understand: a couple of drinks now and then isn't such a big sin. It's hardly even a little sin. Or maybe it's a virtue. "Oh to be back, to be back, to be back, to be back in your arms once again" . . . because a fine lunch with a good friend does a lot more for a person than all of the machines that strip the bark off of trees and whose very refined parts are diagrammed with long, compli-cated names, right Swede? The office can go to hell; death to the rotary blades and the angular transmission and to the goddamn water spigots and the damn worm gear and, long live the oyster in its shell, beer, sardines smothered in butter, the barracudas and trips to the Yucatán or to Chiloe; up with all of the faraway islands filled with seafood and fragrant, juicy clams that curl up with a drop of lemon; up with the unfortunate lobsters chosen with implacable fingers to fill an anxious belly; ah, Swede, long live the fish and the shell fish and death to the hunt, long live the wanderers looking for truth and death to the lazy hippies, long live whisky on ice in the late afternoon and death to the son-of-a-bitch liver, long live the hunchbacks and death to the yankee tourists, long live the good peo-ple in the world and death to the shiteating bourgeoisie, a long life to euphoric conversation and a quick death to reception rooms, long live the lively ones like us, death to all the serious fools, long live booming laughter, death to snide smiles, long live life, Johanson, and death to death!

And right when I was going to throw my question out to the gringos, the hunchback entered.

"Look, Johanson. Look at them!"

Distinct expressions of disgust were painted on their faces. She appeared to be horrified; and what irritated him was his pride: how could they endure the entrance of such a creature in a place where *he,* he and his sweet *darling* were trying to enjoy a good lunch. *Disgusting!* Sickening. Nauseating.

The hunchback was a beggar, dressed in a kind of robe that came to his knees, covered with grease and completely filthy; three pairs of shoes and a small cotton bag hang from the rope tied about his waist. His long hair was uncombed, grimy and dusty; he had a black beard, black shining eyes and brilliantly white teeth. And his hump was magnificent; even, symmetrical, of rarely seen perfection. I felt the immediate urge to touch it because it brings good luck and that was something I needed relatively soon. He leapt a couple of times as though playing the boxer and then approached, stretching his hand out to the gringos' table. She looked at us imploring for sympathy, compassion, asking us to join forces with them, a little tenderness for the poor people, look at what was happening to them! The man first glanced around the room for Tongolele or anyone who might have the authority or audacity to kick that monstrous abortion of nature out of there, but then, because the hunchback was insisting with a formidable throaty groan, he put his hand in his pocket willing to take care of everything with a crisp dollar bill.

"Look, Johanson. Look at that!"

Almost at the same time that our oysters and beer arrived, a waiter appeared dressed in a white jacket, who took the beggar by the arm, addressing him with some derogatory remark and pushed him towards the door. The hunchback glanced at our table and our eyes met. He betrayed no fear, nor anger. It was as though he always knew that he deserved no better, that mistreatment and punishment were the first sentences registered in his destiny. Something in his gaze seemed to project a beatific state; his beliefs, steadfast in the face of all trials, a kind of cruelty, of a soul's lodging in places beyond good and evil. And I felt a shiver snake up my back, because his eyes reflected the intuition that I was his equal, that it was up to me to give him a hand, to throw him a lifeline. When I stood up, his expression broke into a thankful, wide-open smile, as though he had sensed beforehand why I had left my seat.

"No!" I told the waiter, grabbing his arm. "He's my guest. His name is Nicodemus and he's come to join us. Tell the waitress to bring another order of oysters and two more beers."

"As you wish, señor," answered the waiter.

I don't know why I chose the name Nicodemus. A man like that couldn't possibly have a name (another one of his talents) but if any name might fit him, it was Nicodemus, the name for people mistreated by nature and humanity, those nocturnal outcasts whose macabre bursts of laughter could be heard in the shadows of the sordid wasteland. A name brilliantly invented to point out the forsaken.

I looked at the pair of gringos on the way back to our table. They didn't speak to us again, didn't even dare to give us one last look before beginning to comment about the horrible things that happen here; what kind of a country is this! And so, staring at them, I said through clenched teeth but without raising my voice: "assassins!"

The hunchback sat down. I offered him one of my beers while we waited for the new order to come. He finished off the foamy glass in one shot and filled it up again, alternating his suspicious glances between the Swede and me. Later, he noisily slurped down the bland oyster meat from each shell, always watching us, but without speaking. What could he talk about? Then an eloquent burst of laughter rang out and for the first time I felt quite comfortable and wanted to tell them both about some things, but my voice got bogged down in the horror and I saw myself mouthing mute words; but in their eyes I could perceive understanding and companionship even though they couldn't hear the screams, the fear, the howling pain that wanted to speak for me, for those nights in the stadium, the rapid machine gun fire, the smell of burning flesh, the knowledge that death was nearby; Swede, Nicodemus, you don't hear me, but I'm speaking to you. One guy, about twenty-eight years old, skinny, blonde, almost angelical-looking, approached me in the locker room and said, "I don't think I'm going to make it out of here, compañero. If you do, please try to see my wife. Tell her to be strong, to take good care of the children" and he made me memorize how to find his house. One of those cool and clear September nights, they called his name along with five others in the locker room and I never saw him again. After they read the names you always heard the machine guns—do you know, Johanson?—always the machine guns. One day they interrogated me. The electric blow feels as though they're pulling out all your teeth at once. You withdraw completely, Nicodemus, you contract like a mollusk, you feel that you've run out of air forever and then you get nauseous and a drowning sensation overcomes you and your chest tightens in desperation, and later, you still keep trembling, very sensitive, your morale in tatters. But I wasn't subjected to many blows nor was I the victim of other tortures that still make my spine tingle to think about them. A couple of jabs with rifle butts and a broken rib were my only punishment. And of course, the electric shocks. It was nothing. Afterwards, Nicodemus, when they were convinced that I probably wasn't hiding an arsenal, they made us get into a truck and tied us to the floor. Cracking jokes, the soldiers walked on top of us and during the journey one of them even urinated on our heads. They took us to the outskirts of the city and released us in an open field. There were about twenty of us. "Here's where you get off," said one of the soldiers, "Get out and start running." I fell face down in some thorny bushes and listened to the shots. Then the engine roared and the truck disappeared. It began to grow dark and I thought these bushes were going to be my resting place for the night. To go out into the street meant sure death if it was after curfew. I didn't dare call out anyone's name. I didn't know who had fallen and who was trying to save themselves from death like I was, under a much friendlier prickly roof than those groan-filled locker rooms in the stadium. What a shame, Johanson, that you can't hear me. Even though I was afraid, I looked for the wife of that young blonde in the stadium. When I arrived at their home, an old lady told me that such a woman didn't live there, she had no idea where she might be living nor how to find her, but if I wanted, I could leave a message because who knows she might . . . I told her that the woman's husband had been shot and the old lady fell to her knees and burst into tears. I decided to leave; I was filled with shame, nausea, fear, and almost without thinking, without knowing, as though some strange force had inspired me with energy, I arrived at the Swedish Embassy and requested asylum. The hunchback finished his second beer, looked at me and, without saying a word, got up from the table, burped and with little hops, went on his way, the three pairs of shoes bouncing against his thighs, against his buttocks. I would have liked to have touched his hump.

Johanson remained where he was, observing me somewhat bewildered and astounded. My eyes followed Nicodemus until his image had disappeared.

"Have you heard anything about Kirlian?" the Swede asked me.

No, I hadn't heard, but yes, I would listen, yes, Johanson, one of those geniuses who by pure luck provoked enormous changes in the history of man. Newton and the apple? Well, something like that. And this one? This one had invented, or discovered, the photography of luminous discharges. Did I realize what that meant? No, honestly, not really, luminous discharges? Yes. Yes, every living body emits radiations, did I understand? Even the definition of death will change when they perfect Kirlian photography, because—was I listening?—the fact that the heart stops beating and breathing is cut off, does not mean death, aha! What did I think about cutting off the edges of a leaf with scissors and then electrophotographing it so that the image of the complete leaf would appear including the parts which had been cut off? Could I comprehend it? Well, if I was curious to know why he was telling me all this now, he was going to explain. It was because some experiments using photos of luminous discharges emitted by the fingertips of several people had revealed that the energy fields were similar to those of a magnet: attracting or repelling each other. Did I see, did I really understand? That's why, at times, when two people shake hands they know instinctively if they like each other, wasn't that incredible? And perhaps you might convince me that the same thing can happen with the eyes.

"Listen, Johanson," I said. "Let's not talk about that. Right now, only the little things in life are important to me. I had wanted to talk to you about your country, about Stockholm in the winter, about the snowy lakes, the boat trips through the icy regions, the sunlight in the mornings, and the green reflections of the roof tops, the moving sadness of Strandvagen when evening closes in, the lights illuminating the winding, medieval streets in Gamla Stan at three o'clock in the afternoon. I wanted to tell you many, many things about your country that you probably haven't seen for quite a while now. But, that's not important to me either, please understand me. What's important is the meaning of a sunny morning, the significance of a plate of oysters, or the insistent memory of a dead woman; or maybe, the music and the words of some song that, by simple repetition, penetrates the conscious mind; the flight of a butterfly, Johanson, patting the hump of a hunchback so we might have a little, just a little luck, like I've had today, eating so many oysters, drinking so much beer—how many have we had so far, Johanson?—and meeting you. Now I feel a bit heavy, I probably can't move around very easily, but let's make the effort; twilight is just around the corner, the swan has trumpeted his last song for the day; let's go, take me to the French Cemetery; one more laugh for the hyena; it might not be such a bad time after all to meet Sybila."

St. Elizabeth

(Chapter from "F.", a novel in progress)

By Claudio Giacomi

Translated by Jo Carrillo

Torrential downpour, the traditions of a half hour. I came to the Pot of Gold hoping to find Barbara, but she wasn't free. Anyway, I stayed and ordered a roast beef that was dry and inedible. I'll need a bottle of Pepto Bismol to get rid of the gas. The worst thing of all is that it's still May.

Dusk with rain. Large grey streaks fall over the city. I don't know how long it will take these clouds to clear. Here in these rainy afternoons, like over there, you stay on your guard, eating *picarones* if it's winter, with kind relatives and the atmosphere of friendship.

I've never liked the place where I work. The institution is the most rotten imaginable . . . they call it Union Paramaricones.* The office where I work gets the bureaucratic jungle's worst waste. I can't stand Gordo's presence, least of all when he wakes up in a bad temper panting in the big leather chair. I accept the infection, because after all, everything that surrounds me is decadent and senseless, but here at least I'm doing something about the well-being and education of my son, even though I can't say anything about that to him or his mother, not

---

*Play on Union Panamericana (Pan American Union) and Union Paramaricones (Union of Faggots).

112

even to F. There are secrets that I keep to myself, so that I can hear myself tell the truth once in a while.

If I appreciated my work more, if I gave it more importance, if I had something lasting and dignified to look for in these times, some stimulus, some attraction, the future of the children, of humanity, etcetera, although humanity is reaching its own limits.

Yesterday, F remembered the man in the underground. We were in the Pot of Gold. He did his thinking by talking to himself in English, so that no doubt would remain: "Rationality, sirs, is an illness, an illness in every sense . . . " Even Ingrid turned around to look at him.

My present rationality comes from the fact that I have time, a lot of time to think. The result of a good financial situation is a clear mind and insomnia. Before, when I lived from hand to mouth, I didn't have time to think, but now, the foul-smelling waves that Gordo and the bootlegger Iturbide send to me, I protect myself from behind my desk, behind the curtain of smoke of three packs of cigarettes a day. First they ruin my health, and now they want to get rid of me. I know them . . . Now that I have a halfway comfortable life, consciousness of time comes back and with it, there's nothing but vertigo.

Sunday. A cockroach came down the bridge of my nose this morning to wake me up. I called F to tell him, but Eliane answered: *"Attends."*

With great sadness, F told me that it has to do with an unequal war and that it's useless to worry too much. He let me know that cockroaches surpass the human population 200 to one. "They've survived atomic bombs, it's common knowledge." I answered that D was his musical note. F told me that he didn't understand the connection between cockroaches and D. "We'll take it a step at a time." I answered. "D—*re* in Spanish—also means king in Italian and G major—*sol*—the zenith, it's clear as day, like Eliane; G minor—*sol menor*—has to do with the stars, the sun at its lowest point, like you . . . " F interrupted me: "Don't tell me that I'm the king Sun of the night and Eliane, the moon of the day . . . "

Sometimes it's like that . . . *duro di testa,* hardheaded. I explained to him that D major, loved by all the musicians and held in their esteem as the most brilliant, is considered the same as the kingly tone . . .

"Queen, you mean, Queen tonality . . . "

"*Re* means king in Italian, and also D, as you'll learn and that's what I think you are, like me, the same as you, in the now ancient and age-old *liason* that unites us, *in somma* . . .

"Go on, go on . . . " was the response that he gave and he excused himself saying that he had to hurry and leave.

Thursday. An electrical storm and echoing thunder that seems like a bombardment. These downpours don't last more than half an hour, they end quickly because they get tired of themselves, and then the air comes back newly washed. Umbrellas keep opening and closing and there are others that the wind takes away. People who pass with an air of panic covering themselves with the *Washington Post.* The hurricane-like winds sweep them away, down the avenue. I'd like to see an umbrella running after its owner, but no, you never see that and that's the trouble with it.

Existence here is without any pleasure. Too much concentration of power, that's F's diagnosis. Deceived from all corners, they come to the city as if they were drawn by a magnet to propose ideas to change the world, but the city changes those who propose the changes and, in the end, nothing changes. According to F, there are two armies: the army of frustrated ones and, on the other side, the army of opportunists, and there is always someone who will take advantage of the confusion.

Monetary grief is the worst disgrace that can fall on an alert mind here. To be poor is a crime. Impotence is more notorious when it rains in the summer with fully orchestrated thunder, a torrent choking itself while the year grows old and its teeth and hair fall out. Their eyes seem to be looking for an outside equation and they see only decadence and the end of the world. That's how you start to prepare for the end of life, that which will conclude a universe of appearances. The rain is going to pass quickly, it don't last more than a half hour. On rainy afternoons here, the same as over there, you stay on your guard and wait, but over there you talk about poetry in a friendly atmosphere, eating fritters if it's winter.

Dusk is almost here, upset faces and dripping eaves. Meanwhile, Barbara thinks it won't be possible. So do I. And then . . . "will you call me later?"

Today I decided that the solution lies in becoming a millionaire overnight, in a brilliant way. Instead of writing biographies of inventors, I discovered that what I should do is invent toys for children from five to eighty, or perfectly useless inventions, to test my inventive talent, nothing more. We'll cultivate olive trees in the ashtrays, like I used to do alone before, I said.

Lunch with F in the Go-Go Girl bar on Pennsylvania Ave. Since we've come in, the woman who contorts herself on the stage to the rhythm of rock, has been winking at me. The place is packed. What if there were a fire? Overhearing my thoughts, F immediately wants to leave, he suffers from claustrophobia. "Let's go across the street, to the Pot of Gold," he tells me. But I say, "I'll pay."

Finally, we settle down in front of the small stage and we order lunch, meat loaf. The next act comes and they announce Cindy, who rubs against me as she passes. Cindy climbs the steps, she fills the entire stage with her presence. The same thing happens . . . From the time she begins her swaying, she doesn't take her eyes off of me and every once in awhile she sends looks my way, like in porno flicks. Full of shit as usual, F tells me to be careful: "Careful, don't get messed up, she smiles at everyone, it's part of the show . . . "

No, he doesn't realize. F can't understand and, as always in these things, he gets in a bad mood. A curious thing happened afterwards, when Cindy called me with a finger gesture . . . It was in the most cat-like part of the go-go dance. F came back to tell me that I should be careful, that the cat moves were for everybody, that they didn't mean anything, but I didn't pay any attention and I left him raving at his plate. Naturally, I got up and stretched my hand toward the white bottom that gave me a wide smile from the stage. F yelled for me to sit down. Sometimes I don't understand him with all his chatter and theories.

Friday. Memorandum and scribbled poem at noon in the Pot of Gold, which I transcribe properly corrected:

Chile: Humiliation with witnesses? Never.

Return: Don't even think about it, or maybe returning only for a while (in parenthesis).

Europe: Impossible.

Montreal: Possibility of a more pleasant life.

Skills: Office work, translations.

Need to make more money. Urgent complement: Translations. Make a file of clients and send the shit to Gordo, before he sends it to me.

Love life (sentimental problem, in the original): Abolished. I'm alone with some responsibilities and very little time to make capital.

Not to lose anymore time or energy. To defend myself from F's negative waves. To recover a more economical sense of the days. And to make a file of clients.

USA

Too much money
Too much poverty
Too many cars
Too many tantalizing girls
You can never
        never
            never
                touch . . .

I had thought of making a *caligramme* and having the three nevers take the forms of fingers that reach towards the stage, where Cindy was waiting for me with a gorgeous, smiling and trembling rear, I heard a loud voice: "Hands off". . . Some steel hooks grabbed me by the neck and with a strong kick they threw me out into the street in the middle of a laughing crowd. The paid cromagnon in short, proved to be a troublemaker. But F was furious, and on top of that, terribly ashamed because he had to go out to look for the money that the cromagnon wanted and go in again to pay the bill in front of all the regulars, among them executives from BID, from OMS, and a misguided one or two from the Union Paramaricones. All people whom F hates with a passion. I've never seen him so angry. When he left, he glared at them and, even with the door half open, he yelled at the people inside. "Bunch of slaves! Bootlicking parasites! . . . "

This afternoon I went to the bank and took out some money, I took a taxi and when I saw that F was going down Pennsylvania Avenue with long strides, I made the taxi driver stop. The driver was a sweaty Black man with bulging eyes.

I paid him with a hundred dollar bill and I told him to keep the change. He gave me a strange look and floored the accelerator, leaving me the unpleasant odor of burnt rubber.

F and I went to the Pot of Gold to eat a pastrami sandwich. When we went in, we met Ingrid, who was leaving right that minute, dressed in a Hindu shirt.

F invited her, but she answered with a smile more unfathomable that Gioconda's and without saying a word, she passed us, grazing us with the *frou-frou* of her flowing shirt.

Three days later.

Ingrid walks as if she'd swallowed a broomstick. F says that she is purging the crimes of her race and that's why she has cropped her hair, as if she were coming out of Auschwitz. She has blue skin, violet rings under her eyes and finally, a face deformed by a permanent grin of fear that produces a horror film inside her brain. F's diagnosis is concentrational catatonia. Sometimes a half choked smile comes from the bottom of Ingrid's face. She could even be pretty if she fixed herself up, if she at least put on a wig to cover the bald spots. She is always afraid of the slightest physical contact. She spends entire days in the Pot of Gold and no one can pull a word out of her. If you ask me, I guess she is in love with Barbara, cropped hair or not. F told me that her father raped her when she was ten. "*Viola* is all a mystery." He knows because Lester, the psychiatry student who is an intern at St. Elizabeth told him. Wealthy family from Dusseldorf. The father is a fat fish in the academic world; he teaches German idealism. Professor Emeritus, but he has had to spend most of his personal money on sanatoriums to cure Ingrid from the trauma he caused when she was ten. Herr Professor had her admitted to a Swiss sanatorium her last semester, from there she came out with the idea to chop her hair off. F told me that he had visited her once, on the eighth floor, where she has a studio with thirteen cats. "Before she gave in to the scissors she was a model" F informs me. "Maybe that's why she's so stuck up," I said. "She showed me the cover from a *Cosmopolitan* ... She was the cover girl, sexy, silky, long hair, stupendous ... She invited me over to show me her paintings, the ones she hung on the walls at the Pot of Gold, remember?"

How could I forget ... a few small squares pierced by a swarm of minute brush strokes.

"Imagine a transistor inside ... "

The pure truth. The squares were a stack of twisted cables and disconnected ribbons of every color. Her father lives in the same building, on the sixth floor. By explicit orders from his daughter, he never goes up to see her, but calls her on the telephone twenty times a day trying to dissuade her from this or that. He wants to marry her to one of his disciples, an aspiring professor at Princeton. The night that F visited, her father called nine times. They have an agreement not to see each other, on the condition that Ingrid doesn't reject his phone calls. This evening, Ingrid is bothered because she accidently bumped into her father in the elevator. It had been 199 days since she'd last seen his face. The night that F visited, he could hear Herr Professor's heavy breathing on the phone, but Ingrid would always end it by dryly cutting him off in German. Each time she'd hang the receiver up with disgust, as a result of what he said, as if the phone was full of some poisonous material that came through the wire, the paternal breath rotten from black tobacco and *kummel,* all of which put her into an extremely bad mood. Lester, the one who does his internship at St. Elizabeth, said that rape was a current thing among Germans after the war and that when he studied in Fribourg he was told that Germans needed four times the normal dose of anesthesia to lose consciousness. It's because they never relax. By day they are model citizens and animal lovers, but by night they dream of revenge, and in the end they all go completely crazy, and those who aren't declared so, go on to occupy government posts.

Suddenly, F said to my face that I went to the Pot of Gold because I was in love with Barbara. It's the opposite, I answered and, if he doesn't believe it, to watch when Barbara passes obsequiously close to the table shaking her hard, raised ass.

Tuesday. In the Pot of Gold with F, hungry and broke as usual. In two bites he devours the pastrami that Barbara brings him. Ingrid is in the corner. She has spent all afternoon looking at her coffee cup. F wants to approach her but she clips his wings with a furious look. She is more blue and monstrous than ever. F tells me that last time he visited her, he tried to interest her in romance: for example he asked her why she had changed so much from the front page of *Cosmopolitan* to now. She told him that the *Cosmopolitan* photographer wanted to make a fortune off of her and thrust her into the market, and everything was going well, until he made her pose nude and tried to seduce her. F whispered that making love could also be a beautiful experience and, putting his words into action, he approached her smoothly, measuring the distance, but the thirteen cats jumped on him. They didn't scratch him, but it seems that suddenly they got bigger and were waiting for a signal from her to go for his throat, and all the while she laughed coldly, but he couldn't hear her because of the enormous commotion that the mad cats made. "I begged her to call off the furies please! But she made me first promise that I would behave well, and I did . . . then I told her that I wasn't serious about her cropped hair and trained cats, then without any bad intentions I suggested that she let her hair grow, like on the cover of *Cosmopolitan.* At that she got furious and the cats pounced on me again . . . "

The way I see it, it was F who made her go crazy, or at least he gave her the final push. Now, F never takes his eyes off Barbara. I asked him how the visit to the eighth floor turned out. "She told me that she had become disillusioned with me . . . let her stay with her scissors and her cats," he said, and after a long pause, "You can see your Cunegunda comes from the steppes of Asia, with her firm grapefruits . . . " From Silesia I corrected. "It's the same effect, with her blonde braids and her country air . . . "

F has become a fool since I told him that Barbara had asked to borrow five hundred dollars from me to finish her art studies. I told her I would think about it . . . Since then, F calls Barbara my Cunegunda. Very funny, but to me it isn't

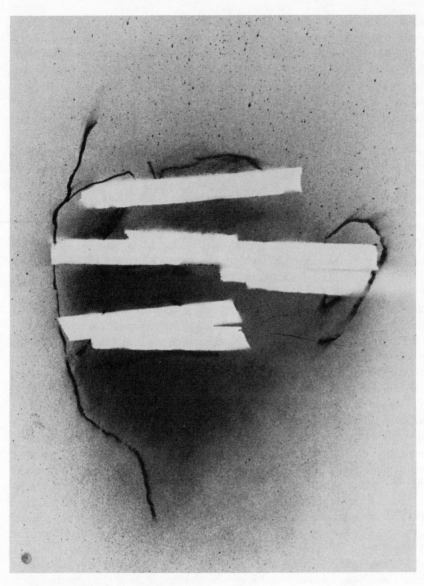

Untitled, drawing by José Balmes.

at all humourous. "Be careful, appearances can be deceiving," F warned me. I feel like giving him the same shit. If it weren't for me, he would have starved to death. Who would have imagined, the nerve?

Friday. Half dizzy from the puffs of marijuana and the thunder of the tom-tom that lifts out of the blackness, I cross Dupont Circle. From a distance I see F sitting, dejectedly reading the *Washington Post*. At times I know whether the news about Chile is good or bad just by looking at his face. F reproaches me for not reading the paper. He tells me that Hegel's reading of the paper was his daily philosophy lesson. That I must read the paper daily to anchor myself in the real and concrete world. But it doesn't help him to anchor himself so much. To cheer him up, I tell him the story of the taxi driver with the bulging eyes. Hearing me, he stops his philosophy lesson and holds his head. At the end of his exclamations and fuss, he looks at me wildly and says it was crazy for me to be throwing away money, and to finish off the argument, he made the following point: that that money could have been put to better use. Next time those foolish instincts hit me it would be better to let the bills fall into his mailbox at 2521 Pennsylvania Avenue. With that amount he could have eaten for two months, etcetera. I replied that that isn't all, that I had passed out three hundred dollars to three sleeping winos while I was crossing the street, at one hundred dollars a head and that the thing is to plant cows and reap feathers with a butterfly net, you understand? He looks at me with his mouth wide open. I told him that you take *coño* with *caña* and *colmo* with *calma.* * Upset, F makes me listen to his lecture about Hegelian philosophy again. He shows me one of the headlines: OFFICIAL CIRCLES WORRIED OVER THE NATIONALIZATIONS OF THE U.P.; I remember that I have to stay in the real world, that I can't keep on like this, that we live in hard times, etcetera, but I invite him for a pastrami sandwich in the Pot of Gold and his rage passes as if by magic. "The *como* looks for itself in the *cama,* it's clear that each time the water passes through the colander it changes color," he answers.

"Strange language for a *Washington Post* reader," I say.

As we move away from the furious African tom-toms, F tells me that before I arrived, he had imagined that he was in the plaza of Dar-es Salaam. We hurried down New Hampshire Avenue and when we got close to the Pot of Gold, his face returned to normal.

"A little hungry, *compa* . . . ?"

"I'm really hungry, not just a little hungry, dear Sancho of the complicated sayings."

"The *palo* peels itself with the *pala*."

"And the *pera* stops with the *pero* . . . "*

We burst out laughing, making our way through the racing engines, indifferent to the clouds of carbon monoxide, to the staring people, and to the jeweled butterfly glasses of two women with violet hair that look us over from top to bottom with absolute horror.

---

*play on sounds, only nonsense syllables.

Saturday. I am tired of the custom of dying and being buried. So much land in which you could lift up another song to love, full of kneeling headstones, scarcely a sign of decaying bodies. Why should you accumulate so many tombs? *Anorexia nervosa* is twisting my bowels.

Last night I took a walk by the 14th Street Porno District. It is the worst sight you can imagine. The waitress that brought me the Bloody Mary started yelling because I grabbed her sweaty ass, but I passed her a fifty dollar bill and nothing happened. "My whole body, for double that," she told me. Because she was black, I could only see the whites of her eyes in the darkness but she wore a florescent skirt and she was topless.

I can't stand vodka. Seeing that I don't like the stuff, it's not so bad in the porno district since they fill the glasses with tomato juice and only a couple of drops. I called F, who, from a sociological point of view is more interested in the pornographic slum than I am. He called it the epitome of Western decadence, but he couldn't come. He was with Eliane, who had arrived from Pittsburgh to see him. In the morning I ate three eggs, and three spoonsful of Pepto Bismol to pass them, but after an hour the gas had me feeling like an inflated balloon bumping against the ceiling.

At times they save themselves, thanks to the humility and nobility of country cemeteries, generally set up in lines and shaded by trees. On the fences they always hang flags. But these masses of stuffed concrete, these monuments to the lack of imagination should simply disappear by permanent edict. Abracadabra.

I asked the black prostitute at the bar if she was interested in art. She laughed with her huge mouth and the whites of her eyes joined the white row of her teeth. "Art? . . . Art? . . . of course . . . " And she showed me the screen, where at that moment a young man, who was playing a gynecologist, ejaculated into the obliging face of . . . The paid cromagnon calls the black woman from the bar. She leaves in a hurry excusing herself because the cromagnon is scolding her: "He's a weird one . . . " She doesn't realize that the only weird one is herself and this whole nauseating place that stinks of semen. F is right . . . decadence of the West, and what do you say about poor Hegel, he would be so frightened if he saw this he would forget his daily philosophy lesson forever . . . If I was sure that I was doing something for my son, what would it matter about Gordo and the bootlegger Iturbide . . . history is coming near its end. I have been a witness and nothing more, a witness of a terrible illusion at that. In this city, power is excessive, the spirit is broken, there isn't one cure that wouldn't be part of the same lie. History is coming to an end and I pity the person who crosses its path. Rationality is a sickness, a sickness in every sense, without any possible escape, except at lunch hour, which lengthens to two hours without worrying about Gordo's curses and the bootlegger Iturbide's hypocritical grumbling. Gordo takes his siesta sprawled in the big leather chair snorting like a bellows, and when he wakes up, he becomes hateful.

"And what has that shit-eater done all week? . . . He still doesn't have the bulletin ready."

Crazy diplomats of contagious diseases, I'd stick their bulletin up their ass. I am in the hole more, without hope and getting bad feelings, but isn't something always possible . . . I'm saved by being nobody. It was better in the Galapagos when they rode turtles . . . Elegance can save anything; let's go to France, Barbara. Last night I dreamed that I was in Caleu with M.H. and J.Z., taking a walk below the wild plum trees in the orchard . . . Or no, I had gone to Caleu because M.H. suggested it to me.

"What are you going to do this summer?" he asked.

"I don't know . . . "

"Where are you going, or are you staying in Santiago? . . . "

"I don't know, I don't have anywhere to go . . . "

"Go to Caleu," he told me with a shrewd wink.

"Don't worry about the money. Don Carmelo is in the pear harvest, and you offer him help, see? Free lodging . . . "

It was a bad joke. There wasn't any such pear harvest, nor were there many pear trees. It seems to me there were only green apples and many golden plums that grew wild like weeds. I don't know if it was because of the plum trees but for us Caleu was like a version of Arcadia. Those were the years we hung around M.H. and J.Z., who was as deaf as an adobe wall when he wanted to be. In an old, convertible Packard, with three rows of seats and luggage racks along the running board, the chauffeur of Caleu and the owner of its only motor vehicle arrived to pick us up at the Prince of Peace Station. The fact that the car was still running was proof of Manuel Godoy's mechanical abilities, that was his real name. Behind the enormous steering wheel, busy with the levers, Manuel Godoy picked us up, but he looked at us with astonishment, surprise and something of suspicion to hear himself questioned as Prince of Peace and Duke of Alcudia when J.Z. explained the courage of Manuel de Godoy in the court of Carlos IV. M.H., who never seemed to get tired, went out at dawn, near the streams, to look for the blue flower of Novalis, and in the afternoons he walked through the halls of Don Carmelo's rambling house, reading *Les Nourritures Terrestres* in a loud voice. In their endless interlacing monologues, M.H. and J.Z. each bragged of outtalking the other. Both dotted their bold eloquence with mythological names and references to the Hellenic period, and because of the lullaby rhythm of their speeches, we let ourselves be carried to a timeless reality in that valley settled in the Coastal Cordillera, said valley of Caleu. *¿Qué se fizo el Rey Don Juan? ¿Los infantes de Aragon, qué se ficieron?** Suddenly, I saw myself in Paris, a city I know only in dreams, in the middle of a carnival procession, dressed in a long silk shirt with colors like the murals of Pierro della Francesca. All of those in the procession were women, and they all looked like Josephine Baker and F and I were in the middle dressed like harlequins. The procession advanced slowly towards the Elysian Fields. It was dusk. Nobody talked and nobody looked at each other, everyone walked in formation to the Follies Bergere. Finally, we arrived at a

*From Jorge Manrique's *Coplas* (1440-1479). What became of the King, Don Juan? And the Infantes of Aragón, what became of them?

water trough with silver siphons. There all of us bowed and treated ourselves to the magic potion. Then the procession dissolved, breaking up into small groups looking silently for each other, yet not able to get back together. One small group, F and I amongst them, went to the twisted back alleys of the Latin Quarter. They looked at us questioningly. We asked *de quoi sagit-il?*, but nobody knew how to respond, nor were there many who could hear us, they just looked at us with wondering eyes. "They are the artificial paradises," a tall mysterious woman who looked like Vera Korene said. "Do you want to come in?" And we followed her. We went down to the sewers and lay on the dike watching the waters go by. From the other bank Don Carmelo was looking at us, as if he were asking why we were there. We had been left alone and the rising water had started to lap at our feet. I wanted to stop, but my tired arms and legs wouldn't move. With disgust, I saw my penis, the symbol of my manliness, disappear slowly into a hole and a small stain of blood. At that moment, someone from the procession arrived to whisper in F's ear that Eliane was in another artificial paradise. "But she is with you, she waits for you." Still disgusted, I looked at the hole, but F didn't seem to notice.

Be careful of Gordo and the bootlegger Iturbide. Don't get close to them. I know what they have up their sleeves. I know they want to get rid of me. All of their insinuations about the lack of money, bureaucratic trash, I already know, I already know . . . I know them . . . They want to get rid of me and keep the money for themselves. Above all, avoid turning your back on the bootlegger Iturbide, watch out for the shot of curare, and the prick in the shoulder. Last week he hugged me with a sad expression because I had been gone for three days. I know that he had the syringe up his sleeve, and while Gordo tried to shake hands with me, he made a sign to the bootlegger and . . . zaaaasss! I felt the prick from behind.

After the porno bar, I went to the Speakeasy on 14th Street. Adieu, Adieu, I said goodbye to the cromagnon and the black prostitute as I left. They looked at me strangely. If F is worried about the decadence of the West, he should see what has come to the Speakeasy since we were here three years ago during its peak, when the biggest attraction was a fat woman with blonde curls, dressed in a corset, who balanced on a trapeze above the customer's heads. There is no longer a trapeze artist, but Slim Joe is still around, dressed as usual in the United States flag, and playing ragtime songs on the upright piano. The people have also changed in the Speakeasy. They are no longer poor students getting drunk on beer, but talkative Cubans, tourists dressed in immaculate polyester suits, and executives with cold eyes and crew cuts. I sat next to the restrooms, at the same table we were at the night before Christmas eve, three years ago, oh, how time passes. That was the period of fat cows for F, and the period of thin cows for me, when I earned a few miserable dollars running a copy machine. F had come to see me from Pittsburgh in a flaming red sports car. A little later he left his post as a professor with high hopes to go to Chile, but it didn't go well for him. He came back with his tail between his legs. That was when things got hard. He couldn't find work. Rejected on all sides. They looked at him suspiciously because of the nationalizations. He told me that it wasn't the best time to be Chilean. He even had to wash dishes at $2.25 an hour. It was good to touch bottom, he said, there at the bottom he was learning things. He could swear it again and again until he went hoarse and I still wouldn't have believed him. Anyway, he didn't stay down there at the bottom learning things for very long, after a few weeks, he said to hell with it, he would live on the streets. He didn't want Eliane to be a witness to his hard times and when I went to Pittsburgh to wait for him at the Greyhound station, it was 40° C outside. The first thing he said to me was, "This seems like the capital of Senegal!" If only it were true . . . I don't think he will be able to forget that night before Christmas Eve. At the next table there was a surly Irish man who made more noise than a battalion. He seemed to want to talk with us, like those dogs that wag their tails begging for a word of recognition or sympathy. He made various foolhardy attempts, but F rejected him with a cold look warning him to stay at his table and stop pestering us, but the giant kept at it. The waitresses no longer wanted to serve him, he had followed one of them into the restroom, but the woman came out after a moment having a fit. Four cooks went into the restroom to get it over with and throw him into the street, but he showed them a card. They let him go and let him return to his table. Slim Joe resolved the situation by attacking the beat of *Ain't Misbehavin* with spirit, and soon everything returned to normal, upset occasionally by an incoherent remark from our neighbor, in which we could only make out the words gook, fuck and a sound very similar to the rattle of a machine gun. Once again he started at it, and he came towards our table to start a conversation saying he was of Irish origin: "I am Irish American . . . "

But F stopped him in a second: "And so what!" I thought the man would try to hit us. I saw him grind his teeth. But nothing happened. Like a scolded dog, he flattened his huge body against the wall and continued his seething monologues. When we left the bells were ringing, it was midnight and it was snowing hard. We went to look for the car and I remember we walked two blocks sliding through the snow in the middle of the commotion of 14th Street. We stopped in a bowling alley to have coffee. Coming around the corner half an hour later, in front of the Speakeasy, we saw that there was a crowd of onlookers and police cars were arriving, cutting the night with the howl of their sirens. We went over and asked someone what had happened. He replied that some man had shot himself in the temple in the restroom of the Speakeasy. F turned pale. "Maybe if we had talked with him . . . " but he didn't let me finish. He told me that the man had a gun and had to use it against someone, that he could have shot him or the woman in the restroom but he finally shot himself. Early the next morning I woke up when F left to buy the daily paper. Opening the door he told me that violence is as American as apple pie, and with a calm voice he added that he hadn't been able to sleep.

Where are the poor students of days gone by? Slim Joe plays with less enthusiasm. He seems to miss them too. The polyester tourists and the talkative Cubans and the executives with cold looks and pincer hands grasping their glasses of Scotch, talk only of dollars, dollars, dollars . . .

Monday. I woke up at noon. All morning the telephone rang, and I let it ring. Let it ring . . . For sure it is Gordo or the bootlegger Iturbide. I go to the pharmacy for Pepto Bismol, but the pharmacist tells me that I am taking the wrong medicine, I should take Serpasil he tells me. I told the pharmacist that it takes a long time to fall out of love. He looked at me strangely and said, "One dollar fifty five . . . four tablets daily, after meals." There go the spring women scattering flowers through the golden valley of Caleu . . . We were all going to be queens, of four kings from the sea . . . When your stomach falls, the same as over there, you stay on your guard, but there it's in the company of friends. A few officials from the Union Paramaricones live in the building and when we meet each other in the foyer, they move faster or slower so as not to have to go up with me in the elevator. Other times it is me who moves faster or slower. Bureaucratic cow dung, I know them all . . . I don't have the slightest doubt that they hide the syringe under their sleeves like the bootlegger Iturbide. A thin Columbian woman who is a secretary at BID also lives in the building and she doesn't look at me any more since I told her that she looks like Nefertiti. Passing by the Pot of Gold I saw F, sitting talking excitedly with a pale young man. F asks where I have been. He tells me that Iturbide called him in the morning, that they worry about my health, that the Bulletin has to go to the press and it's still not ready, etcetera. He tells me that Ingrid has disappeared and he thought perhaps she and I . . . Barbara comes over and asks, "Where have you been?"

"In Orinoco," I said. But she didn't seem to understand. She asks me what I want and I respond, "When?"

She says, "Tomorrow." For six months she has been saying the same thing. F tells me what they were talking about before I arrived, and I realize that only intelligent beings get melancholy and perhaps that is because they live in two times, the past or the future, the present they suffer through like purgatory.

"We were talking about Durero's engraving *La Melancolía*," F explained. "Ingrid looks like . . . when she had long, thick hair . . . The same serious expression, the same intense look." I responded that the only thing melancholy is Tiffany's at six in the evening, and the Empire State Building in New York. "But we are never in New York and six in the evening is never six in the evening," F comments.

And Lester adds, "Above all the Empire State Building in the eight hour short film by Andy Warhol." The thought of this young man seemed so hilarious that I knocked down Barbara's tray when she arrived with the pastrami. F and Lester looked at me strangely while Barbara leaned over to clean the mess, it gave me the wild desire to grab her ass. F tells me that Ingrid's problems can be traced to her lack of economic independence and in the way the Herr Professor blackmails her. Lester adds that the father has made her believe that she isn't worth a thing and that without him she'd be lost in the world. Lester tells us that when she gave the exhibit in the Pot of Gold she wanted to use the money from the sales to go to California and buy some property in the San Fernando Valley in order

124

to convert it into a transcendental meditation commune, but she didn't sell anything . . . she was asking three thousand dollars for each painting. F said, "Three thousand? . . . She has to be crazy." Lester: "And who knows, maybe in twenty years her paintings will attract some crazy millionaire's eye and she'll be in style." F agrees: "And then she'll move back into the eigth floor studio to paint and, to keep the Herr Professor from making another move, she'll tie one of his legs to the bed with a chain." Lester: "A gold chain . . . " They laughed until their sides ached. Lester is missing a tooth. F: "But after the exposition fiasco she turned it all on herself . . . melancholic, concentrational catatonia, that's my theory . . . " Lester agrees. When Barbara returns with the pastrami I push her aside with my hand. Her look alone makes my gastric juices flow and gives me gas. In two bites F puts it into his iron stomach. I take out my Serpasil. Before Barbara moves away I ask her, "Tomorrow?" and she asks me if I've thought about it. I answer that I'll bring her *The Theory of the Landscape* by Andre Lothe. She wants to paint simple little landscapes to start with, not like crazy Ingrid with her ribbons and transistor filaments. The pale, young boy gets up and says goodbye.

As soon as we're alone and seeing how he is crazy about *ritornella,* F starts to talk about the taxi driver with the bulging eyes, that it's crazy to go around throwing money away, that I can't go on like this, that these are hard times, that I should take care of what I have. To calm him down, I tell him the plan to make myself a millionaire by inventing toys . . . "Toys?" . . . "Yes, toys for children from five to eighty," I explain. Like a chameleon that swims on its back to see an airplane fly during an afternoon in the Orinoco, F gives me a strange look. As usual, he quickly changed the subject, but then he started to talk about Gordo and the bootlegger Iturbide; we agreed that perhaps Gordo was an ass but that Iturbide was a good person and he worries about me. I've heard it all before. Gordo always insists that my job is nonexistent and that he hired me because Iturbide almost started crying, "Poor man, we should help him . . . " The position might be very nonexistent, but the occupant exists and since Gordo arrived he has been on a campaign of terror, that my position is provisional, that he has decided to slash the budget. I know those budget stories . . . They want to fire me . . . And since when has F become so friendly with the bootlegger Iturbide? As far as I'm concerned, he is part of the conspiracy and he wants to get my job. Is he also in the conspiracy? I don't have any more strength . . . Over there, to run there . . . They would forgive me . . . no it's better not to run away . . . simply arrive, arrive at the branch where the kestrels settle after a long flight. I swear, gentlemen, that rationality is an illness in every sense . . . exiled, homeless, bodiless . . .

"That's why," F told me, "you have to start with your body . . . you have to eat . . . let's be reasonable, you have to pull yourself together." He tells me that when he calls me on the telephone he will use a password so that I can know that it's him and answer without worry . . . He will ring twice, riing! riing! then hang up, then call again. That will mean the coast is clear. "Understood? . . . "

He told me to stay quiet. "And finally what is this story about your Cunegunda and the five hundred dollars?" he asked. "Have you looked at yourself in the mirror lately?" I got up and I, small as I am, grew and I watched him shrink like a twisted pigmy.

"Go to hell right now!" I yelled at him with a thundering voice.

"And do you want me to stay there?"he asked calmly.

"There? . . . where?"

"There in hell . . . "

Then I shrunk again, while everything spun around, and I saw him from below, he was enormous. I said he looks like Polifemo and I sat down again. We looked at each other in silence, and in a short time we began to laugh. F ordered another pastrami and a chilled Heineken and he warned me that appearances can be deceiving. And I told him I would think about the five hundred dollars. Then F said, "That is why your Cunegunda is so friendly to you," and went on to tell me something that had nothing to do with it. Art Studies? But what art . . . don't even believe it! . . . You should see the Cunegunda when she leaves every night with her horde of biker friends who come to look for her at the Pot of Gold and you should see her at closing time when she lets loose her innocent braids and changes from her peasant skirt to tight black leather pants, leather boots and a leather jacket with metal studs. You should see the band of rowdy cavemen with their cans of beer, belching at the people and passing time by throwing daggers to test their aim. Then you should see the Cunegunda when she jams on her helmet and runs out to mount the back of the leader's motorcycle. He uses a Wehrmacht helmet with a swastika. You should see that awful sight . . . the insignias, the goads, the bolas, the chains, the swastikas, the locks, the knuckledusters, and the roar, the roar and the sulfur trail when the gang of Attila moves out . . . I told him he was losing his mind, I told him to go to hell, and this time I really left.

I have finally found a reasonable person whom I can talk to. His name is Abraham Lincoln, he is from Illinois and he was born in a cabin, the same as Abraham Lincoln. He has a thin beard, he is tall and skinny and, the same as Abraham Lincoln, he dresses in a black coat and a top hat, but everyone here calls him Abbie.

When we arrived, F and Eliane came into the park with me and left me in front of the white mansion with my overnight suitcase and my toothbrush. I saw Lester, the one who does his internship at St. Elizabeth's, at the foot of the steps. "And you, what are you doing here?" I asked him. With a grin of complicity he explained that he made up the Reception Committee for Persecuted People and that it was an honor for him to welcome me. Next act, Lester kindly conducts me to a small room where officials dressed in white asked me my name, age, place of birth, they are interested in knowing about my parents, they felt my chest and my back, after which they asked me if I had had any illness. I answered without a pause that rationality is an illness, sirs . . . rationality in every sense of the word. They praised the correctness of my thoughts. I asked the officials in white if there were any disgraced dignitaries in the mansion, to which they politely responded that among the guests there were very few who fell into that sort of disgrace. I should say that the mansion impressed me much more on the outside than on the inside. The next day, I told Lester that I noticed that my room left a lot to be desired and, above all, I let him know that the bed was hard. He explained that it was all for the well being of the guests, so that they wouldn't get accustomed to softness and to the easy life, and in that way they'd stay in better physical condition. I praised the wisdom of his words and I told him that, from now on, I'd take the bed out of my room and sleep on the bare floor. He told me, no, that there was no need to exaggerate, that would only provoke a spirit of rivalry among the guests, which one should avoid in an egalitarian society. At that moment, Abbie came to ask Lester for paper and a pencil to write some important proclamations. Lester introduced us. They gave the impression that they knew each other well. Abbie scrutinized me with a questioning eye and asked me where I was from. Without hesitating, I answered yes, that I didn't have definite plans; I answered no, that from then on . . . I immediately gathered that Abbie was also persecuted and, in the time that we walked on a path under the birches, he told me that I should prepare myself for a war between the Pink and the Pank. For me, it has to do with those same frustrated people and opportunists that divide society, as F puts it. In the time that he had talked, a group had formed behind us that cheered him on. "Give them hell Abbie . . . " they yelled in chorus. Abbie stood on top of a natural platform that the jutting roots of a gigantic birch formed. There he gave a fiery speech against the California growers who preferred the cultivation of *annona reticulata,* not the *cherimola* variety because it wasn't considered profitable. The audience applauded frantically. When he got down from the roots, I talked to him about the cherimoyas of Quillota, close to the branch where the Prince of Peace was going to pick us up in his monstrosity to take us through valleys and ravines of the Coastal Cordillera to the golden enclave of Caleu, but he wasn't interested at all in the Prince of Peace. The *cherimola,* his fixed idea . . .

"*Cherimola?*" he asked me with disbelief and eyes wide open.

"All *cherimolas!*" I answered and he affectionately took my arm and he commented that my country was a civilized one. As we were walking, Abbie led me toward a wrought iron grating where you could see a half hidden door through the wild foliage. On the other side, you could hear the traffic. Abbie told me that above all, I should be careful with the man standing in front of the door. What man? I told him that I didn't see anybody and he explained to me that that was precisely because the man in the door was an invisible man. He asked me to remember so that F would write a protest to send to the House of Representatives. With reluctance we moved away from that place and walked toward the northern pavillion of the mansion, but at that moment, the lunch bell rang. I told Abbie that the *anorexia nervosa* had disappeared. After all, F was right when he said that *anorexia* had something to do with the nerves, which goes to prove, as the saying goes, that the devil knows more because he's old, rather than because he is the devil. Here I even ask for seconds of cabbage soup, and two loaves of black bread, like the bread that we ate in Caleu.

I don't remember when I arrived here. I think that it was in the middle of thermidor F and Eliane brought me, the song of the morning whose key is G major. She told me to be ready, that they'd come by in the afternoon in a Versailles coach, to look for me, but the coach turned out to be a rickety taxi and the coachman a sweaty Black man with bulging eyes. Sometimes it happens that way, strange things. They left me at the entrance of the vast mansion and said goodbye, Eliane sniveling and F looking dejected.

Just in case, and to be sure, Abbie explained to me that the Pink were the patriots and the Pank, the superpatriots, but that the Pank were so super that, in the end, they became antipatriots and responsible for the bad image that the country had internationally. We headed toward the podium under the birch tree, and a group of panting guests anxious to hear the speech followed us. There are young guests and old of every size and shape. There are guests who walk through the park paths without stopping, some who are in a hurry to get to their destinations, and others who stay standing or sitting like statues. There are also those who reason with loud voices with some species of invisible man, and others who smile nicely. There is another who runs, flapping his arms but I haven't seen him fly.

Abbie got up onto the platform and attacked the California growers again, saying that they treated the rest of the nation like second class citizens. He said that in order to reduce costs, they preferred the *reticulata* variety, that it is less bothersome to cultivate and has a longer refrigeration period than the delicate *cherimola.* The group yelled slogans against the *reticulata* and then incited him: "Give them hell Abbie! . . . " Some of them were beside themselves, but not all of them showed enthusiasm. At some twenty feet, a guest with a grim face turned halfway around, dropped his pants and showed us his pimply rear. Abbie hardly changed his pace and continued his discourse, after yelling to the rude person to go back to the caves where he came from. And to me, that the rude person was a Pank. I don't know if the untimely rear in the air was the cause, but Abbie abruptly concluded his speech, not without first assuring the audience that that he'd present a motion for the consideration of the House of Representatives. I didn't suspect that he was saving the juiciest part of the speech for me. We moved away from the group that was cheering him and throwing curses against the *reticulata* and, then, taking me smoothly by the arm, in an eloquent torrent that would have left Demosthenes and Caton green with envy, he emptied the flood of his thoughts. It would be a very hard task to try and repeat his speech that lasted until midnight, but it's enough to say that he traced the country's entire history from the Paleolithic times to now. He took a good hour to explain that this was the only country in the world with organized crime, and one could say, with unorganized crime. According to what I could gather from his words, the country doesn't even have a name . . . it's called the United States . . . United States of what? He said that the country even appropriates other people's names

... and that there are other united states, the United States of Brazil, of Mexico or the United States of Venezuela and that all countries are united states and that the United States designates a form of government, but it is not, nor never will be, the name of a country, that that only reflects the abysmal lack of Pank imagination, from the time the country buried its previous history so as to make a new start. That they could have called themselves Mayflowerlandia, for weren't they the first colonizers, those who landed on the Mayflower? . . . " It should be called Calomega, Micromegas, or Ramona, the Republic of Ramana, a name for a country but not the United States, that is not the name of a country and here we are with a country that doesn't even have the name of a country that bullies the other countries and that divides the world into two categories, the Pink and the Pank, and if you are not Pank, to hell with you . . . That night we didn't eat, and it's too bad because there was chicken pot pie.

I don't know how long I've been here. I vaguely remember a morning. The telephone rang twice, riing! riing! and it stopped, then it started ringing again. The password . . . But it wasn't F. It was Eliane. "Dulcinea speaking," she sung to my ear with her crystal voice. I answered that her note was G major. She talked quickly and she told me that poor F was on nails and he had been looking all over the city for me, where had I been sleeping these days, that they had let the police in on it and that they were afraid that something had happened to me in the middle of the street fighting with tear gas, that they had come to my apartment and they had found it open, miracle, miracle that they had not stolen anything . . . that I had gotten lost in the demonstrations on Constitution Avenue. Immediately afterwards F got on the telephone and asked the same questions. A little later they came to the apartment to look for me. F stared at me in silence. I had never seen him so sad. He spoke with a tired voice and he made me realize that I was starving and that I could hardly hold myself up. "Just look at how you are," he told me. He told me to shave and we could go to an Italian restaurant on Novena Street. "I'll pay," he told me, but Eliane made a grimace; that no, that that section depressed her, she said. That we should go instead to the Trieste on Pennsylvania Avenue. I suggested that they move away from the window, that it wasn't an accident . . . I brought them up to date, that my enemies had made a pact with Voodoo Witchdoctors. "But where have you been?" F insisted. I assured him that I hadn't been lost and that I had run into Jesus Christ and it was him who brought me to the house. I told them that I wasn't lost, that I had been through meadows and gardens, that close to me there had been strange pastoral scenes, with people giving water to goats, hanging next to the blackberry bushes, reclining in the shade of the pastures. As far as I was concerned, everyone was Pink and they were in artificial paradises. You could hear the flute of a young blond boy playing sweet Lucca Marenzio tunes. To my surprise, the young blond boy turned out to be Jesus Christ and he offered to accompany me home. There was a great crowd . . . in a park.

F used to like to go to Trieste because it is one of the few places left that doesn't play "confusing music at 100 decibels," (as we went in, the Wurlitzer was playing *Una Furtiva Lágrima)* but also because he believed that his knowledge of

Italian astounded the customers and the owner, an opulent woman who made eyes at him from the coat closet. The owner would approach one table or another moving through the isle with the jingling of her jewelry in her zig-zagging trip toward the kitchens in back, and she'd stop walking to share an Anisette or a drop of coffee with us. The customers would look at her greedily, and resentful faces would turn toward our table when she would pass by. In those occasions, F and Eliane were in their element and we always ended up making fun of the clientele who were wealthy but obviously yokels.

The waiter asked me very formally what I wanted and I told him: *"Picarones."* F explained that they didn't have *picarones* there and he took the menu away from me. He ordered shellfish for me and they ordered *ossobuco* and *calamari* and a carafe of Bordelino to wash them down. I didn't even want to touch the shellfish, I was sure that it was poisoned, but Eliane swore "no." "So you'll see," she said, "I'm going to taste it . . . See, nothing happens to Dulcinea . . . oh, and it's delicious . . . " Ah, she licked her lips . . . then, I let her serve me four spoonfuls, for no other reason than to appease her.

A little later, the owner approached our table to say hello. She and Eliane had become good friends. The owner would tell her life story to her favorite customers. She explained that she came from Udine and that she had met her dead husband, who was a native of Trieste, over there, and that they had married in Udine and later lived for several years in Remini where they started a restaurant and in the beginning, they were inclined to name it Udine or Trieste, but in the end, they opted for Trieste because it was a better known name; but Silvio *il mio marito,* always said till the end of his life, that Udine had more elegance . . . then came the happy ending, the trip to America, and they brought the whole Trieste, to the last fork and the last crystal goblet from Murano. We had heard the same story five times, and now I'm not sure if the thing is backwards, if they married in Remini and they put the Trieste in Udine. In any case, she has the thick, sun-tanned skin of the Adriatic navigating people, but this time, when she stopped to have the goblet of Anisette, F spoke first and told the story of the unfortunate affair between Paolo and Francesca de Remini, and moreover, Eliane, the lynx, started to talk with me about Genoveve de Brabante. The trick had excellent results and in that way we avoided the already overworked story of her geographic migrations. When she moved away, we began to laugh like crazy. F suddenly became serious and he made me realize that the time had come to grab the bull by the horns and, since I was persecuted, it wasn't the time to be putting myself there within reach of my enemies. I told them that they were everywhere, but he put my mind at ease when he told me that he knew of a mansion where clerks worked, whose only job was to protect me from my enemies and keep them in place with constant vigilance. He led me to understand that they couldn't enter there. "Impossible! They can't enter, they can't," he told me and Eliane added: "Impossible, they can't." I thought about the sense of their argument. Eliane asked me to be ready, they would come looking for me in the afternoon in a gold Versailles carriage.

130

Today, if they would put me in front of the shellfish that I didn't want to try in the Trieste, I would lick the plate clean. The moment to pay arrived, the hilarity abruptly died down when F saw that the owner had included the three Anisettes, which at other times she had offered as a *beau geste,* in the bill. And that wasn't all. She had also included the shot that she herself had taken. But it seemed that F quickly got over it, deciding that nothing would ruin his high spirits. He paid without joking and in the end, in a big uproar directed to the Italiana, he raked *"nel mezzo del camin di nostra vita"** to the boorish, proper and fatfaced waiter who wasn't listening to him, but who nodded with an understanding air, his eyes nailed to the bill. As soon as the waiter left, F became somber again. He explained his paying for the drinks as a supplementary test of the decadence of the West: "And us, the geniuses who were so happy! She charged us for the story that we saved her from telling, the harpy! She charged us the drinks!" To underline his displeasure he hit the table softly with his fists. Eliane agreed. She said that, in reality, the boss was a *degueulése*** and that she is in the perfect country for *degueulése* like her. In the minutes in which the owner was making her raid through the kitchens in back, we slipped out the door. For F that was the end of the Trieste . . . he'll never set foot in the place again.

Once in a while they come to see me. The last time, F brought me a fragrant camelia and Dulcinea a truffle-paté that she bought in the imported food store on Wisconsin Avenue, because she knows that I like it. They told me that they'd come by to see me on Saturday so that we could speak more calmly, but I told them that on Saturday, Abbie has to go to Gettysburg to give a transcendental speech on the abolition of slavery. He asked me to go with him and I told him that I'd go.

---

*"in the middle of the road of our life," from Dante's *Divine Comedy.*
**foul-mouth

My Beautiful Buenos Aires

By Leandro Urbina

For the first two weeks, I took cold showers at night, because my body was soaked with perspiration and the sheets weighed heavily, twisted around armpits and neck, bringing on dreams about death, and the temperature shot up with 90% humidity, and in the room next to me, on the other side of the thin wooden partition, a blond exercised her trade, alternating groans with boleros by Eydie Gorme and the Panchos in a precise rhythm, while downstairs, a typical orchestra I never saw shook the Boite Malevaje with a thick syrup composed of concertinas and drums, in the style of Astor Piazzola. I closed my eyes and a cloud of brilliant colors passed regularly from left to right; a sabre, a crown, my grandfather's face, teeth clenched like bone eyelids through the glass of the coffin, the lapis lazuli veins running down from the eyes to the chin, ah, my love, I'm all alone here on the beach. The dirty jet of light from a small bulb streams through the transom in the door that opens onto the corridor, illuminating the plaster ceiling; then the mosquito buzzes a long, peninsular Z, as if from the small shops on Reconquest Street that sell bread, cheese and olives, and I cover myself with the wrinkled, damp sheet and play dead, but its stinger pierces my thigh and sucks up a long stream of bitter red tea and before I can squash it it flies heavily to a dark corner to digest. The blonde and I whine and the woman in the room across the hall screams out who do you think you are, I'll get you booted outa here tomorrow, you tryna drive us crazy (I am half-crazy, madam), and that Chilean who takes baths at this hour of the night, the horny bastard, and you just sit here and don't say a thing because you're scared shitless. Well, next month I'm going back to the village and you'll be left alone. I can't go back, I can go down to Lavalle and plunge into the frenetic multitude of heat, cinema and gin, look for a café table where I can talk about James Caan, Lacaan and Peroon, eat a ham and cheese special, drink an espresso.

Besides, I'm hungry. My father gave me the fifty-dollar inheritance my aunt sewed into the lining of my jacket collar so the cops wouldn't leave me broke if they stopped me crossing the mountains, and I've spent 25 in two weeks and I haven't found a job yet and I don't know what to do, I always go to sleep around 5:00, when the air loses some of its load of barbecue-and-sweat-smells and the aroma of water and oil rises with the breeze from the River Plate and runs through the streets gathering papers and plastic bags into little blind flurries while somebody arranges his tie, whistles and staggers, and I mount the rotten hotel steps to sink into the cold humidity until past one in the afternoon. But the heat doesn't let me. You understand, I come from the mountains, from a dry wind that puts roses in your cheeks, here I suffocate and I get excited and angry, too, even angrier. It's the old thing about veins expanding with pressure, Julio, this is the harbor, here people don't eat spicy foods because if they did they'd blow up. Just steaks with salt, but what steaks, see? That could be it too, eating a lot causes nightmares, it's a kind of restlessness. I wrote my father an eight-page letter telling him all about it, I'm the first of the family to go abroad, you know? I bought some white, fibrous paper, very thin. On the little table in my room I rearranged the few books I brought with me, along with some German pencils I bought in Punta Arenas, and I added two pads of paper, one for letters, onionskin for weepy letters, and the other heavy brown paper for my novel. You understand, I also want to get to know the cultural environment, browse through the bookstores, read all the newcomers, and write what I have to write with an impeccable style, terse but bloody and complex. Maybe I won't be talented enough, but it's like a duty, even if I fail. Still, I only have 25 dollars left and that won't be enough for my project. We'll see, I have some friends around, as poor as church mice though; they get upset when you come to the door, they get nervous, either he's come to sponge food or he's going to ask me for money. My friend Pedro Gutierrez is an actor, he complains that every complimentary remark of mine costs him dear. He's one of the few doing something concrete and I like to have conversations with him and encourage him, but it's hard to relate to people here, with doubts and suspicions nagging away at you, whispering filth in your ear like a police informer. I take a drink, go ahead, have a shot. That's it, love, that's it. At 12:30 I go out to the street and I cross the Plaza de Mayo to reach Lavalle, I buy a magazine, a newspaper, I settle down with a cup of coffee beside a window and I read.

The morgue was overflowing with bodies. When I reached my sons I hardly recognized them. Hurry up and get these sonsabitches out of here, we need the room, a sergeant said to my uncle and he was more afraid than angry and he said yes, sir.

I need a light jacket, around here people put a lot of store in how you look; good thing I know how to wash and iron. The mirror's a bit wavy but it's not bad for shaving. I have delicate skin. I look older, about thirty; I'll be 23 in March. Sometimes I spend a long time looking at my face, flattened out by the quicksilver, and I feel like crying and I cry for a while sitting on the toilet and then I pull the chain. My hands start to tremble. I remember you, my hand circling your circumspect nipples, your lips half-open, and my mouth slides towards your thighs, leaving an opulent, pearly track upon your brown skin. You got me used to all those things. She (the blonde) sings, warbles too, tacky boleros, she perfumes her armpits with Jean Lapin. Of course, I don't tell any of this to you, nor that they kicked my brother to the point of nausea, nor that they broke my father's jaw; I don't want to go crying to anybody, I don't want anybody's sympathy. I wanted to have a coffee and you said you were just leaving and I sat down and thanked you and we remarked on how many people were out at that brilliant hour of the night and you noticed my sing-song accent, you're Chilean, eh? and you ordered another coffee and we talked. Was it very terrible? I had to go into exile, I can't tell you what happened there because my tongue stiffens and dries up in my mouth. Make way for the new government. The dog went crazy whining, howling and whirling around because the old man and my brothers were lying on the floor with their hands behind their heads and my mother was choking with sobs and my second brother and I were hiding in the attic. Then, at night, when they had taken them away, we cut our hair and shaved dry, that is with spit and a rusty Gillette. Then my brother left and I lit a cigarette. In the light of the match I discovered, a couple of feet away, the skeleton of a cat, gnawed by worms. My nose was full of dust, the smell of rain and cat piss and I thought, "this is like a bad Poe story" and I went out onto the roof and lay down on the shingles and contemplated the timeless stars as the night echoed with the sound of machine gun fire from downtown, come on, come on friend, to the front, come and find me, I want to join the fight. It was a cool night at winter's end. I think it's better to tell, see? What good is silence, you're choking on so much accumulated crap it's coming out your ears. You don't understand, it's not a matter of just sitting down and turning on the tap. I should have put on a different shirt, but I never imagined I would meet her here, I came for a coffee, besides I haven't unpacked yet, I can't manage to get settled, my money's running out, I haven't got a job, no use going around packing and unpacking every two weeks, I prefer to use a few clothes, wash them and leave something for special occasions, when my situation is more stable, not now. I have a poncho my mother gave me, a book of flora and fauna, a cookbook and a map of Santiago, my city; pure romanticism, you feel like carrying away with you something of what it was, reconstruct a piece of that ideal country, the mythical space we all had in our heads and whose signs we hardly managed to catch a glimpse of or thought we did, or dreamed we did because things are a lot less clear right now, do you understand me? Helplessness. That's why I like your legs too, the hint of thigh under the skirt and the little whisper of the stockings when you cross one leg over the other that I hear over the sound of the voices and the clinking of glasses and cups and the happy murmur that comes in the window from the street. I like that style of stockings, kind of old chocolate, like the women from my street who heard mass with their knees pressed together. Then it occurs to me that I don't want you to go just like that, that I'd like something to happen, that your shoulder might be soft and smooth if I rested my head on it, and that those tense lips, so well disposed to the irony required for psycho-analytic sexual sparring in a Buenos Aires café, might even turn out to be hospitable. So I say that I'm hungry, and that I don't know of any place and could you accompany me to some place where the food is good, and you smile and say why not? And I leave a bill beneath the coffee cup and we go out.

That was when we plunged into the floating column of white shirts and necks and bare arms and wet armpits and foreheads so shiny they reflected the rapid neon lights of the cinema and the restaurants exhaling their warm breath through tireless fans to the hot, humid, stagnant air like the water of the pond at Avellaneda in the middle of the night in Lavalle and Florida and Esmeralda as we advance elbow to elbow so that the tense tide, the ebb and flow of muscles, cannot break, as it would like to, this fragile alliance born of curiosity and the trembling vision of a scrap of perfumed flesh on the pupils that tell all; fear, absence, desire, that which is not and that which draws near; because undecipherable omens are being described on the sky: Armandia lidderdalei, Platessas, swords and ships; because the implacable clocks still frighten me, the idea of "curfew" and "state of emergency," even though Peron came back and even though the democratic and popular process of construction of Argentina-World Power has been set into motion like the multitude; suddenly, so much shoving and exophthalmos and strangled mouths and feet and hands and the serious murmur of voices, give me the shivers.

You put your hand on my shoulder and indicate the oasis of the next street, and as we turn the corner, jerkily, into a sudden, momentary silence, I hear your voice announcing the choice of "The Hunting Horn," not too expensive and not too cheap, so that we can look into each other's eyes across two glasses of Riojan wine.

We sit down in the middle of the dining room, at a little table with a red table-cloth and a candle, your choice because I prefer corners, and when the white-jacketed waiter sets off towards the kitchen with the order of French bread, veal cutlets à la napolitaine, souffléd potatoes and red wine, I looked around for the first time and realized we were being watched. You moved your chin slowly, slightly, with a notoriety that would like to pass unnoticed, like one of those Metro Goldwyn Mayer princesses who have left their castles in search of adventure and hope that their chosen escort won't recognize the greatness of their company. From one side, a guy about forty was watching you, seated at a table beside the window with two young men and a woman. One of those old guys with gray at the temples and a little official's moustache, he dispatched me a contemptuous glance and then lost himself in you; you ignored him. Then, as we were drinking our first glass of wine, one of the young men passed you on his way to the bar and "How are you, my little flower?" he said by way of greeting. "How's it going, turkey?" you answered drily. At that time I found Buenos Aires aggressiveness strange, even though I had the feeling it was a way of relating by hiding real affection beneath the verbal barb. Anyway, just then the waiter arrived with an array of dishes, and as we got into the rituals of digestion, clink go the glasses, our surroundings vanished and there was only the shine of your pupils and your teeth and your lips, which had swollen with the wine and the candlelight. Really, I want to say it but I can't, that there is a woman in Chile who is part of my neurosis, who comes to me at night with sleep, the sound of gunfire and the cold sweats —you're starting to look more and more like her, the way your eyelids fall and the languid gestures, and something about that verse by Goll: "Why are you never alone with me/Deep woman, deeper than the abyss/To which the sources of the past are attached?" But better just forget it, it's not only that. The thing is that when we left the half-empty restaurant, we were like two old friends, arm in arm and silent because they've said a lot to each other and they still have a lot to say. We walked along Corrientes and all of a sudden you stopped and we looked long at each other and something moved in the depths of your eyes and you took my hand and we went down into the next subway station. There, under the sleepy dome, as the flash of light from a train rushed by in the opposite direction, I first breathed the perfume of your hair. It was a slight, but electric contact. You looked at me, confused, and you tried to say something, but our train was arriving and your words were lost in the squeal of the brakes and the burst of air against the tiles of the platform

A crowd got off the train, and it astounded me that people kept coming downtown at this hour, when other cities were sleeping the sleep of the just and the repressed. What would Buenos Aires be like with a curfew? An immense and mute skeleton, with its muzzle buried in the riverbanks, with ten million inhabitants behind its windows, across from the television, the radio, or a cold bottle of beer.

The lights went out suddenly as the train started to move and when they came back on you were looking at me. "Does all this seem very strange to you?" "It's hard to say." "Do you know what a symbolic wound means? . . . You're like a symbolic wound. I think I would go crazy in your situation, I think I'd run to a psychoanalyst." "Do you think I'm crazy?" I wouldn't be surprised, after all this talk, after telling you that I have showers at midnight and that I dream about my dead grandfather. Fortunately I didn't say everything, fortunately there are still mute spaces in my consciousness, steep spirals where you can go around forever without ever reaching the great plain of the fundamental columns, of our fetishes and our shadows, the place where our gestures and our words are resolved and stagnate. "Do you think I need a psychoanalyst?" "You don't have to be crazy to go to a psychoanalyst; on the contrary, they're a great help, you know?" As for me, I'm used to group therapy. We got together, a million guys, and we yelled: Allende, Allende, the people believe in you. We resolved our little lunacies in a place bigger than an office, it's true that now we're left with nothing, with nothing more than screams and dead bodies and aches in our bones. "You're a good psychoanalyst, Mariel. During these hours with you I have been able to keep the anxiety and the fears at bay, I've recovered a little of my sense of life." I can't deny that while I was talking I had the feeling I was writing a bad novel, but I had to do it, I had to get emotional. "It's strange, it's all very strange." I felt your hand on mine and when the train stopped at Federico Lacrozce, lights winking on and off, you pressed up against me, saying "Don't lose me."

And we went out into the street through the arches of the railway station and there was La Chacarita with her illustrious dead and the pizzerias and the little grocery stores and the damp earth smell of the green parks and we were walking down the wide, treed streets with a strange joy of the body. I even heard the tinkling of a waltz in the rhythm of your legs. "With roses in her cheeks and jasmine in her hair/gracefully went the cinnamon flower." Because that's what I'm like when I fall in love, like the Wurlitzers in my neighborhood, and because even now there are no other sounds of the soul, and I hadn't yet learned the love gestures of Buenos Aires. That's why I could not decipher the pathos of your smile as we reached the door of the building where you lived and you said you were glad to have met me and that you'd like to see me again and why didn't I give you my telephone number; and I was all shaky and I made some kind of gesture and I thought that you should have given me a chance, a coffee and a gin, since the moon was so beautiful and Buenos Aires must look so majestic from the balcony of your apartment on the tenth floor. Then I shrugged my shoulders, beaten, and I was walking towards the desolation of the streets and the hotel when you called to me to come back, maybe you'd like a coffee, I have some gin, shall we go up? I'll go up if it's no trouble, of course I'll go up.

The marvellous thing is that I had imagined almost to the last detail the place where you lived. The sofa in front of the picture window, a coffee table in the middle, a shelf with a small record player and some best sellers and a compendium of psychoanalysis and dream interpretation, a black silk negligée trimmed with lace hanging behind the bathroom door, a large brass bed glimpsed in passing by your bedroom. "I'll sleep in that bed tonight," I said to myself and I could smell the perfume of the sheets, of your body and mine, of the pillows where our heads would be lying in the morning. This must be how it feels to have grace, that gift of God that raises me above ten million others, that sign that showed me the café door and the way to your table. Then, as we drink our gin, I tell you that it's been a long time since I felt so happy, that you are my first girlfriend in Buenos Aires, but it's hard to explain what that means because I had never experienced anything quite like it, that my generation has oscillated between the most absolute superficiality and the fiercest commitment with history and with life, that now we must struggle against a lachrymatory frustration, for once we were the golden youths who were to direct the most significant political project of the century in Latin America, only now we go around in circles, beaten from head to foot; our rituals and our language lost; that reality has become flat for us, and when the time comes to get back to earth, far from our streets and our mountains, to find a girlfriend is the first healthy opportunity to start picking up the pieces. You smile and your fingers sink into my hair and you rest your head on my shoulder and you say something to me with your hoarse little voice but I only hear its music because I've already begun to lose myself in you, to perceive the soft purr of your interior movements. You say that one must stabilize oneself, that equilibrium is indispensable, why kick up such a fuss just to suffer afterwards; then I kiss you on the neck and I feel you tense up and you keep on talking and I kiss you, my hand caresses your legs and you talk and sigh and little by little we slip into a horizontal position, until you suddenly remember that you left the coffee on in the kitchen and the moment is broken. But I have time, I would like to make love to you on the sofa, slowly, raise myself up on my elbows contemplating you without breaking the dense rhythm of the moment at which the sun rises out of the River Plate and the first bluish light comes in the window to illuminate the contours of our bodies. But you are in the kitchen putting out coffee and crackers and cutting a bit of cheese, and I am sitting with my arms resting on the back of the couch and my eyes half-closed and all of a sudden I realize that none of that will happen. Because my ear, intent on your movements in the kitchen, also perceives the sound of a key in the lock and I open my eyes to see the figure, silhouetted against the hall light, of the grey-haired guy with the military moustache.

At first I felt panic, the first thing that occurred to me was that it was a trap and that both of them were police officers and that the window was behind me but it was the tenth floor, then I see the man's face change from its first spiteful expression to one of infinite pain. He closes the door behind him and goes into your room. Then you come out of the kitchen with two cups of coffee and a question in your eyes. I look at you, overwhelmed. You say: Did he come in? and a sob answers you from far off. You put the cups on the coffee table and, without looking at me, go towards your bedroom. I hear both of you talking as if through clenched teeth. The man is crying. I get up off the sofa and for at least five minutes I stand there like an idiot. When I hear your shoes fall to the floor, one by one, and the rhythmic squeak of the bedsprings, I look around for something worth stealing. Then I feel sorry for you. I hear you moan softly. I pick up my old tweed jacket and, with one last chivalrous gesture, I leave your apartment on tiptoe. Outside, Buenos Aires is luminous. Upon reaching the subway station, before going in, I stop and look at you face to face, city of the Plate. On the stairs to the tunnel a drunk is singing: Oh, my beautiful Buenos Aires. We'll have to wait until six, when the station opens. Hey you, come on down for a shot and gimme a butt, yells the drunk, brandishing a bottle of grappa. I go down.

Putamadre

By Ariel Dorfman

Translated by Stephen Kessler

"It's not time yet, " declared the putamadre. "They never get started before eight."

The three slowed their pace, took on an easier rhythm without giving up that proud bold something in their stride, as if their very legs could tell they were on the right track, that this night would go especially well, so why hurry, boys. As if to emphasize their arrogance, their irreproachable freedom, their masterful command of the pavement of this unknown city in a strange country, the two bigger ones had sunk their hands deep in their pockets, enjoying the touch of the secret sinewy fluidity of muscles accustomed to so much military exercise, muscles going up this gringo hill effortlessly, working easily now, and which later would do some serious working and sweating, at a man's job. The third, on the other hand, a little less sure of himself, couldn't keep still. He kept moving back and forth beside the others, trying to figure out where he belonged. First he'd walk on one side, then he'd move around beside the putamadre, finally he'd elbow his way in between the two, raising his head as high as the shoulders of the other two cadets so as not to miss a single lively syllable of the conversation. He was about to jump in with a couple of his own opinions when the putamadre made a quick turn like a bullfighter, stopping short, smiling with a flash of his straight white teeth. A platinum blonde went by swinging her ass as if some inner hurricane propelled her agitated thighs. The little guy turned his head too, and did his best to break his momentum and stop as suddenly—but he couldn't. He bumped the putamadre, lightly.

"You clumsy twerp!"

The putamadre brushed off his uniform with a dignified seriousness, so not one speck of dust would dirty the immaculate navy blue cloth. He studied the extraordinary bouncy ass of the blonde disappearing down the street; his eyes skilfully surveyed her down to her suntanned legs, clinging to that skin, covering her body like a distant sweat.

"On account of you, Valdés," the putamadre asserted, "we've lost that piece of ass you see right there."

Chico Valdés had no desire to debate the strength of this judgment. What mattered more to him was the woman. "You mean she . . . ?"

The putamadre waited for the blonde to disappear completely into a crowd before answering. "She is," he sighed. "She and every other woman are for that, turdbrain. Right, Jorge?"

Jorge's hands were still in his pockets. He gave the impression of not being particularly interested in the woman. He calmly agreed: "All women are whores. Except my mama and my sister."

The putamadre let his mouth drop open like a fish out of water, and then he stretched his lips just so, a little twisted, squinting his eyes in more of a sneer than a smile. "Of course, of course, I forgot. Your mama and your sister are different. You'll have to forgive me." He took off his cap and made a bow. "Allow me to congratulate you, your majesty."

Chico saw his opening. "All women are somebody's mother or sister," he said. He'd heard the putamadre say that already while they were surveying the east coast of Colombia, waiting for the chance to go ashore, two weeks ago—two weeks and now at last here they were, *the United States of America.*

Jorge looked him up and down. "And what do you know about these things, huh? What do you know?"

"Let's go," urged the putamadre. "We're blocking the sidewalk."

Jorge didn't budge. "Huh, Chico? Huh? What do you know?"

"He doesn't know shit about this stuff," said the putamadre. "That's why we came ashore, asshole, so he could learn something."

"All right," declared Jorge. "Fine. But first he ought to get his dick wet, then he can carry his tool like a man, and then he can have opinions about whatever."

"He can have any opinions he wants to," said the putamadre. "It's an important night in his life. Let him have a good time." He made a gesture that included the bay below, the Embarcadero where the aristocratic silhouette of the ship could be made out, the big concrete buildings. "And what better place than San Francisco? It's like being in Valparaíso again. Just like home. And the people here are nicer than you can believe. Losing your cherry here is like doing it in our little Chile itself. And more romantic . . . "

Chico was absorbed in looking at a map he'd pulled out of his pocket, trying to get his bearings and locate the corner they were standing on.

"What do you need a map for, asshole, when you have me," said the putamadre, snatching it away. "I know this place like the palm of my hand. We're going to Fisherman's Wharf, but instead of going along the waterfront like the rest, we're making this detour through downtown, we're taking a walk across this fine turf, and you guys can have a chance to ride the famous cable car." He pointed uphill and kept walking in that direction. "It's this way," he asserted. "Geary or Powell Street, I don't remember which, but that's what I've got a mouth for, to ask—to suck too—but for now it will serve to ask the million dollar question, precisely." He lurched off in the direction of a tall young woman waiting on the corner for the light to change, and—winking an appreciative eye in the direction of his two friends—asked her in English: "Excuse me, miss, but we'd like to take the car to Fisherman's Wharf. In what direction?" They were impressed by his pronunciation.

While she was answering, the putamadre didn't take his eyes off her face. Chico started to feel uncomfortable seeing how he fixed his gaze on the depths of those gringo eyes, so blue, too pale, too transparent to support such a gaze. "Thank you," the putamadre said finally; and after a pause: "You're very nice." The girl threw them a Colgate smile and crossed the street. The putamadre stood there watching her. "It's where I told you."

"So let's get going," said Jorge.

"Of course we're going," said the putamadre. "First stop: Fisherman's Wharf, very picturesque, like Puerto Montt only cleaner and more modern, and then we'll go down to Ghirardelli Square. Lots of nookie there, showing it off all over the street. But the hippies don't bother you like they used to." The putamadre led the way toward the street in question. He took Chico Valdés by the arm. "I'm going to tell you a secret, Valdés. I'm going to tell you that the best moment of any encounter is when you realize the chick is hot for it, she wants it, she tries to push you a little, sort of panting, and everything's set up. There's nothing like that moment, Chico. In that moment you know the whole plot of the movie, you know how the story's going to work out. The rest is anticlimax. *You get me?*"

The putamadre had taken his first steps in English, more or less British, at Mac-Kay's Prep in Viña del Mar. Later he'd perfected the idiom during the two years his parents had lived in Chicago. But a few months before the September coup, the putamadre had returned home, newly enrolled in the Naval Academy. "What a nose my folks had, eh? They wanted me to have a good education, and they knew the score, that the days of the gentleman were numbered, were about to be cut off. That's why I had to go back. It's a shame. I'd been stung by a little widow. I'd never gone to bed with a woman that big. A gigantic gringa. As soon as I found myself in her grips I asked myself what I was doing with her. But between the legs they're more or less the same, whether they're dwarfs or elephants. What counts is how they shake it, and if you know how . . . "

"How much time have you spent in San Francisco?"

"Not much. I've been here twice. Once on the way to L.A., once on the way back. Enough to memorize the schedule that matters."

"And if you know so much, how come we don't look for some good girls, ones that aren't whores," Jorge insisted. It wasn't the first time he'd said it. "With this uniform on, it's a piece of cake. Come and get it."

"With this uniform on, it's a piece of cake." The putamadre raised his hand with two fingers extended to his open mouth, as if he wanted to yawn, making gestures and grimaces as if he were wiping off drool. "A piece of cake. Come and get it. Right this way—sure. Don't you see we're with Valdés, that we promised Valdés's uncle that we'd get this stud back to Chile made into a man. Don't you see that they didn't let us go ahore in Colombia, nor in Ecuador, that we never even docked in Acapulco, because it was full of chickenshit loudmouths and traitors, and we couldn't get laid anyplace. Can't you see we're overloaded as a bazooka and we've got to score for sure, because we've only got one night. Or how about if I take off on my own and find a little friend, like that beautiful gringa we just met, eh, and you guys can fend for yourselves?" They'd reached the car stop and the putamadre stood there looking at them, hands on his hips. "The one who decides here is Chico Valdés. His opinion goes."

"It's okay with me," said Chico, but that's all he said, because just then the cable car pulled up, bells clanging.

"This is it," the putamadre announced. "Climb aboard, boys." He kept talking while they boarded and pulled out some coins to pay the fare. "I'm going to take you to a special spot, a bordello with a special feature. It's called Lucia's. Bilingual, no less."

"Bilingual?" said Jorge. "Bilingual?"

"It was started by an old girl of Mexican descent. I think she named it after her mother. A little surprised, aren't you?" The putamadre set down the money. "Three, please."

"Getting laid in Castilian," said Jorge. "You're a genius, putamadre, sometimes you're full of shit but your genius has to be acknowledged."

"That's where you're going to unload, Chico," the putamadre informed him. "In a Pan-American atmosphere. We're going to pick out the finest honey they've got, we'll get them all lined up first, you take your time and pick one out, and then, you show her what Chilean quality's all about."

"Can they . . . do they, do they refuse sometimes?" Chico Valdés had a hard time stating the question, but it finally came out, weekly, shyly, but it came out, like a periscope in a rough sea. "Because all of a sudden I think it's better. . . "

"They never refuse," Jorge concluded.

"All you need is good money," the putamadre agreed, rubbing his fingers together significantly. "Everything's bought and sold in this life, old man, including love. That's what whores are for."

"What gets you down and dirty," said Jorge, Belmondoesque.

"What are you talking about, down and dirty? This is a high class joint, good reputation, the girls are hand-picked, medically checked-up and tried-out by the police. Here Chico Valdés is going to fuck to his heart's content without a worry and come out spotless." The putamadre gave his shoulder an affectionate hug. "That's why it was entrusted to me. I keep my promises, like a good sailor."

"Fine, fine," said Jorge. "Defend your little whores, if that's what gets you off. You give the orders, captain. This boat's going to Lucia's. But afterwards I'll give you my opinion about the merchandise."

"You can give any opinion you want," said the putamadre. "That's what we live in a free country for. We're going back to the academy ship Esmeralda with our nuts good and empty, it won't even matter that we won't get fucked again till we get to Tahiti—pure native meat in those parts."

Jorge turned around in his seat. He studied Chico carefully. "And you, Chico, do you feel very nervous?"

"What's there to be nervous about? He's a chip off the old block. With an uncle like his, he won't have any trouble."

Chico didn't answer. Out the window he saw the sweet warm evening coming down over San Francisco. People were walking their dogs, doing their shopping, going home, all as if they weren't in the least hurry, as if they felt themselves masters of the universe. "United States, fuckhead." It was the jubilant voice of the putamadre, and his hand on Chico's shoulder shook with feeling. The putamadre expounded, bewitched. It was the center of the world, the most powerful nation on earth. And on top of that, the country that had saved the fatherland, because when the rest of the cowards gave up the fight there would always be the yankees, manning their battle stations, with their missiles and their destroyers and their aircraft carriers, the putamadre personally assured them of this, because he knew them, because he'd lived for years on such hospitable soil, the gringos were the only allies you could trust, they were tight with Chile, and with that kind of a giant by your side nobody was alone in this world.

As for that, Chico's eye had been caught by a poster on a wall. What irresistibly attracted him was the very name of Chile in red letters, dripping, like a warped echo of what the putamadre just said. He couldn't read the rest of the words, but the other colors were those of the flag, white and blue. The car was moving too fast. They'd already reached the top of the hill and now they were on the way down, the immense bay of San Francisco glittering at their feet.

"Look," he blurted out—but he needn't have. The putamadre had swallowed his eulogies all of a sudden. Now they could all see several more posters, like a series of identical windows all the way down the street, culminating in the last exhibit, the identical design just being posted on a new wall by a little group of gringos—two young men and a blonde woman—with nervous efficient movements. The car stopped a little further down. They could sense how the woman was gluing the edges of the poster with special care, almost with affection. There was no doubt about the message. It wasn't exactly what you'd call a welcome. They recognized their vessel, the academy ship Esmeralda, steering its blue prow through a stormy sea of blood, its holds and its masts crammed and hanging with corpses, twisted figures, a howling mangled agony of men and women. Equally impressive were the words. STOP THE TORTURE SHIP, they read. BOYCOTT CHILE.

"Mother . . . fuck . . . ers," the putamadre snorted, savagely accenting each syllable. "Right here in the USA. Motherfuckers."

"They never give up," said Jorge.

With a sudden jerk, the car got going again.

The putamadre took command. "We're getting off," he ordered. "Quick."

They stumbled toward the rear door but the conductor dryly indicated they'd have to wait till the next stop. Something dangerous gleamed in the putamadre's eyes, but he contained himself. Not a word for two more blocks.

They barely touched the street and the putamadre took off resolutely in the other direction, back uphill.

"What are you going to do?" Chico managed to ask.

But the putamadre kept on, composed.

"Hey, putamadre," said Jorge, "what do you think you're doing?"

"We're going to kick some ass," the putamadre announced without slowing down. "We're going to show the sons of bitches we won't put up with their dirty posters while the academy ship of the Chilean Armada is in this port."

"Wait a minute, cool down a little," said Jorge. But the putamadre didn't seem to be listening. The other two had all they could do to keep from breaking into a trot. "Listen, psst, you asshole, wait a minute, will you."

The putamadre didn't stop. He didn't even look back. He shook off Jorge's arm which was trying to slow him down.

"Tell him, Chico," begged Jorge. "Tell him he shouldn't make trouble, that he's in uniform."

"You're in uniform," said Chico. "We could get in a mess."

"The commander said we shouldn't let ourselves be provoked," Jorge asserted, now almost running alongside the putamadre, a little ahead of him so he could speak to his face and catch his reaction. "If we get in a mess, all the newspapers will find out, and we'll be the worse for it."

The putamadre stopped as brutally as he'd set out, and turned to face them both. "Shit-eating cowards, faggots, yellow-bellied scum-bags. Can you just stand there while some bearded cocksuckers sold out to communism take the name of Chile and shit on it? A few lousy bastards that hate our country because we knew how to liberate ourselves. I don't hang around with fags. All right, they're going to find out that our battle for liberty's still going on. And they're going to find out through these arms, these fists. We're going to rip down every poster and then we're going to stomp every bone in their bodies. They're filling the city with . . . with . . . " Words failed him . . . "with shit," he said finally. "We don't have to put up with insults to our Armed Forces."

Jorge spoke slowly, trying to keep his voice from shaking. "If we touch a single hair on one of their heads," he said. "Imagine what would happen if we even laid a hand on one of those types."

"Or the woman," said Chico. "We can't beat up a woman."

"I'm asking you to think it over, putamadre, just calm down a little. This business, man: forget it! The city is full of people that love us, admire us, who understand what happened in Chile, people who support us. We have to think of them and not these others, they're in the minority. We're in a friendly country, see?"

The putamadre said nothing. His face was less red than before, but his eyes still had the same ferocity he'd spewed out in the torrent of his words. He looked up the street, where he could see the three people putting up another poster. The sun's rays at that moment shone on the long blond hair flowing down the woman's back to her waist. She was wearing a long skirt that reached all the way to her sandals. Her companions had beards and long hair and one of them had on a pair of those wire-rimmed glasses the hippies wear.

"Let's at least go talk to them, set them straight," the putamadre said finally "We can't let them lie and trick people like that."

"There's no time, don't be a jerk," said Jorge. "They'll figure it out soon enough, when they're on their own, when they're not living off daddy's money and they have to work. That's what my mama told me, and she's right."

The putamadre still wasn't giving up. "We're going to walk right in front of them. So they'll see we're not scared of them. I speak English, you know."

"It'll end up in a slugfest," said Jorge. "And if anything happens to us, we won't get Chico taken care of. Imagine the look on his uncle's face. Captain Valdés will be furious."

Suddenly the putamadre smiled, like they do in the movies, with the bitterness of the defeated but the superiority of one who possesses the truth. He raised his head, took a deep breath, and looked at his buddies with a pained expression. "Okay, we won't do anything to them. I promise. But . . . "—and he closed his eyes to a squint, thinking it over—"but . . . I want to find out where they live, I want to know in case we ever have a chance to get even. Don't worry, I swear, I keep my promises. I'll stay here, I'll follow them home. You take a little walk, if you keep going down this street you'll come to the Wharf and we'll meet up later in Ghirardelli."

Jorge and Chico saw that the people were getting away, they turned the corner.

"You think you're Sherlock Holmes," Jorge protested. "It'll take hours."

"I'll make you a deal. If I can't find out anything in an hour and a half, I'll give it up. At a quarter past eight, what do you think, in Ghirardelli Square, on the upper terrace." The putamadre was already on his way, radiant, sure of himself, in control. He turned around. "I promise to behave myself. I won't fuck the slut . . . not this time, anyway." Without their being able to stop him, he ran toward the corner and turned in the same direction the North Americans had gone.

"This asshole's crazy," Chico muttered.

"He may be crazy, but he'll get the addresses. Names and addresses both. Just wait."

They didn't have to wait long. He arrived at 8:25 at the place agreed upon. Jorge and Chico were sitting at a table on the terrace.

The putamadre greeted them from a distance with his arms upraised.

"Sitting pretty, eh? So how goes it without your favorite guide to San Francisco?" And he took the third seat.

"Did you track down the info?"

"Did I track it down? What are you drinking? Phooey! Don't bother with the milkshakes, you've got to get into the chocolate sodas, they serve the best chocolate sodas in the world here. It'll get us in shape for the night. Calories!"

The putamadre got up to order them personally.

"Take a look at the view, turkeys," he said with a merry excitement. "In Chile it's colder than shit right now, and here the boys are watching the last rays of sunlight fall on San Francisco Bay—what do you think?"

"You didn't do anything to them, did you?" said Jorge, uneasy faced with so much unexplained exuberance.

"Eat your chocolate, pay what you owe," sang the putamadre. "I keep my promises, right? Ever see me lie? Does a sailor crap out on his honor? Well? I didn't even touch that lady's little left tit. And her tits were little enough, believe me."

"And the guys?" asked Chico.

"Them? Faggoty jerk-offs, I wouldn't dirty my hands on their kind. Those guys spend their whole day stuffing themselves with reading, their only muscles are in their eyelashes." He dipped his long spoon into the glass and fished out a glob of ice cream. He popped the whole thing into his mouth. "Wow, it's like being in Valparaíso, but Valparaíso in the year 2000, when we'll have buildings and bridges like these. Check out the blue of that water, yes sir, the Golden Gate. And over there, across, that's called Sausalito. They throw terrific parties."

"Just tell us already."

"There's nothing to tell. Her name's Marlene Jennings. Single, she lives alone. A student. You want to visit her? She lives at 126 Dolores Street, number 2E. Dolores Street. Here everything has a Spanish name."

"But how do you know?"

The putamadre slapped him lightly on the cheek. "Poor kid. Because I followed them, shithead. These gringos eat early. I know their customs. They waste a day like this eating at home."

"And then?"

"And then? And then, and then, and then. Then I followed them, asshole, they went into this house, and I asked a few questions in the little store downstairs."

146

Chico cleared his throat. "And they just gave you the info, just like that?"

"Just like that, well no, Valdés, nothing comes free in this life. I had to con the little old lady on duty, I buttered her up with a bit of *Chilean charm.*"

"And she spilled everything."

"Almost everything. Her name, which is what mattered. The little gringa's schedule, which also counts. You want to know what time she gets home tonight, for example?"

Jorge followed the course of a sailboat cutting across the bay. "And their names?"

"Theirs?"

"Her companions."

"I shit on the names of those faggots. They couldn't shake the dust off their own dicks. It's the girl who's the vocalist in that trio . . . And if you want to know how I know, it's because she's a pretty hot little woman, not one of these dumb-ass gringas with a horse's teeth. Thin, with a strong voice, a fine chick . . . I wouldn't mind having her naked under a shower. Too bad she's such an agitator, the commie, but we could try to change her mind, right? Why not? Once she's tried out a good thing she won't be so quick to put down her *Chilean boys.*"

Jorge sucked the last of his chocolate through the straw.

"Okay, you had your fun, you know where she lives. Now let's get on with ours."

"Yeah," said Chico, "it's getting late."

"You go pay, Jorge," the putamadre ordered. "I'll treat, but you get in line."

Jorge didn't object, although in fact there was a long line inside up to the cashier. As soon as he walked away the putamadre leaned over toward Chico.

"Well, Valdés, how do you feel?"

"I feel fine, why shouldn't I?"

The putamadre bit his lip, thoughtful. "After you fuck for the first time, you change, see. You're never the same."

"I'm not scared."

"Academy cadets are never scared," said the putamadre. "It's your mama that couldn't take care of you, that's what happened." It was getting dark. Some lights were coming on in the little square. "I want to ask you something, Chico. Now, beforehand, you know?"

Chico said nothing.

"I'm your friend, Chico. I'm a grade ahead of you, but you can trust me. You know that I don't go sticking my nose into anything that's not my business. If what I say to you hits you wrong, okay, just tell me, man to man, and we'll forget it. But in order to help you out, tonight, so everything goes smoothly, there's just one question I'd like to ask."

"We've already talked a lot," said Chico. "During the voyage, all day long, all we've talked about is women."

"You didn't get me."

"I'm tired of listening to stories. It's been how long, about forty days since we sailed from Valparaíso, and every day you've told me a different story."

"I thought it would be good for you to hear an expert, that you'd get into the details, see how natural it all is, so you'd get over any shyness."

"Okay, my shyness is gone. I know exactly how you fucked that country girl in the ass, the first one, out on your grandpa's property, and that it's always good to have a handkerchief handy just in case she's a virgin. And Nilda, the shopgirl with the incredibly big tits and ..."

"Ease up a little. I don't want to tell you anything else. You don't understand. I just want to ask you a question."

Chico got up from the table. Jorge came back, and they walked off toward the stairs.

"What's with Chico?" Jorge asked. "Did you say something to him?"

The putamadre took him by the arm. "You blew it, asshole. You came back too soon. Leave this to me ... Look, you follow us, lag behind a little, as if you're paying attention to something else. A few magic minutes and ... presto! we'll have Valdés ready for the big blow-out."

Jorge gave the putamadre his change, coin by coin, dropping them into his open hand, looking him in the eye. He did it slowly, deliberately.

"You've got a big mouth, putamadre. What did you say to the kid?"

The putamadre didn't flinch. He put away the change, letting the metal ring in his pocket. "Look, Jorge, I helped you get your rocks off right there in the Academy, you don't have to teach me any lessons. I just have to find out something, that's all."

"What?"

The putamadre signalled in Chico's direction, he was leaning on the railing, absorbed in the sumptuous sunset over the bay. A light breeze was cooling things off and at the same time driving the sails scattered over the water.

"There's something he never told us about, that little problem he had."

"Oh, so you're still on that?"

"On that, right. The girl, what was the girl like, I mean physically, what was she like?"

"You never give up, do you, putamadre. We don't know what she was like. I thought Captain Valdés finally managed to find out."

"Captain Valdés insists that Chico doesn't want to talk about it. Of course, since Chico feels ashamed, the way things went that night ..."

Jorge lit a cigarette. "And Chico's never told you about it?"

The putamadre took a deep breath, filling his lungs with the soft sea air— warm air cooling down, air still carrying traces of the sun's taste, where you could feel the first night-smells. "Of course he's told me about it. He's told me everything."

"Everything?"

"Almost everything. We know this much: he didn't want to fuck her. That it wasn't fair, or something like that, that she was defenseless, and so he couldn't do it. That she had a right to her own ideas. What bullshit! He was with this chick a long time, talking I suppose, he must be an idiot. Afterwards he could have fucked another one."

148

"But he didn't want to describe her to you."

"He's keeping his mouth shut. He won't let loose. Besides, that night was pure chaos, remember. I myself don't know if I laid the same one twice or two different ones. I gave Chico his turn and he didn't want to." The putamadre looked over at Chico, still wrapped up in the shimmering blue of the bay, in the cities whose first lights were breaking the calm on the other side, the green and coffee-colored hills piled up behind them. The shadow of the San Francisco skyscrapers was moving out over the water like a slow dark lightning. "But he's going to tell me, he's going to tell me everything. You can't keep this putamadre in the dark. Everything'll come clear."

"If I were you I'd leave him alone. He's already edgy. Don't put so much heat on him."

"The fact is I'm not you. Maybe you haven't figured that out yet. I'm me. We'll handle the kid very gently." He winked a big eye at Jorge and walked over to Chico, parking himself by his elbow. For a while he didn't say a thing, sharing the view, the boats, the noise of the passersby, the skirts of the females going by below for the eternal delight of eyes like theirs. "No need to sulk, Chico."

"I'm not sulking."

"Yes, you're sulking, and with good reason. Look, Chico, I know myself, I know myself, I might as well be looking in a mirror. I always go around shooting my mouth off, it's true, I don't give anyone else a chance to express themselves."

The other had his eyes on a sea gull and managed to follow its endless dreamy flight till it disappeared. "Everybody has their own personality, you can't always help the way you are."

"I don't want to just be talking to you for its own sake, understand. I'd rather listen to you. I need to listen to somebody."

"The thing is, putamadre, that you have too much to tell, and that's why you talk so much. Me, on the other hand—I don't have any experience, I haven't lived. Especially since my old man died, it's like my life stopped. Just my mama and me, in that house."

"Okay, but enrolling in the Naval Academy was a big break. It was a great move on your uncle's part."

"My uncle always wanted me to be an officer in the Armada, like him. It was my father who thought there was no future in it."

"With all due respect, there's nothing better, Valdés, it's the best you can do. Nothing but future." The putamadre looked around, almost as if he were looking for an audience for his next words. He put his hands to his neck and stretched his body skyward, delighting in the crackling of his muscles, the tension in his thorax, his elbows intently thrust into the air.

"It's all the same to me," said Chico. "It's a career like any other."

"What do you mean like any other? It's the queen of careers, no, I lied, I lied. It's the empress. And now, more than ever, we have to take care of our country."

"Our country," Chico repeated.

"Our country, asshole. What you don't understand, Chico, is that we're heroes, national heroes . . . With your intelligence, Chico, with your sensitivity, you could

"Letter from Chile," drawing by Nemesio Antúnez.

turn out to be Minister of Education some day. We'll be running everything."

"And you'll devote yourself to Foreign Affairs, right?" asked Chico, sarcastically.

"I devote myself to all affairs, asshole, foreign, domestic, up, down, whatever I'm offered."

They laughed, and a certain tired electricity hanging between them dispersed as if someone had broken the circuit. They started to walk, in no particular hurry, and soon were descending the top stairs. Behind them, Jorge was coming along, seemingly absorbed in watching a little boy chasing a bouncing ball.

"You know, putamadre, I don't feel a bit nervous," said Chico.

"Of course not," the putamadre answered.

"What's happening with me is that I don't believe much in words. Just talking, talking doesn't get anything accomplished. It gets to be a drag, you know? We were going to go ashore in Colombia, then we were going to go ashore in Ecuador. And Acapulco, Acapulco wasn't an official visit. Acapulco couldn't fail. Everytime I got myself worked up, like you advised, I thought about her, I went over her beforehand in my head, from top to toe."

"Slowly, very slowly," urged the putamadre. "But without paying attention to the most important thing."

"Without paying attention to the most important thing. I let myself go, that's all, I was getting ready, relaxing, breathing deep, so everything would go just fine. Sometimes I couldn't sleep, putamadre, at night. That tropical heat. But we never went ashore. Just official receptions. And you know something? In one of those dances, in Colombia, I really liked one of those girls, one of those young ladies."

"But those weren't for fucking," the putamadre objected. "Those are fine people, daughters of people like ours."

"I liked one of them so much," Chico insisted. They kept on down the stairs leading to the street. It was a long way. Their footsteps sounded almost militarily, in unison, perfectly timed. Their black shoes, shining, gleamed as in review. "We never went ashore," Chico repeated. "We stood there looking at the land, the houses, the goddamn dock. Shore leaves cancelled, boys. It's dangerous, boys. There's a demonstration against Chile, boys. National security, boys. And you, talking about your adventures." He looked at him sideways and quickly added: "I like it, putamadre, deep down I like it, but imagine how I feel, how I felt. The shit was building up in me with no way out. Even when we did exercises and you were showing us how to wiggle our asses, flexing, moving your ass as if your favorite honey were under you. I felt like a jerk."

"It's true," the putamadre lamented. "You're absolutely right. I've got a prick like a prod, but my mouth's more like a bullhorn. I was born this way, what do you want me to do?"

Chico pulled himself together and looked accusingly at his watch. "You said eight o'clock, and now it's nine. We'd be there by now if you hadn't taken off after some idiot gringa."

"She wasn't an idiot gringa. She was pretty foxy, if you got a look at her."
Since Chico didn't answer, the putamadre took advantage of the opening.
"That's just what I wanted to talk to you about, I wanted to ask you just one
question, and then we'll go, we'll leave the Academy out of it, and that'll be
that."

Chico didn't smile this time. They'd already reached the street, and he
stopped walking, as if they'd had some previous agreement.

"It's essential that you know how to choose the right woman tonight," the
putamadre went on. "And I'm missing a few details."

"She has to be a woman, that's all," said Chico. "Let's quit going around in
circles."

"You've got to feel comfortable with the girl, Valdés. I'm telling you up
front. I don't mince words. I need to know what that girl was like, the one that
night. That's what I have to ask you."

Chico took a deep breath. "I already told you that I just didn't feel like
making love with a woman who didn't want to. It seems old-fashioned, sure, but
it was like raping her, and I'm not into that."

"But nobody's telling you you should be. Every man to his own tastes.
That's why we live in a free country. The way I see it, those chicks get whatever
they deserve. I sure don't need to fuck any feisty women. I've got bites of my
own."

"Maybe, but that night you went to bed like everybody else."

"They were giving it away, asshole, fresh meat, for free. What I'm saying is I
didn't need it. It was a good opportunity, so I grabbed it. These things always
happen in a war. It's the winners' spoils. If they'd won, any old scummy prick
from the slums would have been fucking our cousins, and not in the Naval Academy but in our own houses."

"I just couldn't do it," said Chico.

"So who says you had to, asshole. It just seemed to me like you passed up a
golden opportunity to get your cherry busted. And it wasn't much of a favor
you did the girl, because finally somebody else fucked her. And I assure you he
didn't have any second thoughts . . . And those girls that night didn't do so bad,
they got off good in fact, later we let them go, I know what I'm talking about."

"They got off good?" asked Chico.

"They're all a bunch of whores," said the putamadre. "The one I had ended
up loving it."

Chico put his hands in his pockets and kicked a little rock that bumped a
lamp post. It made a metallic sound and bounced off. "Putamadre, I don't believe you, that one I'm just not going to believe."

"Believe me if you want to and if not, go fuck yourself. I'm telling you it's a
biological thing. If you work the little button right, and if you know how to rub
it, if you move your ass nice and slow, if you can keep it up, the sweet Eve explodes, explodes, man, that's all there is to it. All these dumb broads are whores.
They love it, old man, they love it."

"Putamadre," said Chico, "can I ask you a big favor?"

"Anything you want, Valdés. Your wishes are granted."

"Putamadre, let's get going already."

"Okay. Let's go. It's not far. Near Nob Hill." The putamadre tried one more line of attack. "But it would help me a lot if I knew what the girl looked like that night . . . It's a way of getting over that experience, understand? Her hair, Valdés, at least that detail, so I can tell your uncle I knew how to make the right choice."

"Why not let him make the choice?" Jorge's voice said suddenly—he'd caught up with them and had overheard the tail end of their conversation without their knowing it.

The putamadre turned around in a rage. "You stay out of this."

"I'll get in it if I want to," said Jorge. "Valdés is my friend too. I can give him advice as well as you can."

They were the same size, but the putamadre looked a little taller. He spoke from above, like an admiral giving orders. "Captain Valdés spoke to me. He entrusted me with this mission. I'm responsible, I gave my word of honor as a cadet and I'm going to make good on it. And more than that, I'm going to make it perfect. That's why you're staying out of this, and you, Chico, you're going to spit out the color of that girl's hair. Right now, you little hothead, we want to settle this. With this detail, victory is assured."

"None of this matters," said Chico. "Let's forget the whole thing."

"Valdés," said the putamadre. "Valdés, I want to know if she was a blonde. It may seem like an unimportant detail, but it's enough for me. You tell me, and we'll go."

"Leave him alone."

"You shut up. This is something between Chico, his uncle, and me. If we brought you along, be satisfied with that, and keep your trap shut . . . Valdés!"

"It was just a stupid mess, that's all," said Chico. "There's nothing to describe."

"Was she blonde? Was she blonde or brunette? Tell me that much at least."

Chico hesitated for an instant. It had gotten dark and by the neon lights boiling swarms of little black flies could be seen.

"She was blonde," Chico said, finally.

"She was blonde." The putamadre's face broke into a big grin, and he smoothed back his slick hair. "All right, Valdés, that's just fine, because it's going to make our mission easier. Let's get going, shitheads, what the fuck are we standing around here for." They started to walk. "A natural blonde?"

"Natural," said Chico. "A student at the University. She had been anyway. They'd kicked her out. It seemed like she had some foreign blood."

"I see you know quite a bit about her," said the putamadre. "If you'd only fucked her . . . okay, but that's over with. Over and done, and a clean slate. Whoever's got the guts can follow me."

They walked along in silence for several minutes. The putamadre whistled, hummed, shadowboxed the lamp posts, recited the wonders of San Francisco.

He was drunk with joy, overflowing with a power that shook him electrically. The other two followed, not saying a word.

"Here it is, didn't I tell you," proclaimed the putamadre, exultant. He'd just made sure by checking with a band of little boys sadly watching a pick-up basketball game on a playground. "What a memory your daddy has . . . "

The building was tall, modern, imposing. Behind the immaculate glass doors was a plush lobby: a tasteful row of plants and ferns arranged alongside a wall-length mirror enhanced the impression of an exclusive and distinguished ambience. All that was missing was a doorman.

"Apartment 3B," announced the putamadre, and pressed the appropriate button.

"It's here?" asked Jorge, dazzled.

"The place has class, I'm not going to take you to any old whorehouse."

Just then they heard a woman's voice over the intercom: "What's the name?"

The putamadre answered in English that he'd been there a couple of years ago, and that they were a party of three.

"Okay," said the voice, and a buzzer rang letting them in.

"You wait here," said the putamadre, crossing the threshold. "I'll come back for you."

"I'm going with you," said Chico Valdés.

"We're all going up," Jorge asserted, "or we don't go up at all."

The putamadre didn't answer. The elevator was spacious, quiet, fast. The door to apartment 3B was ajar. The putamadre knocked softly, and they went in.

No one was waiting for them in the dimly lit entry hall. In the half-light they could see two doors, both closed. From the other side of one they could hear the sound of glasses, a steady murmur, and over the conversation a woman's sharp clear laugh. As if from a great distance, the first few bars of a song reached them. In Spanish. *Cuando te veo con la blusa azul* . . . Whenever I see you in your blue blouse . . . It was a happy song, but there was something nostalgic about it, a weakened or possibly defeated joy, that came across in flashes. My eyes reach out to you, not wanting to . . . *Mis ojos sin querer van hacia ti* . . . The putamadre surveyed the hall with a gesture, radiant. But his voice came out low and fragile, as if they were in a cemetery or a hospital.

"What do you say, eh? That's the bar and the salon where we can dance a little and examine the merchandise. We have to treat the girls to a drink. For that we have a fat bankroll, the good old dollar. Then we go in there," and he pointed toward the other door, "where we try out the mattresses."

"What are we waiting for?" asked Jorge. "Let's go in."

"Wait a second, have a little patience, studs. We have to wait here. I'm sure Lucia will receive us personally. She always comes out to have a look first."

At just that moment the door to the bar swung open. The brunette who came into the hall was tall, tall and slender, dressed in fairly dark colors, but very stylish, and her age was hard to determine, as if she'd decided, on reaching

154

maturity, to stay that way forever and get no older, but there were also certain parts of her body that hadn't completely obeyed. "Come in, come in," she said in English, "make yourselves at home."

"We speak Spanish," said the putamadre. "Hablamos español."

"Welcome in Spanish, then," said the woman, with a heavy Mexican accent.

"Lucia's not here?" said the putamadre.

The woman suddenly looked at them differently, they felt themselves scrutinized by those intense eyes in the dimness. It was as if she'd suddenly remembered something. "No, Lucia's not here," she said. "She's in Bakersfield." But her words came from some other place, empty, as though she were thinking of something else. She still had her fingertips on the doorknob, but she didn't open the door to let them in. On the contrary, she pulled it shut. The already dim light grew dimmer; so did the fragmentary sense of music, smoke, the special density circulating inside, where they'd caught a glimpse of men and women dancing, drinking, laughing. The only thing they could still hear clearly was the imploring, urgent voice of the singer: *Por Dios no te pongas más, la blusa azul.* For heaven's sake, don't put your blue blouse on. And the chorus of voices: *Por Dios no te pongas más, la blusa azul.* "You came into port today?" asked the woman.

"We got here yesterday," Jorge answered. "But we couldn't come ashore till just a little while ago."

"Of course," said the woman, "and you came straight here." Something strange was happening, something vaguely cold was covering the walls and filling the corners of the room. The woman went toward the switch and flicked the lights on. They blinked with the brutal glare, and suddenly saw themselves in a mirror that covered the space between the two doors. There they were, their uniforms immaculate, custom fit, the perfect gentlemen. Handsome, faultless, irreproachable. The putamadre was the first to break the silence. He saw himself speaking in the mirror and admired his own serenity.

"Straight here, no," he said. "We took a little walk first. They never get started before eight, so there was no hurry."

"You were here before," said the woman. "I don't remember you."

"I was here twice," said the putamadre. "Both times with Tomasa. I don't remember you either."

The woman stood still. She had an unlit cigarette in her left hand, but she made no move to light it. She didn't approach them, she didn't open the door. The distance between them was cold and awkward, as if some obscene dead cat were hung up, stiffening, between the three of them and the woman and none of them wanted to take the first step toward crossing that space.

"Is Tomasa here tonight?" asked the putamadre.

"Tomasa went back to Mexico."

"All right, there must be others," said the putamadre. "It's too bad, I liked her a lot . . . Okay, let's go in." But he didn't move, waiting for her to invite them.

"You're Chileans." It wasn't a question but an assertion.

"Chileans," declared the putamadre. "And proud to be. Chileans with plenty of cash and ready for a good time." He looked at the others. "Isn't that so?"

"We've been aboard ship for a lot of weeks," said Jorge.

"And that uniform, do you always wear it? Or do you leave it home sometimes?"

"We're cadets," Jorge explained. "Don't think we're members of any crew."

"Sure," said the woman. "I see you're quite the gentlemen and you know how to treat the ladies. You came on that ship with such a pretty name. I had a friend in Mexico by that name. Esmeralda."

But she didn't budge, she didn't make even the slightest move toward opening the door, smiling at them, nothing. It was as if the four of them were waiting for a bus and chatting to kill time.

The putamadre decided to take the bull by the horns. After all, he was the one responsible for this expedition. "What's going on? Aren't there any girls? Are they all busy?"

"It's not that," she said.

"Because if they're busy, we can come back later. We're in no hurry."

"It would be easy to tell you that," she said, with her slightly harsh Mexican voice. "But that's not it."

"Terrific," said the putamadre. "Then, it's agreed."

Just then the other door opened and a couple appeared, crossing the hall, laughing, toward the salon. On the arm of a balding gringo about fifty was a fantastic blonde, strong, phenomenal, wrapped in a green dress that looked like a second skin, she was a white panther, awash in perfume, each feature rippling with hot waves of energy—mouth, breasts, hips—a regular monument to nature's work. The three stood there staring till she disappeared.

"You can't," said the woman. "I'm sorry, boys."

"What?" said the putamadre. "What do you mean sorry?"

The blonde stuck her head out the door. "Hey, what's the matter? Everybody's asking for you, Sylvia. You're the life of the party."

"It's the Chileans," said the woman.

"Ah," said the blonde. "The Chileans. The sailors." She slinked into the hall with an incredibly catlike motion. They looked at her goggle-eyed, one by one, and it was as if someone were bathing them in champagne, as if they were bubbling warmly in someone's throat.

"She doesn't speak Spanish, but she understands," said the woman. "She can explain. You want to tell them."

"It's a strike, boys," said the blonde. "Sorry." She approached Jorge, took his hand, examined it as if it were some strange object. She traced his life line, and then made an X in the middle of his palm.

"Say it in Spanish," said the woman. "Tell them in their own language."

The blonde swung her other arm around the putamadre's neck. She balanced like that a little while, with both hands occupied, like a bridge between the two cadets. "Come here, you, lonely boy," she said in English to Chico Valdés, who wasn't holding on to anything. Chico Valdés didn't move.

The putamadre took her by the waist. "And you, my love, what's your name?"

"Huelga," said the blonde, like that, in Castilian. The word came out with a yankee accent, but clear as a bell, or like a wheatfield in the sun, as if she'd studied the pronunciation for hours in front of a dictionary.

"Huelga?" Jorge repeated, as if he didn't understand the language.

"Huelga," the blonde insisted. "We're on *huelga,* don't you know what that means?" She drew an H on the chest of his uniform, and then the other letters. "Huelga, that means strike."

"But how?" protested the putamadre. "The ones inside, how come you're serving them?" He pulled his hand angrily away from her waist. "I've never heard of anything like this before . . . It's, it's . . . ridiculous."

"It's not a strike against everyone," said the woman called Sylvia, slowly. "It's only against you."

"Against us? Against sailors?"

"No, against you, the Chileans of the Esmeralda. That's all."

"Nothing tonight for any of you boys, not here in Frisco," said the blonde, playing with the lock of hair on the putamadre's forehead. "Nada, nada."

The putamadre shook his head, he took a step away from the woman. "Against us? Only against us?"

"If you want to come another day, when the ship's gone, we'll be happy to have you here again. Any time you're not in uniform, it's your house whenever you come to San Francisco. But not tonight."

For the first time, Chico Valdés spoke. "When the academy ship leaves," he said slowly, "we go with it. We can't stay here once it's sailed."

"That's just it, that's what I'm explaining to you." The woman studied them with her steady eyes, that had seen it all, that had done it all. "This way out, fellas." Since nobody moved, she herself crossed the threshold and went out toward the elevator. She pressed the button. "We're on strike. The whole staff decided two days ago. Boycott the Esmeralda. We abide by our democratic decisions."

"Democratic," the putamadre exploded. "Whores, democratic? The world's crazy . . . "

Inside the record was ending. The blonde was singing along in a low voice, with an atrocious accent. *Por Dios no te pongas más, la blusa azul.* For heaven's sake, don't put your blue blouse on.

"Are we going to go?" asked Jorge. "Are we going to let them throw us out like this?"

The elevator had arrived. The woman called Sylvia opened the door and for the first time smiled at them, more maternal, more like a madonna smiling at a baby, than anything else. With her long dark hair and black eyes and that skin, she almost looked like a Chilean woman. "That's life, kids," she said. "You learn something every day."

The putamadre walked to the door of the apartment. His fist opened and closed violently and his lips were trembling. But when he spoke, his voice came out slowly, strong and deliberate, like a cowboy baritone. "It doesn't seem the best way to keep your clients," he said.

The blonde let go of Jorge's hand. "Bye bye, boys."

"It doesn't seem such a good way to keep your clients," the putamadre repeated, looking at Sylvia and the blonde by turns.

"There are more important things," said Sylvia, and motioned toward the elevator. "Go home already, fellas. We're wasting time. Not tonight."

The putamadre turned his back. He looked at his two friends and raised his voice. "You see what happens with a soft government, don't you? Even the whores revolt and turn communist." He made a signal with his head, as if he were directing a combat squadron. "We'll find someplace else. Frisco's full of whorehouses."

He heard Sylvia's voice, weary, resolved, tough. "You won't find any place that will take your business. There's not a girl in San Francisco who'll go to bed with you. Even if you offer them a fortune. Not the oldest hag, not the cheapest streetwalker. Nobody. Now, go see a good film, then hit the sack, boys."

The putamadre took his time. He walked up to the blonde and said to her: "Some day I'll come back here and show you what's good, baby. I hope you don't get ruined in the meantime." Then he walked slowly toward the elevator. Like a gentleman, he let his two friends go in first. Then he followed, and Sylvia closed the door behind them. For a fleeting instant they were captivated by the brown maturity of her face in the round window of the elevator, like a portrait of some forgotten Aztec goddess. "We'll be seeing each other," the putamadre promised. Then, totally dignified, he pressed the button, and she vanished. They descended in silence.

"What gets you down and dirty," said Jorge suddenly, and he opened the door with a kick.

The putamadre didn't say a word. He smiled with a strange calm.

"We should have said something to them," Jorge went on. "We should have shit on them somehow, putamadre, we should have said something."

"You think it's true what she said?" asked Chico. "Is it true that in the whole city . . . "

They stepped out into the street. The putamadre threw a look up toward the third floor, but they couldn't hear a thing, not even music. He lit a cigarette, striking the match on the wall. "What time is it, Chico?" he damanded.

"Whores shitting on us," said Jorge. "Whores shitting right on our faces."

"The time, Chico asshole," the putamadre ordered again.

Chico showed his watch so they could all see it. It was almost ten. The putamadre stopped under the light of a streetlamp. He kept looking up toward the third floor, watching the smoke from his cigarette drift up toward the balconies of 3B.

"Letting them dump on us like that," said Jorge. "The trash, the worst garbage, the lowest of the low, doing that to us—a whore, a whore."

The putamadre shook his head reflectively. His composure was extraordinary. "So her hair was blonde, right?"

Chico Valdés didn't answer him.

"Like our gringa, eh Chico? Answer me just this: did she look like the gringa?"

"Gringa?" asked Jorge. "What gringa?"

Chico paid no attention to Jorge. He looked straight at the putamadre. There was a chill in his voice. "Right, something like her. Same length hair."

"Was she about that size, more or less, Chico? Thin, with a nice ass, plenty to grab hold of, little tits?"

Chico didn't answer.

"But who are you talking about?" Jorge interrupted again. "Who the fuck are you talking about?"

"You don't have to answer my question, Chico," the putamadre continued. "I know she was more or less like that, wasn't she?"

Chico said, very quietly: "Yeah, more or less."

"Could you kindly inform me who you're talking about?" asked Jorge.

"The gringa from this afternoon, asshole—Marlene," said the putamadre impatiently. "Who else would we be talking about? The one with the posters."

"Oh, that gringa," said Jorge.

"Right," said the putamadre, "you figured it out, you win a prize. That very gringa."

"I don't get you, putamadre," Jorge said. "We've never let anyone insult our flag, our country, like that."

The putamadre ignored him. "It's not late," he said. "It's not far either." He placed his hands on Chico Valdés's shoulders and took a deep breath. "What do you think, Chico?"

"I don't think," said Chico. "I don't think anything."

"If it's the uniform you're worried about, forget it," said the putamadre. "Nobody'll know the difference in the dark."

"I don't think," Chico repeated. "And it's not on account of the uniform. It has nothing to do with the uniform."

"Valdés," said the putamadre, "Valdés, I promised your uncle."

Jorge jumped in again. "Can you tell me what you're talking about. I don't understand a goddamned thing."

The putamadre didn't look at him. "Chico, are you going to fail again? Do you realize what those motherfuckers are trying to do. They've even corrupted the whores. Do you realize, Chico, do you realize? And all your compassion, what good does it do?"

Chico shook his head.

"Think about the voyage home, Chico," said the putamadre. "Another forty days, and nights too. You'll go crazy, brother . . . We can't let them shit on us like this. They have to pay for it somehow. Look, I'm telling you, we don't even have to turn on a light. It's a matter of not saying a word. Real quiet, Chico, just like that."

Chico kept shaking his head, as if he didn't trust the voice that might come out. Like a stubborn horse that's forgotten any other gesture.

"It's not far, Chico. Your dad here will set it all up. Barrenechea here and I will arrange everything. Right, Jorge?"

"Arrange what?" said Jorge.

"Since you haven't figured it out yet," said the putamadre, as if he were explaining it to a retarded person, "the topic of conversation is the gringa. That's what it's about. We have to help Chico here. We gave our word that he'd come back to Chile a man, and we have to keep it."

"You're the one who gave your word," said Jorge. "I didn't make any promises."

"But you don't desert a buddy in the middle of a battle . . . " The putamadre threw down his cigarette. "Chico, she lives alone. I know everything, I know how to go up the back way, how to get in. These gringos leave their windows open in the summer. Chico, we'll wait for her in her own apartment. Tonight she'll come home alone, about eleven. It's no sweat. And nobody can connect us with her. We don't even know her. It's easy, right, Jorge?"

"It's not easy," said Jorge—his voice was trembling. "But it's not impossible."

"Think of your uncle, Chico, I want you to think about that. The triumphant minute we dock in Chile, and you feel like a real man. Chico Shitkicker, don't you see that when you're dealing with the enemy you can't think twice. Charity begins at home. That's exactly what needs to be done to teach these whores. If you always turn the other cheek, they'll just keep slapping the shit out of you. They spit on us, they insult us, they hate us. How long are we going to put up with it, Chico, how long? An eye for an eye, an ass for an ass. That's my philosophy."

Chico kept shaking his head, looking at the ground, avoiding the putamadre's eyes. He kept his gaze fixed on the cigarette burning at his feet.

"Barrenechea," said the putamadre. "This is no longer a matter of friendship. This is a patriotic duty. Barrenechea, you tell him, explain it to him."

Jorge smiled slightly. "Let's go, Chico," he said. "The day comes when we all have to be a man. You'll feel much better. The putamadre's right: it's easy."

The putamadre crushed out the butt. Then he took Chico firmly by the shoulders till he had to meet his gaze.

"What do you think, Chico? Shall we get going? Huh? Are we going to have fun with the gringa, with the blonde Marlene?"

They waited for an answer.

About the Authors

Fernando Alegría, novelist, poet, and critic is the author of more than twenty books, some of them translated into several languages. Among his books translated into English are: *My Horse Gonzalez, The Chilean Spring* and *Instructions for Undressing the Human Race. Coral de guerra,* his latest novel, was published in Mexico by Editorial Nueva Imagen (1980). He teaches Latin American Literature at Stanford University.

Poli Délano has written several books of fiction, among them *Mask Change (Cambio de máscara,* which won the Casa de las Américas Literary Prize, 1973), *No Dying Completely (Sin morir del todo,* 1975), *Two Lizards in a Bottle (Dos lagartos en una botella,* 1976), and *In This Sacred Place (En este lugar sagrado,* 1977). He lives in Mexico.

Ariel Dorfman is the co-author of a widely known book: *How to Read Donald Duck,* 1971. He has written also a number of studies on the ideology of comics such as *Superman and his Dear Friends (Superman y sus amigos del alma,* 1974) and *The Last Adventure of the Lone Ranger (La última aventura del llanero sol-*

itario, 1979. He has published two novels: *Beware of the Enemy (Moros en la costa,* 1973*)* and *New Tourist Guide for a Country in the Third World (Nueva guía turística para un país del Tercer Mundo,* 1979*).* He is a professor of literature at the University of Amsterdam, Holland.

Juan Armando Epple, author of several articles on Spanish American literature, has published short stories in literary magazines and anthologies of the new Chilean narrative. He is currently Assistant Professor of Romance Languages at the University of Oregon.

Alfonso Gonzalez Dagnino, physician, has published numberous articles in the field of medicine and public health. *The First Days (Los primeros días)* is his first piece of fiction. He lives in Madrid.

Claudio Giaconi, the author of a book of short stories, *Difficult Youth,* 1954 *(La difícil juventud),* was awarded the Municipal Prize in Chile. *Amadeo's Dream (El sueño de Amadeo),* a collection of short stories and essays, 1959; *A Man in the Trap (Un hombre en la trampa, Gogol),* a long essay on Gogol, 1960. Giaconi is a free-lance newspaper man and translator working and living in New York. At present he is writing a long novel called *F.*

Aníbal Quijada has published only one book, *Barbed Wire Fence (Cerco de púas),* considered by many critics the most moving testimony on the persecution suffered by Chileans during and after the military coup of 1973. He is in exile in Mexico.

José Leandro Urbina is the author of *The Bad Company (Las malas juntas,* 1979*)* and several short stories published in magazines and anthologies in Spain and Latin America. He teaches in Canada.